"I'm going to tea

Everett lifted Joey onto a saddle on a freestanding rack where it awaited cleaning.

Joey gasped with excitement.

"First, hold on to this." He patted the saddle horn.

Joey gripped it tight with both his hands. He was much too small for the saddle, but that didn't seem to matter.

Everett then moved Joey's legs into position. "Keep these straight, okay? Not all bunched up. That's how cowboys do it."

"I'm a cowboy."

"Just like your dad." He patted Joey's shoulder, keeping his hand there to steady the boy.

Joey gazed up at Everett with undisguised hero worship. The ping Macy had felt earlier turned into a stab of pain. She suddenly realized more was at stake here than just her renewed attraction to Everett. Her son was also becoming attached to him. And if Everett left, which he well might, he'd break Joey's small heart. That would hurt worse than Macy's own disappointment.

Dear Reader,

I love starting new things, and *The Rodeo Cowboy's Return* is book one in my latest Harlequin Heartwarming series, The Rocking Chair Ranch. People often ask where I get the ideas for my stories, and I usually have an interesting answer. But I'm not sure where the original inspiration for this book sprang from. I only know I've wanted to write about a charming and quaint independent senior living community for some time. And because I love writing cowboy romances, of course it had to be a Western setting.

Everett and Macy's romance is a second chance for both of them in more ways than one. Years ago, Everett let Macy down, and she doesn't trust him with her vulnerable heart, or the one belonging to her adorable young son. Only by taking a chance, and Everett proving he's not the same man who once abandoned her, can their newfound love bloom.

The Rodeo Cowboy's Return is also populated with some charming secondary, elderly characters who will make you smile and even sigh. I hope you enjoy reading Everett and Macy's story as much as I did writing it.

Warmest wishes,

Cathy McDavid

PS: I love connecting with readers. You can find me at:

CathyMcDavid.com
Facebook.com/CathyMcDavid
Twitter.com/CathyMcDavid
Instagram.com/CathyMcDavidWriter

THE RODEO COWBOY'S RETURN

CATHY McDAVID

Harlequin

HEARTWARMING

Harlequin®
HEARTWARMING™

ISBN-13: 978-1-335-05114-1

The Rodeo Cowboy's Return

Copyright © 2024 by Cathy McDavid Books, LLC

 Harlequin Enterprises ULC
22 Adelaide St. West, 41st Floor
Toronto, Ontario M5H 4E3, Canada
www.Harlequin.com

Printed in Lithuania

Recycling programs
for this product may
not exist in your area.

MIX
Paper | Supporting
responsible forestry
FSC® C021394

New York Times bestselling author **Cathy McDavid** has written over forty-five titles for Harlequin. She spends her days penning stories about handsome cowboys riding the range, busting broncs and sweeping gals off their feet—oops, no. Make that winning the hearts of feisty, independent women who give them a run for their money.

Books by Cathy McDavid

Harlequin Heartwarming

Wishing Well Springs

The Cowboy's Holiday Bride
How to Marry a Cowboy
A Secret Christmas Wish
Her Surprise Cowboy Groom

The Sweetheart Ranch

A Cowboy's Christmas Proposal
The Cowboy's Perfect Match
The Cowboy's Christmas Baby
Her Cowboy Sweetheart

Visit the Author Profile page
at Harlequin.com for more titles.

CHAPTER ONE

THE RUSTED IRON gate stood open, inviting anyone who approached to enter. Some things, thought Everett Owens, never changed. And, unfortunately, some things did.

Ignoring the stab of guilt squeezing his heart, he drove his late-model cobalt blue pickup truck onto his grandfather's ranch, the tires shooting plumes of dry red dust into the air. A few hundred yards later, the dirt road curved and pasture fences came into view. Three years ago, a herd of Arizona's finest quarter horses would have galloped alongside the fence line, escorting Everett to the outbuildings. Today, the pastures sat empty.

A dozen broodmares and one stallion were all that remained of his grandfather's once thriving horse breeding business. In the wake of the older man's recent heart attack, Everett assumed that the horses would soon have a new owner. The ranch, too.

Help selling off. That must be why his grandfather had summoned him home. Only a few reasons could convince Everett to set foot in Wickenburg,

Arizona. His grandfather's health. The ranch and horses. A funeral.

Another funeral, Everett amended.

He shoved the sudden flood of unhappy memories aside and focused on what, according to his mom, might be required of him during this visit. Liquidating Pop's few remaining business assets. Making any necessary repairs and then putting the ranch on the market. Eventually, overseeing the sale. Finding a suitable eldercare facility for his grandfather.

How long would all that take? Everett had no wish to prolong his stay or keep returning. He didn't miss his hometown, and he was sure his hometown didn't miss him.

The outbuildings came into view, shabbier than the last time he'd seen them and crying out for fresh paint. He counted at least a dozen missing roof shingles on the mare barn and stallion quarters. Doors hung crookedly on loose hinges. The hay shed housed at most thirty bales. Barely enough to feed a string of pregnant broodmares and a big, hardy stallion for a week.

Everett's mom had either downplayed the situation or lacked a full understanding of it. She and Everett's aunt Laurel would have been here if not for Pop's objections. Everett was the only one his grandfather had summoned. According to him, a phone call wouldn't suffice. The two of them needed to talk in person.

Aiming the truck in the direction of the house,

Everett reduced his speed to a crawl. Pop must have been watching from the back window, for the kitchen door opened, and he shuffled onto the spacious back porch. Shuffled? What had happened to his robust stride? His worn work shirt billowed at the waist where it once strained against the buttons, and his formerly square shoulders now drooped.

Swallowing his shock, Everett parked in front of the freestanding garage behind the house and climbed out of his truck. His mom's worry hadn't been exaggerated.

"Hey, Pop," he hollered and waved.

Most people in town called Winston Connelly by his nickname. If asked, he couldn't remember how or when it started.

"Everett, my boy. Mighty good to see you."

They met on the porch where Everett enveloped Pop in a fierce embrace. Feeling his grandfather's slighter frame gave Everett another shock.

"Good to see you, too, Pop." He fought the sudden tightness in his chest. "I've missed you."

"Missed you something awful." Pop clapped Everett on the back before releasing him. "You hungry? Thirsty? Can I make you a sandwich?"

It was too early for lunch. "Maybe later," Everett said. "I'll take a cold drink in the meantime."

"You fetch your stuff from the truck and come on in. I'll round us up a couple of root beers."

Pop's favorite beverage. That much was still the same.

Everett did as instructed and carried his duffel

and laptop satchel into the house. He passed Pop at the kitchen counter, struggling to pry the lid off a bottle. Everett resisted offering to help—Pop was a proud and independent man—and headed down the hall instead. His cowboy boots echoed on the wooden floor only to be muted when they reached the carpeted guest bedroom.

The quilt that had won his late grandmother first place at the county fair two decades ago covered the bed. Like everything at the ranch, it had seen better days. After setting his duffel and satchel on an old chair in the corner to be unpacked later, he returned to the kitchen.

Midway down the hall, Everett came to a bone-jarring halt. How could he have forgotten about the photo, one of many in a vast collection that stretched from one end of the long wall to the other? Feeling like he'd been kicked in the gut, he stared at the image of his younger and happier self. He and his best friend, Brody, had their arms draped around each other in a congratulatory side hug. Their grinning faces spoke of a good day. A good rodeo. They'd both finished the weekend with first place wins, Everett in bulldogging and Brody in bareback bronc riding.

Eight months later, Brody had died, the result of a head-on collision. Everett's fault. Because of him, the finest man to ever walk the face of the earth lay six feet beneath its surface. Worse, his beautiful wife became a widow, and his yet-to-be-born son was left to grow up fatherless.

Everett attempted to draw air into lungs that refused to function. He shouldn't keep coming back, even as seldom as he did. Too much time had passed for him to make good on his broken promise.

A loud clatter jerked him from the dark hole he'd disappeared into, and he hurried to the kitchen.

"You okay, Pop?"

His grandfather stood over a bottle of root beer lying on its side and emptying its contents into a puddle on the floor. Pop's wizened features twisted into a frustrated grimace.

"Dang blasted bottle slipped out of my hand."

"Don't worry about it."

Everett bent and retrieved the bottle, which he set in the sink. He then ripped a long length of paper towels off the roll and sopped up the mess, disposing the sodden paper towels in a trash bin beneath the counter.

"It's my arthritis," Pop said with a note of dejection.

"I'll lend you this new ointment I've been using. Pretty good stuff." Everett suffered his share of aches and pains. Rodeoing was a physically demanding way to earn a living.

Pop reached for the refrigerator door handle. "Let me grab you another soda. Then we can tour the stallion quarters and mare barn."

Right to business. Okay.

With their drinks in hand, they walked from the

house to the barn area at a more sedate pace than in days gone by.

"What did the doctor say at your last checkup?" Everett asked.

"I'm fit as a fiddle."

"Pop, I'm serious."

The older man's chuckle lacked mirth. "I'm doing well enough for a man who almost kicked the bucket. Could've been a lot worse."

"He's satisfied with your progress, then?"

"*She's* satisfied. And young enough to be your sister, iffin' you had one. Says I'm recovering nicely. Then again, I should be. She's got me taking more pills than a grizzly has teeth." He snorted in disgust. "Insisted I give up all my favorite foods. Steak. Bacon. Fried potatoes. Salt, for Pete's sake. Now I have broiled chicken breast and salad for dinner prit near every night."

That accounted for some of the weight loss, though not all. Pop had the appearance of someone who'd been gravely ill for an extended time.

"You sure you're allowed to have root beer?" Everett asked, only half-jokingly.

"Give a poor man a break, will you?"

He supposed they could bend the rules this once. "I won't tell."

As they neared the stallion quarters, a magnificent chestnut trotted out the stable door and into the paddock. Snorting and shaking his head, he came to a standstill at the paddock fence and emitted a shrill whinny that let everyone in earshot know he was king of his domain. With a well-defined head that might have been chiseled from marble, his heavily muscled form displayed a strength and athleticism inherited from the best quarter horse lines.

Pop reached out a gnarled hand to the horse, whose personality instantly changed from that of a lion to a lamb.

"How's my good boy?" He ran his palm along the horse's prominent jaw.

In turn, the horse pressed his nose into Pop's shoulder and nickered with contentment. There was no doubt of the close bond the two shared. A chip in Everett's carefully constructed armor fell away.

"Champ looks good," he observed.

"He's a beaut."

Doc Bar None Better was the stallion's registered name. After his first win—a halter competition as a yearling—Pop had started calling him Champ, and the nickname stuck.

"I've had help looking after him. And the place," Pop added with a tilt of his chin.

"Your neighbors?"

"Them and some of the folks in town. They keep things clean and tidy for me."

Everett was glad to hear that. Champ was a valuable asset. Selling him and the dozen mares would bring in a lot of money that could be put to good use. Such as nice accommodations in a reputable eldercare facility. A clean and tidy place would also help obtain a good sale price when they sold the ranch.

After Champ had his fill of being doted on, Everett and Pop made their way to the mare barn. Half the stalls were occupied. To Everett's relief, he found the mare barn in the same well-kept condition. Even better, the pregnant residents appeared healthy and content. Pop was fortunate to have such kind neighbors and friends. No way could he care for this number of horses on his own. Cleaning the stalls alone would do him in. Not to mention hauling hay, watering and the countless other labor-intensive chores required with running a ranch. Even with a limited number of horses.

"I need to rest my feet a few minutes."

Without waiting for a response, Pop eased himself down onto one of two worn wicker rocking chairs sitting just inside the barn's wide entryway. Most likely, he needed to catch his breath rather than rest his feet.

Everett joined Pop, taking the other chair. They chatted while finishing their sodas. Everett caught Pop up on his parents' doings and his rodeo career.

"I'm proud of you, sonny."

"Thanks. That means a lot to me."

Where they sat afforded them a clear view of the distant mountains, their gentle slopes a soft green gray typical of late summer. The hot afternoon sun bore down on the parched ground, trying its best to drive all manner of man and beast inside. No wonder Pop felt winded.

After a moment, he said, "There's something I need to talk to you about."

Everett sat up straight. "Yeah?"

Finally, he thought, the reason Pop had summoned him home. Asking for help, admitting he was too aged and infirmed to keep up with the ranch, had to be hard for a proud man like his grandfather. Everett didn't push and let Pop make the request in his own time and own way. It was the least he could do.

"I could use a hand with some things."

"Sure, Pop."

"As you can guess, this place is a lot of work, and my ticker ain't what it used to be."

"Whatever you need. You just have to ask."

The older man relaxed. "All right."

"I've got a job lined up. A youth rodeo coach. But that won't start until January. I have to finish the year out first." And qualify for the National Rodeo Finals in four months. If he did, he'd receive a nice signing bonus. "I told my buddy Rusty I'd rope with him at the Big Timber Rodeo later this month. In the meantime, I can carve out a week or ten days at the most. We'll get this place in order and maybe even ready to put on the market. I can also reach out to a few breeders I know and see if they're interested in Champ or the mares. If you can dig out their registration papers, I'll take pictures with my phone and—"

"What in blue blazes are you talking about, sonny?" Pop drew back and stared at Everett. "I'm not putting the ranch on the market, and Champ isn't going anywhere."

"What are *you* talking about?"

"And as far as the mares go, they aren't mine anymore. I sold them a while ago."

"Sold them!"

"Didn't have much choice. Property taxes and insurance were due. But I still own twenty percent of the foals they're carrying. That was the deal I cut with the collective."

Everett shook his head in confusion. "Collective?"

"I don't want your help selling the ranch. I want you to *manage* it for me. In exchange for half ownership. Only fair your mom and aunt get the other half. Champ would be yours, however. You'd have to keep working with the collective and allow the mares to remain here. That's part of the deal. My hope is you can rebuild the breeding business."

"I don't understand." Everett pushed to his feet. "You're not making any sense."

"What's not to understand? A horse collective bought the mares. I bred Champ to them in exchange for an ownership percentage of the foals. More'n that, they help me with the chores, and I let them keep the mares here. It's a business arrangement."

At that moment, a white pickup truck appeared and drove slowly to the barn, its tires making a crunching sound. Everett went still. He knew that truck. Four years ago, he'd been with Brody when his friend bought it brand-new off the lot in order to surprise his bride.

Not her, please.

"Well, lookie there," Pop said with a happy grin. "We got us some company."

"Why is she here?" Everett choked out the question.

"She drops by most days. She's head of the collective."

By then the truck had come to a stop. The driver's side door opened, and a young woman wearing jeans, boots and a baseball cap emerged. Her long blond ponytail had been threaded through the hole in the back of the cap and swung jauntily when she turned to open the rear driver's side door.

Macy. Brody's wife. No, *widow.*

Everett felt the weight of his guilt, as if he'd been stomped on by a two-thousand-pound bull. That was nothing compared to the blow he suffered when she opened the rear door and lifted out a little boy with dark curly hair and who was the spitting image of his father. With an easy, natural grace, she hoisted the boy onto her hip.

Everett grabbed the rocking chair, feeling disoriented and unsteady from the force of being thrust back in time. When he and Macy had last spoken, they'd been at the cemetery, her pregnancy just starting to show in the somber black dress she'd worn.

She caught sight of him then and reached for the side of the truck, her reaction an exact mirror of his.

No, not exact. Everett's expression was no doubt contorted into a mask of agony and grief. Macy, however, glared at him with undisguised anger.

Her mouth moved. From this distance, he couldn't hear her words, but he could read her lips.

"What are you doing here?"

MACY SOMMERS REMINDED herself to breathe. Five counts in, seven counts out. The coping mechanism was one she'd learned during grief counseling sessions, and it usually worked to restore her calm. Today proved no exception.

Her blurted question to Everett had been purely a knee-jerk reaction. She'd known he would be here. Pop had informed her of Everett's arrival days ago. Still, she'd been unprepared for the shock of seeing him in person after all this time.

Anger bloomed anew inside her. He'd been Brody's best friend and rodeo partner. And then, he'd abandoned her, breaking his deathbed vow to be there for her and the baby. She'd forgiven him, hard as it was. But she didn't trust him. Not for a minute.

"Put me down, Mommy."

Her young son, Joey, kicked and squirmed and wouldn't stop until he got his wish. Still, she held on, wanting to protect him from…from what? Everett? The past? Her own uncertainties?

"Now, Mommy. Please."

Joey was strong for such a tiny human being. He'd wear her out before long, and the last thing she wanted was for him to throw a temper tantrum. Not in front of Everett.

She lowered her son to the ground, and he immediately took off running with the fearless confidence of a two-and-a-half-year-old.

"Pop. Pop."

"Hello, there, youngin'." The old man opened his arms.

Joey plowed into him. Pop hoisted the boy onto his lap and enveloped him in a fond hug.

"I want to ride a horse."

"That depends on your mom." He glanced at Macy and winked. "She's in charge."

"Not today, honey. We don't have time."

Macy sometimes led Joey around the ranch on one of the older broodmares. It was a treat for them both. Joey was a natural and would no doubt grow up to be an avid, talented horseman like his father. If she could just keep him from rodeoing. She couldn't bear it if another person she loved left her behind for a life on the road.

She walked toward Everett, wishing she possessed a fraction of her son's confidence.

"You made it," she said when she neared.

Did he hear the challenge in her voice? Truth be told, she'd half expected him to bail on his grandfather. More than half. He'd bailed on her, after all.

He nodded. "Just got here. Pop was showing me around."

"Don't let me stop you." She retreated a step. "Come on, Joey."

He curled against Pop. "I want to stay."

Her son had a stubborn streak that landed the two of them in frequent power struggles. He also melted her heart with his silly antics, charming personality and sweet bedtime kisses.

Pop chuckled. "I'm happy to watch him while you check on the mares."

"I can't keep imposing on you," Macy insisted.

"He'll only get underfoot." Pop tweaked Joey's nose. "Won't you, youngin'?"

Joey burst into giggles. This was one of the many games he and Pop played, and reason why Macy adored their visits to the ranch. Joey had two sets of grandparents, but Pop filled the role of great-grandfather.

Glancing at Everett, she was struck by his expression, a mixture of tenderness and sorrow and grief. A far cry from his stoic, almost unreadable countenance on the day of Brody's funeral.

Wait. Macy looked closer. Grief, yes, but also guilt shone in his ruggedly handsome features. Did he feel bad about breaking his promise to Brody and staying away? Did he miss his friend and feel like a chunk of his heart had been ripped out? She hoped so. She hoped, like her, he spent restless nights tormented by regrets.

As much as she wanted to, Macy couldn't go back in time and change what she'd said to Brody that last fateful day. But it was different for Everett. He purposely chose not to honor his commitment to Brody by checking on her and Joey, and his actions hurt. She considered asking him why, only to clamp her mouth shut. This wasn't the time or place.

"I have an idea." Pop grinned in a way that had Macy convinced she wouldn't like what he proposed. "I'll keep an eye on Joey. That way, Everett can help you with the mares while you tell him about the collective. I was gettin' ready to do that when you pulled up."

Macy hesitated, absorbing this latest surprise. Everett didn't know about the collective. She had to wonder what else Pop hadn't mentioned.

Suddenly, she wanted to tell Everett everything. Not only about the collective but also her job and school and how well she'd managed these past three years—all without his assistance.

"Fine." She spun and returned to her truck, refusing to give him a chance to object. From the floor of the back seat, she removed a heavy brown medical bag that resembled a suitcase. Carrying it by the handle, she returned to where Everett stood. "Ready?"

His hazel eyes had always been easy to read. He didn't want to accompany her. Didn't want to be alone with her. But as much, if not more, he wanted to learn about the collective. The latter won out.

He extended his hand. "Let me take that for you."

She tugged the bag closer. "I've got it." As an afterthought, she added, "Thanks."

Assured that Joey was behaving for Pop, she

made her way into the mare barn. Everett followed, his slower pace another indication of his reluctance.

"You got your vet tech certification?"

He'd known that was her ambition. "Not yet. I'm close. I'll finish in the spring."

"Good for you."

She stopped at the third stall on the right. A chunky sorrel hung her head over the half door, her ears pricked forward inquisitively.

"Hello, Miss Roxie. How are you today?"

The mare snorted and blew out a gust of warm air that grazed Macy's cheek.

"Better, I take it?"

Roxie swung her head around to nip at her neighbor, letting the well-pedigreed and too-nosy palomino know that her interference wasn't appreciated.

"Quit squabbling, you two," Macy warned as she bent to open the case and remove a stethoscope. When she straightened, Everett stood beside her. Unable to stop herself, she retreated a step. "Oh."

"I didn't mean to startle you."

"I'm not sta… It's…" *Five counts in, seven counts out.* "I've had a stressful morning." That was an understatement. "I'm preoccupied."

"What's wrong with the mare?"

Horse care. A safe topic. Macy slid open the latch and stepped inside the stall, closing the door behind her. "Roxie had a concerning case of colic yesterday."

She ran her hand along the mare's belly, feeling Everett's gaze on her like the glow of a heat lamp.

Roxie, along with most of the mares in the barn, was about four months along in her pregnancy. Horses generally carried eleven months. Sometimes less. A year or longer wasn't uncommon. An ultrasound recently had confirmed Roxie's baby was developing normally, but things could, and sometimes did, go wrong. Colic in horses was always concerning and could be quite dangerous for a pregnant mare.

Relieved that Roxie exhibited no signs of distress, Macy pressed the stethoscope's diaphragm against Roxie's belly and listened. Hearing only typical gut rumblings, she moved the diaphragm around, then repeated the process on Roxie's other side. The mare amused herself by nuzzling Macy's ball cap.

"Enough," Macy chided affectionately and stepped away.

She gave Roxie a thorough visual examination, satisfied the mare appeared healthy. Next, she surveyed the stall. Roxie had eaten all of her breakfast, as evidenced by the empty feed trough, and done her business in the corner. Both good signs.

Still, she'd ask Dr. Beck his opinion at the clinic and stop by the ranch after work for another well check. Roxie was much more than a valuable broodmare and a key to her and her son's financial future. Macy treated all the collective's mares like they were her personal pets, spoiling and fretting over each one.

"You still work for Red Hills Veterinary Clinic?" Everett asked when she emerged from the stall.

She relatched the door and turned to face him. "I do. I manage the office. For now. Until I complete my certification."

"How's Dr. Beck?"

"Good. He's very accommodating with my schedule. In fact, I'm on my lunch hour right now. My mom watches Joey when I'm at work. I picked him up on the way here and will drop him off on my way back."

"They still live right down the road?"

"They talk about moving but haven't yet."

He'd been a regular at her parents'. Brody had brought him to the house often for birthday parties and cookouts.

A quick glance assured her Joey and Pop were doing fine. The older man was attempting to teach Joey the names of coins. Penny, nickel, dime and quarter. Which meant she couldn't use her son as an excuse to escape Everett.

"You were going to tell me about the collective," he prompted.

Okay. Business. That was fine with her. "Pop needed money to meet some of the ranch's expenses."

"He told me that much. Before you got here."

"Did he also tell you he'd been selling off horses for years?"

"I was aware of that."

"And you never asked why?" Her accusatory tone sounded harsh even to her.

"He said he was lightening his load. He wanted to retire."

In Everett's defense, Pop probably had said something along those lines. He'd refused to admit he was struggling to make ends meet.

"Your grandfather couldn't keep up with the ranch on his own. At first, he hired part-time help. Then the supply chain crisis drove the price of hay sky-high, and he could no longer afford help. There were repairs and maintenance expenses. The heat pump on the house broke down. The transmission went out on his truck. Eventually, he couldn't pay the back taxes and almost lost the ranch." She noticed a spark of emotion flitter across Everett's face and paused. "Look. It's not my intention to lecture you."

"It's all right, Macy. I deserve a lecture."

She'd heard him say her name a hundred times. Two hundred. She'd forgotten the way the syllables rumbled pleasantly in that low-timbered voice of his and how she used to love listening to him talk. They'd been so young that summer between their junior and senior years of high school.

Then Everett's dad was transferred for work, and he and his family moved to Santa Fe. Time passed. Macy started dating Brody and fell in love. When she next saw Everett after graduation, they were just friends. Nothing more. Now, they were practically strangers.

Clearing her throat, she continued. "Everyone in town loves your grandfather. He's lived here his entire life. Given to the community. Lent a helping hand to whoever needed one."

"Not many like him," Everett agreed.

"We, his friends, didn't want to see him lose the ranch because of being unable to pay back taxes. But he refused the loan we offered him. So, we came up with another idea. We pooled our resources and formed a collective—I used some of the life insurance money I got—and we bought the remaining broodmares from him."

"That must have cost…"

She could see Everett doing the math in his head.

"Yes. A lot. In addition, Pop retains a twenty percent ownership of the foals, which he'll receive when they're old enough to sell."

"What about any future foals?"

"That will depend. Hopefully, the collective will have enough money after the sale of the foals to pay Pop outright for any stud fees. Or we'll strike a similar agreement with him. Meanwhile, Pop allows the mares to remain here. In exchange, the collective members feed and tend the mares. We cover all their costs, including medical. We also keep up the mare barn and clean Champ's stallion quarters, saving Pop the trouble."

"Wow." Everett pushed back his cowboy hat. "That's something."

"It's a good arrangement for everyone. If all goes well, the collective will make a nice return on their investment and Pop, too, on his share of the foals." At the slight downturn of Everett's mouth, she asked, "What's wrong?"

"Nothing."

"You disapprove?"

"It's not that." He shifted uncomfortably. "Can I ask who else is in the collective?"

"There are five of us altogether. Me, Kinsley Karston, Sheriff Andy, Glynnis Pottinger, and the Hays family. They're the new owners of Hayloft Feed and Tack Store and a valuable addition to the collective. They supply our feed at cost, which is a huge savings."

"The local sheriff is a member?"

"No, no. Nothing like that." Macy shook her head. "His real name is Roy Gleason, and he's a retired real estate broker. But everyone calls him Sheriff Andy. You'll see why when you meet him. He looks just like Andy Griffith from the old TV show."

"Thank you," Everett said, his demeanor changing. "For helping Pop. None of us realized how bad his finances had gotten."

"You know your grandfather. He's very private and not one to talk about his problems. The only reason any of us found out he owed back taxes is someone spotted a notice in the newspaper. If he hadn't paid the back taxes, he'd have lost the ranch."

Everett gave a start, the news clearly unexpected. "I wish he'd told me."

"What would you have done?"

He hesitated. "I'm not sure."

"That's what I thought." Returning the stethoscope to the case, she grabbed the handle and started to walk away.

Everett stopped her before she got two steps. "What does that mean?"

She stared down at where his large, strong fingers rested gently on her upper arm. He immediately let go.

"Sorry."

She nodded, not trusting her voice. Rather than feel threatening, his touch had evoked old memories from their brief period of dating she'd all but forgotten.

"I have to get going." That was only half-true. Dr. Beck had given her extra time off in case Roxie was in distress. "I'll be back around six."

"I can keep watch on Roxie and save you a trip. I'll call if there's any change in her condition."

She wanted to object. But Everett was experienced with horses and would recognize the signs of colic. "Thanks. Guess I'll see you in the morning, then."

"Is your number the same?"

"Yes."

He hadn't deleted her contact info. She'd saved his, too.

They walked to where Pop sat, bouncing Joey on his knee.

"Come on, honey." Macy reached for Joey's hand. "Time for us to leave."

He pouted. "I want to stay."

Pop lifted Joey from his lap and set him on the ground, then, with a low grunt, rose on unsteady legs. "I was hoping the three of us could have a chat."

"About what?" Macy asked, suddenly wary.

Pop grinned. "Our new arrangement."

"I don't understand." She glanced at Everett, who wore a puzzled expression.

"Let's go inside where it's not so hot," the old man suggested.

"Pop." Macy gave him the same warning stare she gave Joey when he was about to reach for something off-limits.

"What arrangement?" Everett asked.

"With you." Pop turned to Macy, his grin widening. "Everett will be taking over management of the ranch and ownership of Champ. The collective will be working with him from now on."

Macy didn't believe her ears. "Is that true?"

She turned toward him, seeing the same shock she felt reflected on his face.

CHAPTER TWO

WHATEVER RESPONSE EVERETT might have given was interrupted by Joey's abrupt loud wailing. He didn't stop to think. He dived forward, grabbed the crying boy and cradled him against his chest.

"Hey, sport. You okay? What happened?" He examined Joey for any obvious signs of injury and found none. Then again, he could fill at most a sticky note with all he knew about kids.

Macy materialized beside him. The medical case lay on the ground where she'd dropped it. "Honey, what happened? Are you hurt?"

With tears in his eyes, the little boy held up his index finger, displaying a small but angry red scratch. "I have an owie."

"Move your finger for Mommy," Macy said.

He did, bending it into a hook. "The chair bit me."

"Bit you? That must have hurt." Her distress visibly drained from her face.

Joey's, too.

"The chair's old," Everett explained. "There's

probably a sharp piece of wicker sticking out. Is that what happened, sport?"

Joey tipped his head back and, for the first time, looked squarely at Everett. His dark eyes widened, and he made a little noise that sounded like the beginnings of a whine.

"It's okay. I'm a friend of your dad's."

Beside him, Macy inhaled sharply.

"Well, I was…and a friend of your mom's." Everett tried again. "I'm not going to hurt you. Just ask Pop. He's my grandfather and will vouch for me."

"I'll take him." Macy held out her arms.

"Sure." Everett released the boy. "You be good for your mom, okay?"

To his surprise, Joey smiled at him, stunning Everett again with his resemblance to his late father.

"I'm a good boy."

Macy enveloped him in a fierce hug and kissed his scratched finger. "Yes, you are."

Everett's chest tightened with emotion. The two of them were alone in the world because of him. He was supposed to have been driving the day of the collision outside of Kingman. Instead, he'd been napping in the back seat, the result of celebrating too hard the previous night and getting too little sleep.

He'd never had the courage to tell Macy. Instead, he'd withdrawn from their friendship and rarely returned to Wickenburg, breaking the promise he'd made to Brody minutes before he died in the hospital ER and two hours before his new widow arrived. When she'd sobbed and clung to him, it was all Everett could do not to push her away and run out of the hospital.

"I've got first aid supplies," Pop said and hitched a thumb toward the house. "We can talk while you bandage him up."

"Now's maybe not a good time for a talk," Everett added. "Macy needs to get back to work."

"I have a few minutes." She balanced Joey on her hip. "And I want to know about this new arrangement."

Everett had been afraid of that.

They made their way inside and to the kitchen. He sat at the table while Macy washed Joey's finger at the sink. Pop returned shortly with some ointment and a bandage. He then retrieved three bottles of water from the fridge, which he set on the table before joining Everett.

When Macy finished with Joey's finger, she put him on the floor to play with an assortment of plastic tumblers and a potato masher she borrowed from a drawer by the stove. He was instantly enthralled.

She'd done this before, thought Everett. Her familiarity with the kitchen told him she was one of those helpful friends Pop had been talking about earlier. It spoke well of her that she didn't hold her anger at him against Pop.

"So, you're taking over the ranch," she said.

"He is," Pop replied before Everett could.

Unscrewing the cap on his water, Everett took a

much needed swallow and willed himself to remain calm. Getting upset with Pop would solve nothing. "We haven't had a chance to talk about it yet."

Pop refused to be deterred. "I'm giving him half the ranch and Champ. In exchange, he'll live here and manage the ranch. As part of the deal, he'll honor the agreement I made with the collective."

Macy turned her gaze on Everett, her raised brows asking a silent question.

"Nothing's been decided."

"It sounds like a fair deal." She sipped her water. "And if you don't help your grandfather, who will? From what he tells me, your folks can't return to Arizona because of your dad's job, and your aunt has a brand-new grandbaby she doesn't want to leave."

"Plus none of your cousins have the first clue about running a ranch," Pop added.

"Neither do I," Everett said. "Not really."

Again, Macy raised her brows.

"Bull riding and calf roping aren't the same as breeding and raising horses."

Her stare didn't waver.

Okay, okay. The truth was, Everett did know much more than his cousins. Their riding experience consisted of annual holiday visits to the ranch and trail riding in the nearby hills. And while inexperienced in business, he was the only grandchild the least bit capable of taking over for Pop.

Under different circumstances, he'd jump at

Pop's offer. The problem was, circumstances weren't different.

"I can't stay," he said. "I'm entered in the Big Timber Rodeo. It's two weeks away."

"You can skip one rodeo," she said.

"I told a friend I'd be his roping partner."

"He'll find someone else."

"I need to maintain my ranking. If I don't, I won't qualify for Nationals."

"Ah. Nationals." She folded her arms across her middle.

"It's fine, Macy," Pop assured her. "If he can't stay, he can't stay. I'll make it until the end of the year. You and the collective will see to it. Then he can return after the holidays."

The guilt feasting on Everett's insides took another giant bite. "I have a job waiting for me. If I qualify for Nationals, I receive a signing bonus."

"A job doing what?" Macy asked.

On the floor, Joey arranged plastic tumblers into an obstacle course and then drove the potato masher through it. His sound effects made it hard for Everett to concentrate.

"Youth rodeo coach for the Oklahoma Twisters."

She glanced away.

"I need a job," Everett said. "I can't rodeo my entire life."

That got her attention. "Taking over your grandfather's horse breeding business would be a job."

"Yes." But in Oklahoma, he could pretend he wasn't responsible for ruining her and Joey's lives.

In Oklahoma, he wouldn't have to see the anger and disappointment in her eyes and be reminded of his failures.

However, in Oklahoma, he wouldn't be caring for his grandfather and returning the favor to someone who had taught him how to ride and rope and set him on a career path.

"Pop and I need to talk—" He started to say in private but was cut off by a buzzing sound.

"Hold that thought." Standing, Macy dug into her jeans pocket for her phone. "It's work." She crossed the kitchen to the other side before answering. "Hello."

Joey paused playing to watch her.

"Look, Pop," Everett said.

"Don't you worry, sonny." The old man grinned, unfazed. "We're gonna figure this out."

Macy returned to the table, but she didn't sit. "I'm needed at work. The vet tech covering for me had a personal emergency and left." She stooped and began collecting the plastic tumblers. "Come on, Joey. Time to go. Give Mommy the potato masher."

Two minutes later, she'd rinsed the items and set them in the sink to dry. Then, she gathered Joey and kissed Pop on the cheek.

"I'll see you in the morning."

"I'll be here." He chuckled and blushed a little.

Everett rose. "I'll walk you out."

"That isn't necessary," she said. "You and Pop have your chat."

"I'll walk you out, Macy."

She lifted a shoulder in a suit-yourself gesture.

Joey dashed ahead of them toward the truck still parked by the mare barn. Macy didn't bother mincing words.

"Your grandfather had a serious heart attack. He can't run this place alone."

"I agree."

"Then, you'll stay?"

Everett wanted to speak first with his grandfather but didn't believe Macy could be put off.

"Pop needs more than help running the ranch. He needs a skilled caregiver. Part-time, at least."

"Hire someone."

"Or I could find a good nursing home."

She stopped in her tracks. "You'd put Pop in a nursing home?"

"I don't want to."

"Really?" she scoffed. "Because it seems like you do. He's giving you the chance of a lifetime. Half ownership of this ranch. Full ownership of a horse breeding business and a championship stallion. How many cowboys on the rodeo circuit do you know who'd give anything to be in your shoes? A lot, I bet. And you're going to turn him down. Why, for heaven's sake? Because your friend needs a roping partner? A possible job? Those are lame reasons." She ground out the last part.

"I gave my word, Macy."

"Your word? When did that become something important to you?"

Her remark cut deep. Deservedly so.

"Or is it only your promises to Brody that you can easily break?" she asked.

"I'm sorry."

Perhaps he shouldn't have told her. But she'd been desperate for a recounting of Brody's last words, and Everett had wanted to comfort her.

"Forget it," she said. "There's nothing you have to say that I want to hear." Without warning, she whirled on him. "But there's something *you* need to hear. If you attempt to sell the ranch, I'm going to do everything in my power to fight you. Not just because Pop deserves more than to be dumped in a nursing home. The collective, and that includes myself, have invested their hard-earned money in the mares. As head, it's my duty to protect our investment. And if we need to hire an attorney to enforce our agreement, we will."

Everett watched her load Joey into the pickup truck and then drive past him on her way out. He had no doubt, if pushed, she would carry out her threat.

"MORNING, SONNY. How'd you sleep?" Pop greeted Everett the next day with a wide grin and a steaming cup of black coffee.

"Not bad."

Everett didn't want to admit he'd slept poorly, spending the night kicking blankets and staring at the ceiling.

His restlessness had nothing to do with the guest

room's ancient, saggy mattress and everything to do with his mind's refusal to shut off. Events from yesterday, as well as the past, had replayed over and over like a video on an endless loop.

With, at most, four hours of sleep, Everett found himself easing into the early morning rather than charging full steam ahead. A long shower had marginally revived him. Enough he could fake it and not dim Pop's jovial mood.

Falling into a chair at the kitchen table where Pop had set his coffee, he took a long whiff. It smelled like heaven.

"Better quality sleep than in your truck, I reckon." Pop chuckled.

"A lot better."

Everett had spent plenty of nights zipped into a sleeping bag and wedged between his saddle and equipment trunk. He wouldn't miss that part of professional rodeoing when he retired.

"Thought I might've heard you tossing and turning." Pop stood at the stove where he scrambled eggs in a skillet. "No surprise, considering things didn't go so well with Macy yesterday."

"No, they didn't."

He and Pop hadn't talked after she left. Not about her or the collective or Everett taking over the horse breeding business. He'd needed time to process. Pop seemed to have sensed that and had chosen to avoid the subject. Instead, Everett had spent yesterday afternoon repairing a break in the pasture fence so that Champ and the mares could be let out during the day for some exercise.

Not together, of course. Everett had released Champ when he finished, and the stallion galloped from one end of the three-acre pasture to the other before slowing to a trot, his long mane and tail flying in the breeze. Pop had tried to hide his misty eyes and claimed watching the stallion was better for his ailing heart than any of the pills in his medicine cabinet.

Maybe he was right. There had been a spring in his step for the rest of the day.

As opposed to Everett's feet, which had dragged. If he was to put Pop in a nursing home, there would never again be days when the old man could watch his beloved horse run loose, his hooves kicking up dirt. Everett's actions would put an end to that. One more reason he'd been awake half the night.

Pop placed a heaping plate of eggs and toast in front of Everett. "Eat up. Folks from the collective will be here soon. They like to get an early start." He sat across from Everett, his own plate holding smaller portions. "That way, they have the rest of Saturday for themselves and their families."

"How long do they usually stay?" Everett took a bite of eggs. "Thanks, by the way. These are good."

"Depends on how much work's to be done and how many of them show up. They don't all come at the same time. The Hays are seldom here. The feed store keeps them busy. They send a delivery truck every couple of weeks with a load of alfalfa and grain. They give me a discount on feed for Champ."

"Macy mentioned that."

"They're good people. Everyone in the collective is. I hate to admit it, but they saved me from going bankrupt."

Pop's honesty surprised Everett.

"I could have lost this place," he continued, his expression sobering. "Then where would I have been? In some county-run old folks' home for people with no money and nothing to leave to my daughters and grandchildren. The ranch I spent my whole life building would belong to a stranger."

"You made the right decision."

Pop had saved his ranch. Except, with only his social security for income and the breeding business at a standstill, he'd be in the same financial straits before long. Property taxes and insurance were due in two months. The collective's resources were limited. Their bailout was a onetime deal.

Everett needed to convince his grandfather to sell the ranch on his terms. If not, the county or the court could force the sale.

Pop stabbed a clump of eggs with his fork. So much for his jovial mood. "We're on the same page, then."

"I'm going to be here a week," Everett said. "Maybe ten days. We've got some time to come up with a plan."

"A plan that includes you staying on?"

He recalled Macy's final words to him yesterday

about doing everything in her power to fight him. "What about hiring a nurse?"

"A nurse? I'm not an invalid."

Everett tried a different tactic. "Me staying is an option. But it's not the only one."

"It's the only one that makes sense." Pop pushed his half-eaten breakfast aside. He wouldn't regain any of his lost weight at this rate.

"I told Rusty I'd be his roping partner at the Big Timber Rodeo in Tucson, and that he could count on me."

"You can go and come back."

True. Everett could. But he'd have to leave Wickenburg again right away. If not, he'd risk not qualifying for Nationals and losing out on the nice signing bonus with the Oklahoma Twisters.

He chewed slowly and swallowed, his appetite also waning. "I made a commitment with the rodeo club. I signed an employment contract."

"I bet they'd understand if you told them why you changed your mind. No one would begrudge you taking over a family business. Heck, they'd probably respect you."

"I'm not sure about that, Pop. They're depending on me."

"I'm depending on you."

"I could run the breeding business into the ground. Leave you worse off than you are now."

Pop frowned. "What's the real reason? You can't fool me, sonny. This have something to do with

Macy? Nothing's been right between you two since Brody died."

His grandfather had always been astute, and Everett considered coming clean. Pop might understand and have some good advice to offer. Then again, he could accuse Everett of being selfish and thinking only of himself.

Why was he such a coward? He regularly climbed onto the back of a one-ton bucking bull without the slightest hesitation. Yet he couldn't bring himself to live in the same town as the woman whose life he'd ruined. A woman who, when they were seventeen, he'd adored and was later brokenhearted when his family moved away.

At eighteen, he'd returned to Wickenburg only to learn she was dating his best childhood pal. Everett had stepped aside, choosing to keep two friends rather than lose them, even serving as Brody's best man when he and Macy wed. He'd believed life had turned out as it was meant to be. And then he and Brody were struck by an oncoming vehicle traveling eighty miles an hour. Had Everett been driving, as he should have been, that might not have happened.

"I'm not a smart man," Pop said.

"That isn't true."

"Not book smart, anyway." He rested his forearms on the table and studied Everett. "But I've always been good at reading folks. Your grandma had some fancy word for it. I just like to think I pay attention." His wizened expression softened. "You're hurtin', sonny. Losing Brody was hard on you. And, maybe, you walking away from that crash with no more'n a few broken bones and bruises left you feeling bad and wondering why you were spared and he wasn't."

A jagged pain tore through Everett's chest. When he spoke, his voice sounded like sandpaper on wood. "They call it survivor's guilt."

Pop snorted. "More of them fancy words. But I'd say that sums it up." He sipped his coffee. "The accident wasn't your fault. Or Brody's. That other driver changed lanes when he should've stayed put."

"I..." Everett started to say he was supposed to be the one driving. It had been his turn. "I was napping in the back seat. If I'd been in the front seat with Brody or behind the wheel, then maybe—"

"You'd have died with him? You think that's what he'd want? What Macy would want?"

"No." But given the choice, she might have wished her husband survived and not his friend. "She misses Brody. And seeing me is a constant reminder."

"That girl is a lot stronger than you give her credit for, and a lot more practical. She has a son to raise. She doesn't waste time drowning in regrets or running away from guilt."

Pop was right. He did pay a lot of attention to people. He certainly had Everett pegged.

They both went silent at the sound of a vehicle driving past the kitchen window.

"Looks like the collective is arriving." Pop shoveled the last of his breakfast into his mouth.

Everett did the same, washing it down with his remaining coffee. He then gathered their dishes and carried them to the sink. "You cooked. I'll clean up."

"Fair enough." Pop ambled to the kitchen door where he tucked in his shirt and hitched up his jeans. "See ya outside."

Once he'd left, Everett checked the window, relieved to see the small compact car that had arrived didn't belong to Macy. He needed time to consider and reconsider his conversation with Pop before facing her.

CHAPTER THREE

ONCE THE DISHES were done, Everett retrieved his favorite cowboy hat from the guest room. This one had a handmade leather band with silver-and-turquoise conchos. When he competed, he stuck a turkey feather in the band for luck. He wondered if he'd need that today with Macy.

By the time he reached the mare barn, Pop informed Everett that another of the collective members had arrived—Sheriff Andy. The retired real estate broker was in the back, distributing salt blocks among the mares.

"Hello, Everett!" Kinsley Karston came from the direction of the stallion quarters, pushing a wheelbarrow with a scoop shovel balanced across the top. She must have been cleaning Champ's stall. "Welcome home."

"Hey, Kinsley. Thanks. How's school going?"

"Oh, I graduated last year." They talked a moment before she headed into the mare barn, the wheelbarrow bumping over the uneven ground.

Everett watched her go. He remembered her as a shy and quirky art student with pink hair and an abundance of piercings and who worked part-time in the local craft store. She'd swapped the pink hair for long auburn locks streaked with purple and lost a few of her piercings, along with her shyness.

Wandering over to where Pop occupied the same rocking chair as yesterday, he sat down and in a low voice said, "She grew up."

"Done well for herself, too." Pop wiped his perspiring brow with a red handkerchief, which he then pocketed. "Makes a lot of money selling those metal sculptures of hers in the tourist shops."

"Sculptures?"

"Animals, mostly. Horses. Wolves. Eagles. Roadrunners. Dang things are half as tall as you and cost a small fortune. Doesn't stop people from buying them to put in their front yards or gardens. She won some sort of up-and-coming artist award last fall. Really boosted her sales."

"I was wondering how she had enough money to buy into the collective."

"Talented gal. And a hard worker."

Sheriff Andy emerged from the back of the mare barn after that. Everett got up to introduce himself. The retiree had moved to Wickenburg ten years ago, and he and Everett had never crossed paths.

"Mr. Gleason. Good to meet you." He extended his hand. The salt-and-pepper-haired man did indeed resemble the iconic character from the 1960s sitcom, just like Macy had said, though much older.

"Same here, Everett. I heard you were coming home." He returned the handshake. "And call me Sheriff Andy. Everyone does. Used to have it printed on my business cards back when I was selling real estate."

"Thanks for helping out my grandfather."

"Are you kidding? Glad to do it. The mares were too good of an investment to walk away from. Their foals will bring a pretty penny one day." He tipped his head in Pop's direction. "I've asked your grandfather a dozen times to let me help him sell this ranch. I'm convinced he can get a good price. But he's turned me down every time. Have to respect a man who knows his mind."

Everett nodded, thinking he would file that piece of information away for later should he convince Pop to sell and move. *When* he convinced Pop.

"Sheriff Andy also handles the collective's finances," Kinsley said. "He's real good at that."

"I try to be useful."

"What can I do to help the two of you?" Everett asked.

Just then, Macy's white pickup drove onto the ranch. She parked behind the mare barn, alongside Kinsley's compact car and Sheriff Andy's luxury sedan.

Everett tensed. He cautioned himself to behave normally and let her take the lead.

Sheriff Andy clapped him on the back, startling him. "You go about your business. There are plenty of us here to handle what needs doing."

"All right. In that case, Pop, I'm going to get busy."

"Kinsley already fed Champ this morning, and I gave him a salt block."

"Good to know."

Everett started toward the stallion quarters. The storeroom was a mess. He intended to start there. Glancing over his shoulder, he noticed Macy watching him. He nodded. She continued walking without acknowledging him, lugging her medical case and with Joey dashing ahead of her as usual.

Okay. It was going to be like that. Everett didn't blame her. He wondered what she'd think of his conversation with Pop over breakfast.

After two visits in two days, Champ was not only accustomed to seeing Everett, he eagerly trotted out from his stall into the paddock, issuing a friendly nickering that turned into a foot-stomping demand for attention.

"Hey, boy. How you doing this morning?"

Everett went through the supply of equine vitamin and mineral supplements in the storeroom and chose two. He added them to a small bucket of grain, the only way Champ would willingly take the supplements. While the stallion munched away, Everett located a screwdriver and tightened the hinges on the paddock gate. Standing back, he surveyed the results, satisfied one less thing on his grandfather's ranch sagged.

Next, he removed pieces of jagged glass from a broken window, swept the aisle with a push broom and nailed down a half dozen loose boards before someone, namely Pop, tripped. When he'd finished all that, he cleaned Champ's hooves and followed that with a thorough brushing.

Periodically, he'd stop in his work and watch Macy, Kinsley and Sheriff Andy. The three collective members seemed to have an established routine and got along well. Joey was in high spirits and amused himself by collecting rocks. Like yesterday, Pop was keeping an eye on the boy. Everett suspected this was a normal occurrence whenever Macy and Joey were there and the reason why Pop had hurried outside right after breakfast. He liked both the company the collective members offered and feeling useful in some small way.

Everett observed Macy returning the medical case to her truck. There, she leaned against the hood and entered information into an electronic tablet. Probably tracking the mares' progress and making notes on their health.

Between caring for the collective's mares, her job at the clinic, vet tech classes and raising Joey, Everett doubted she had much free time. Maybe that was how she coped with her grief.

If so, he understood. He hadn't taken a single break from competing since returning to the rodeo circuit after Brody's death. His schedule provided a convenient reason to avoid returning to Wickenburg and obsessing about the accident.

Finishing writing a list for the hardware store, he decided to quit hiding and ask Macy if she wanted to turn any of the mares out into the pasture. She may be hiding from him, too, but this was business. Giving Champ a goodbye pat on the neck, he started toward the mare barn. At the same moment, another vehicle drove past the house and stopped near where Pop sat.

The collective apparently had a latecomer. Strangely, none of the other members made a move to go over and greet the young woman dressed in scrubs. Not even Macy, who merely offered a distracted hello.

Pop, on the other hand, pushed to his feet with the most vigor and enthusiasm he'd displayed since Everett's return. A broad grin lit his face and took ten years off his haggard features.

"Morning!" he called, a lilt in his voice, and skirted around Joey who played on the ground with his rock pile.

"Hi, Pop." The woman, an apparent health-care worker, opened the SUV's front passenger door in order to assist her unsteady occupant—an elderly woman whose braided white hair reached the middle of her back. At the sight of Pop, her pleasant countenance brightened, much like his did at the sight of her.

Everett ground to a halt, confused by what he was witnessing. He hadn't seen his grandfather this glad to see someone other than family in years.

Suddenly, Macy was beside him. "That's Susan Meyer and her granddaughter Callie. She helps with Susan's care."

"Are they more members of the collective?"

"Oh, no." Macy laughed. "She and Pop are, well, they're sweethearts."

Everett turned to stare at her. "That's impossible."

"Why?"

"Pop doesn't… He wouldn't…" Everett blew out a breath. He honestly didn't know what to say. His grandfather had a girlfriend?

IF MACY WASN'T still mad at Everett, she might have been amused by his surprise and confusion at learning his grandfather was dating. Although, Macy didn't think the elderly pair did much more than hang out together, swap stories about the good old days, discuss their long list of medical complaints and share the latest updates on their extensive families.

Still, they were adorable together. And if all they got out of the relationship was tender companionship, she saw nothing wrong with that. In her opinion, both of them had been widowed for years and were fortunate to have found someone.

Unlike Macy, who had zero intention of dating again. She was satisfied with dedicating her life to raising her son. She owed Joey that. She owed Brody that, too. Especially after the horrible things she'd said to him.

God, if she could only take back their last conversation. All the wishing and tears in the world hadn't changed the fact she'd argued with her husband mere hours before his death, accusing him of being selfish and not caring about her and the baby they'd have in five months' time.

Her throat closed. She couldn't swallow. *Breathe in, breathe out. That's it.*

"How long have they been seeing each other?" Everett asked from beside her.

They continued to stand there, eyes glued to Pop and Susan. Her granddaughter and nurse, Callie Hughes, helped her to the rocking chairs where she and Pop sat down.

Macy found her throat had relaxed, allowing her to speak. "A while. Before his heart attack. She was so cute, visiting him with us in the hospital."

"He never told me when I visited after his heart attack." Or Mom and Aunt Laurel who had stayed with him for several weeks while he recovered. His mom would have surely told Everett. "They mentioned friends dropping by. No one named Susan."

Macy considered. "Maybe he worried you and your family would be upset and think he was betraying your grandmother."

"We wouldn't think that. We loved Grandma and always will. But she's been gone almost ten years. If Pop has found someone who makes him happy, then we'd support him."

"Good. Because Susan's a really sweet lady. You'll like her. She had a mild stroke a few months ago. I guess she and Pop have recent health crises in common."

"Does she live with Callie?" he asked.

"She has a bungalow in one of those senior independent living communities. Callie drops by every couple of days and takes her to appointments or shopping."

Everett continued to stare, his puzzled expression turning contemplative. For her part, Macy contemplated *him*.

"Are you thinking Susan is the reason he refuses to sell the ranch?" she asked.

"She's gotta be one of the reasons. Pop has always been independent. He hates appearing weak and helpless, which is how living in a nursing facility would make him feel. Especially in front of a woman he cares for. He couldn't stand that."

"Then don't move him."

"But Pop needs help. More every day. What kind of grandson would I be if I left him alone to run the ranch and he had another heart attack, this one fatal? Or he fell, broke his hip and lay on the floor for two days?"

"Then don't leave."

He groaned.

"There are plenty of people coming and going who check on Pop," Macy insisted.

"There are also eldercare facilities in Wickenburg. Some decent ones, from what I researched online."

"You said yourself Pop would be miserable in a nursing home," Macy pleaded. "You can't do that to him."

Everett tensed. "I appreciate your concern and your help. I do. Pop would have lost the ranch without you and the collective." He faced her then. "But his care and what happens to the ranch aren't your concerns. They're my family's. Mine, most of all, because my mom and aunt are depending on me, and Pop asked me here."

Hurt, Macy drew back. Perhaps she had crossed the line a little. But that was no reason for him to put her in her place so firmly.

"Sorry," she muttered.

"No, I am. This is a lot to deal with all at once."

"It's okay." She blamed the residual emotions lingering between them. "And not to nag, but he does have a legal agreement with the collective."

"Which will be honored one way or the other. Either by buying you out or transferring Pop's interest to the new owner of the ranch. I won't let him default on your agreement."

Macy frowned. Everett sounded so businesslike. Which, yes, the collective's agreement with Pop was business. But it was also personal. Didn't Everett realize that?

Maybe he did, for he added, "If it comes to that."

"You're right. It's not my place to tell you what to do. But there must be another solution besides selling the ranch and putting Pop in a nursing home."

"Don't think this isn't hard for me, Macy. It is. I hate seeing Pop old and sick. It rips my heart in two. He was always so strong and capable and no one smarter when it came to horses. There wasn't a green colt he couldn't break or a piece of machinery he couldn't fix. Not a problem he couldn't solve with hard work and determination. I wanted to be just like him when I was a kid. Heck, I still do. People love him."

"They do. He's the salt of the earth. Kind. Friendly." Everett chuckled dryly. "And I'm not."

"You used to be, Everett." *You could be again*, she silently added.

"Things changed."

Her throat tightened again. "For all of us."

He reached for her, only to let his hand drop.

She stared at it. "What happened? We used to be close. If I was in trouble and Brody was unavailable, all I had to do was call, and you came. Did I do something to upset you?"

He refused to meet her gaze. "You didn't do anything. It's me."

"You act like you hate me."

"I don't hate you, Macy."

"Am I the reason you've stayed away?"

"No."

He answered much too quickly for her to believe him. The hurt from earlier hit her again, twice as hard. Something had happened. He just wasn't ready or willing to tell her.

She wished he'd let her in. Healing from loss didn't happen overnight. She could attest to that. But pushing away your friends didn't alleviate grief, only deepened it. She could attest to that, too.

"Would you have come home if you'd known about your grandfather's tax situation?" she asked.

"Would me coming home have changed anything? Even if I'd had the money to pay the back taxes and insurance, Pop wouldn't have let me."

"It's not always about money."

"You're right."

"Your grandfather needed his family."

"I'm here now," he answered stiffly.

"Not for long."

Macy reminded herself to resist being judgmental, that family dynamics were frequently complicated. She'd been a teenager the summer she and Everett had dated, and she didn't know his mom well. She'd met his aunt briefly for the first time when she and Everett's mom came out after Pop's heart attack.

Did Everett visit his parents in Santa Fe? Or did he avoid them like he did his grandfather? Why did Macy even care?

For Pop's sake, she told herself. She was fond of the old man. He reminded her a little of her beloved late grandfather, whom she missed.

Everett reminded her a little of Brody. No, that wasn't right. They'd been best friends and rodeo partners, but it was more than that. Being in his company evoked memories. Most, she cherished. Some, she wished she could forget.

"Sonny." Pop beckoned to Everett. "Come on over. There's someone I want you to meet."

"Excuse me." Everett tugged on his hat and retreated.

Macy blinked at the sudden sting of tears. Where had those come from? Mad at herself, she wiped at them with the hem of her T-shirt, ready to claim allergies if someone questioned her.

Thankfully, the collective members were busy finishing their chores: cleaning the stalls, pouring sacks of grain into the feed barrels, cleaning tack and grooming. Macy had given each mare an exam, monitoring their progress and noting it in her charts. To her relief, Roxie had shown no further signs of colic.

"Mommy, Mommy. Look-it." Joey raced over from his nearby pile of rocks, holding out his cupped hands. "I found a snake."

"A snake?" Macy forgot about Everett and their difficult conversation. "Joey, drop it now!"

Snakes were common in the desert, including rattlers. What if her sweet little boy was bitten? Venom would be deadly for someone of his small size.

"No. Look-it." He reached her and opened his cupped hands.

Macy nearly fainted—with relief. Joey had presented her with a yellow-and-black caterpillar. Not a snake.

"Oh, honey." She knelt in front of him. "You scared Mommy. That's a caterpillar. Like in the book Mommy reads you, *The Very Hungry Caterpillar*."

"Can I keep it?"

"I wish we could, but we can't. He needs to eat lots of leaves so he can turn into a butterfly." More likely, given they lived in the desert, this little fellow would transform into a moth. Macy didn't bother to explain the difference to Joey. At his age, he wouldn't understand. "Let's put him over there on that bush. Lots of green, juicy leaves for him to eat."

"I'm gonna call him Stinky."

"Okay." The name Macy used with Joey when she was trying to get him to take a bath. "That's good." They walked together to the leafy bush, which Macy hoped was edible to this species of caterpillar. "Put him on a leaf." She pointed.

Joey did, remarkably careful for a small child. Stinky clung to the leaf, unmoving except for his wiggling back end. Or was that his front end? Macy let her son watch. After a few minutes, he grew bored.

"I'm thirsty, Mommy."

"Me, too."

She took Joey's hand. At the truck, she removed a water bottle for herself and an organic apple juice for him.

"I wanna open it." He reached up with his hands, fingers extended.

"What do you say?"

"Please."

She handed him the squeeze bottle of juice, and he twisted off the plastic cap. While they both wet their whistles, Macy glanced over at Everett, Pop and Susan. Her granddaughter Callie was readying to leave. She did that sometimes, left her grandmother with Pop while she ran errands or visited one of her home health-care clients.

Why, Macy wondered as the nurse drove away, hadn't she suggested Callie's employer to Everett as a possible solution for Pop's care? Granted, convincing him might take some doing. But Pop knew Callie and had a connection to her through her grandmother.

Unless that made it worse. Pop might resist having someone he knew assisting with his personal needs as tasks like showering and dressing became more difficult. Telling him that Callie was a professional wouldn't make a difference. Not with someone as stubborn as Pop.

How would he fare in a nursing home? Despite receiving training, even the most patient caregivers wearied of grumpy, uncooperative residents, and Pop could be grumpy.

Macy smiled as Pop captured Susan's hand and flashed her a besotted smile. His lady friend beamed in return. Too bad, if Everett did convince Pop to move, they couldn't reside in the same nursing home. That would make selling the ranch easier. But she had her bungalow and was every bit as independent and resistant as Pop.

Everett had located an old wooden footstool to sit on. The three of them had formed a small circle and were engaged in lively conversation. Well, Pop and Susan were lively contributors. Everett listened more than talked, his features pleasant but lacking animation.

Giving her head a dismal shake, Macy chided herself for what amounted to spying. The thing was, she cared about Pop and Susan and, yes, Everett.

What was she not seeing? He and Brody had been like brothers. They were together the last moments of Brody's life. That had to have been difficult on Everett. Did he suffer from PTSD? Perhaps. And just because she'd made progress dealing with her loss didn't mean Everett had made progress dealing with his.

Returning home, seeing her, must be stirring up all kinds of unwanted feelings he'd avoid given the choice. Which would also explain why he wanted to sell the ranch and leave Wickenburg as quickly as possible.

She sighed. Such a complicated man.

"Come on, honey." She took Joey's empty juice container. "Let's head home. Mommy needs to finish her chores before lunch." Putting their discarded bottles in the truck, she thought about the overflowing dirty laundry hamper, myriad of toys strewn throughout the house and the chapters she needed to read before her next online class. "First, let's say goodbye to everyone."

Joey bounded over to Pop. "We're going home, Pop. Bye."

"You're not leaving already." Pop braced his hands on the rocking chair armrests and struggled to rise, his knees wobbling. "What about lunch?"

Macy wasn't the only one who noticed his unsteadiness. Everett did, too, and concern knit his brow. The older man had good and bad days. A lot of activity and people put a burden on his heart and tired him. He should probably rest. But he wouldn't. Not until the collective and his lady friend left. At the least, he should get out of the heat. A late monsoon season had sent the humidity soaring, and anyone with a lick of sense stayed indoors enjoying air-conditioned comfort.

"We'll eat at home." Macy thought Pop was referring to her sometimes bringing food for her and Joey.

"Nonsense," he said. "Susan and I are fixin' egg salad sandwiches for everyone. There's plenty."

"Oh, no. That's too much trouble."

Susan gestured to the soft-sided cooler on the barn floor beside her. "I already made the egg salad and brought bread. We just have to throw the sandwiches together."

Pop gave her shoulder an affectionate squeeze. "I have plenty of potato chips and a big jar of sweet pickles. Thought we'd eat early, about eleven, since most everyone needs to get going."

Eleven was an hour away.

Joey tugged on Macy's hand. "I'm hungry. I wanna sandwich."

"I'm not sure…"

"You could take Joey *r-i-d-i-n-g*." Susan spelled out the last word.

She and Pop gazed at Macy with such hope in

their eyes. Yet she held out, caving only when Everett spoke.

"Isn't egg salad your favorite?"

He remembered.

Not exactly an invitation, but near enough.

"Fine, but we can't stay late." She really had a mountain of laundry waiting for her. Weekends were never long enough.

"Wonderful." Susan clapped her hands.

Joey, too.

The hard lines bracketing Everett's mouth relaxed, and for reasons Macy couldn't explain, she was glad she'd decided to stay.

CHAPTER FOUR

MACY WASN'T LEAVING. Everett couldn't decide if he was glad or annoyed. Maybe a little of both. As much as she frustrated him, he liked being with her. More than he should.

Some advance warning about making lunch for the collective members might have been nice. Was that a regular Saturday thing or was Susan's visit the reason?

And speaking of Susan, why hadn't Pop mentioned her? No reason to keep their relationship a secret. She was a charming lady who seemed as fond of Pop as he was of her. Like Macy had said, they were a cute couple. And Everett would feel like a heel if putting Pop in a nursing home somehow caused him to end their relationship.

But Pop struggled to take care of himself. Here it was only midmorning, and he appeared ready to collapse. He may reach a point where he had mobility limitations. Or require heart surgery, followed by a lengthy rehab period.

But then again, here they were, planning on making lunch for everyone and grinning from ear to ear. Quality of life mattered, Everett supposed. Still, that didn't stop him from worrying about his grandfather.

Relaxing his features, he focused on the conversation between Pop and Susan. The two were comparing their different arthritis treatments.

In the mare barn, Kinsley and Sheriff Andy continued working up a sweat, though both had taken breaks to talk on their phones. Everett noticed the first few stalls had received a fresh coat of wood sealer, thanks to Kinsley. Sheriff Andy had repaired three saddle racks, showing himself as capable with a hammer and nails as he'd apparently once been with buying and selling real estate.

Engrossed in each other, Pop and Susan all but ignored Everett. Pushing to his feet, he placed the footstool out of the way where no one would trip over it. He considered seeking out Macy only to veto that idea. She'd tied one of the mares to the hitching rail and, given the way Joey skipped up and down the barn aisle, she planned to take him on that ride Susan had suggested.

"You going to be okay, Pop?" he asked.

"Susan and I are heading inside." His grandfather stood and then helped Susan up.

She showered him with a warm smile, which she then turned on Everett. "I'm so glad we finally got the chance to meet. Your grandfather talks about you all the time. He's so proud of you and your rodeo career."

Everett hadn't thought it possible, but he now felt

like an even bigger heel. She really was a nice lady. "A pleasure to meet you, too, ma'am."

As the elderly pair ambled toward the house hand in hand, another vehicle drove onto the ranch. Pop saluted as the car passed him and Susan. It then continued to the mare barn where it slowed to a stop. Everett decided the place was beginning to resemble a parking lot. Another regular occurrence?

He didn't recognize either the driver or the passenger and assumed one of them was a collective member. From the rearview mirror, a handicapped parking placard dangled. Before he could wonder about that, the front doors opened, and a gray-haired woman emerged from the driver's side. She immediately hurried around the car to assist her passenger, an unsteady gentleman brandishing a cane.

At the sound of a horse's hooves, Everett spun to see Macy leading a sleek sorrel with an almost perfect white diamond in the center of her face. Joey sat atop the mare, holding on to a strap attached to a bareback pad.

"Look-it, Mommy." Joey wiggled his legs, his face brimming with glee. "I'm galloping."

Macy and the horse walked out of the barn and into the open. "Yes, you are, honey. Hold tight. Don't fall."

Disregarding his mom's warning, Joey leaned forward and hugged the mare's neck with one arm, his cheek pressed against the springy mane. "You're a good horsie."

Everett watched, momentarily speechless. How proud Brody would have been to witness his young son riding, even if he was just being led around by his mom on a docile broodmare.

Macy stopped beside Everett, bringing the past forward to collide with the present. "That's Glynnis Pottinger and her brother Abel."

"I should have recognized him." Everett tore his gaze away from Macy and studied their newest visitor. "He and Pop are old friends."

"Don't feel bad. He has Parkinson's disease. It's taken a toll on him and left him gaunt."

"A lot of that going around. Pop lost so much weight after his heart attack, I hardly recognized him."

She started to speak, only to clamp her mouth shut.

"You're right," Everett said, guessing at what was on the tip of her tongue. "If I had come home more often, the sight of him wouldn't have been such a shock."

Macy nodded. "Well, you're here now."

"Yeah. To take away everything that's important to him."

She touched Everett's arm and stared at him in earnest with those expressive brown eyes of hers. "You won't."

"What if there's no choice?"

"There's always a choice. But don't decide today. Give it a week."

He wouldn't lie. He enjoyed the sensation of her

fingers against his skin. It wasn't the first time she'd touched him in a casual way. It was, however, the first time since their breakup years ago he'd felt a small zing course through him.

That was a shocker. From the day he'd returned to Wickenburg after graduation to now, Everett had never considered Macy anything other than Brody's girlfriend and then, later, his wife. This…attraction was new. And unsettling.

"I wanna go faster, Mommy," Joey insisted.

Everett shifted, and Macy's hand fell away. Good. The last thing he wanted was to give her the wrong impression.

"Will you?" Macy asked. "Give it a week?"

"Yeah. I can do that." His temples throbbed. So much had happened in the last twenty-four hours.

Abel Pottinger came just in time, distracting him from his thoughts. "Everett," he called. "My word. Is that you?"

"Excuse me." Everett dipped his head at Macy.

"No worries. I have a little cowboy who's raring to ride." She walked off, leading Joey on the docile mare.

Everett made his way over to greet his grandfather's friend. "Mr. Pottinger. It's good to see you, sir."

They shook hands. Abel's trembled uncontrollably.

"Now, now." He scoffed. "I reckon you're old enough to call me Abel."

"How are you?"

"Been better." He laughed good-naturedly. "Been worse. You remember my sister, Glynnis?"

"I do." He also shook hands with the woman whose resemblance to her brother couldn't be denied—though she was easily ten years younger and a foot shorter. The three exchanged small talk for several minutes.

"Well, I need to get going," she told her brother. "Can I trust you to stay out of trouble?"

Abel made a shooing motion with his free hand, the one not holding the cane. "You run your errands. I'll be fine. Pop texted me and said he and Susan are fixing lunch."

Texted him? When, Everett wondered, had Pop started texting? Or Abel? He grinned to himself, picturing the two old men sitting around texting each other. It was kind of funny.

"All right. I'll be back in an hour and a half. Promise me you won't overdo it." Glynnis gave his shoulder an affectionate pat and then hurried off.

"She's such a mother hen," Abel said as his sister drove away.

"She loves you." Everett wasn't sure how to ask without sounding offensive, so he just asked, "Can I help you sit?"

"I have a better idea."

"What's that?"

"I tag along with you. If you're up to some company."

"All right." Everett nodded. "I'm heading to the stallion quarters."

"Very good. I'll supervise while we catch up." Abel laughed again.

"I need to grab some tools and supplies."

"I'll meet you there."

"You sure?" Everett had his doubts about the older gentleman's ability to travel the uneven ground between the mare barn and the stallion quarters. "If you can wait a couple minutes, I'll just—"

"I'll be fine."

Abel started out walking at a sedate pace, relying heavily on his cane. Everett watched him, wondering if he shouldn't have gone along just to make sure there was no mishap. He didn't leave to fetch the tools and supplies in the mare barn until Abel had safely reached the paddock where he stopped to pet Champ.

Nearby, Kinsley was finishing up with the wood sealer. She had to leave right after lunch to work on a metal sculpture for a client and would return to complete the project another day.

"Take whatever." She made an expansive gesture. "The collective covers all of Champ's stuff, too. That's part of the deal we have with Pop."

"Thanks." Everett gathered what he needed. "Is Abel part of the collective, too? I know Glynnis is."

"Nah. She brings Abel by on Saturdays so he can get out of the house for a while." Kinsley flashed a dimpled smile. "We consider him an honorary member."

Everett hesitated, not wanting his question to

be taken wrong. "Is he okay? Getting around the ranch by himself?"

"As long as he's not climbing fences or digging ditches."

"Okay." Everett felt a little reassured. On his way out, he asked, "Is lunch a regular thing around here?"

Kinsley paused in her cleaning and leaned on the push broom. "Pretty much. We all take turns and keep things simple. I'm vegan and always bring chickpea wraps. Everyone eats them, but I'm pretty sure nobody really likes them." She laughed. "I told Pop changing to a vegan diet would be good for his heart. He's not convinced."

"You're fighting a losing battle with him."

She resumed sweeping. "I'm not giving up yet."

Everett sensed the genuine fondness Kinsley and all the collective members he'd met had for Pop. His grandfather was lucky to have the companionship of these people on a daily basis. Another thing he'd lose if he went to live in a nursing home.

At the stallion quarters, Everett found Abel inside. The sun was heating up by the minute, and he'd probably wanted to get some shade.

"You ready to start supervising?" he asked.

"You betcha."

Abel proved to be good company indeed and a decent helper despite his tremors. He was also something of a gossip.

"Your grandpa is a fortunate man. I had my eye

on the gorgeous Miss Susan for some time. Pop beat me out."

"Can you hand me a rag?" Everett bent over and applied wide swatches of wood sealer to the stall door with a paint brush. Inside the stall, Champ paced back and forth, snorting and shaking his big head. He disliked the strong smell of the sealer and was letting Everett know exactly how much. After a moment, he trotted through the connecting doorway to the paddock outside.

"Here you go." Abel passed Everett a rag and continued with his story. "They met at the senior center. Susan and I have been attending events there for a while. I dragged Pop along with me one day. This was before his heart attack." The older gentleman sighed. "The pair of them locked eyes, and that was that. The rest of us fellows didn't stand a chance with her."

"Looks like you two are still friends."

"Are you kidding? She wasn't interested in me to begin with. Gotta accept what you can't change. Besides, your grandfather is the only one willing to put up with my shenanigans."

The next hour flew by. Everett caught several glances of Macy and Joey on the horse. Parkinson's disease clearly didn't interfere with Abel's eyesight, for he noticed Everett noticing Macy.

"She's doing well," he said. "All things considered. Raising that boy. Working at the vet clinic. Going to school. Donating her time to the collective. Staying busy is how some people keep the sad memories away."

Everett wanted to ask Abel if he was referring just to Macy or him, too.

"It upset her when you didn't come home after Brody's funeral. She needed you."

"I know." Everett stood, his back aching as well as his heart. "I'm a jerk."

"Maybe things can change now that you're back."

"We'll see."

"She's fond of you. Always has been."

"The feeling's mutual."

"Is it?" Abel grinned. "Because the way you've been watching her, I was thinking your feelings run a mite deeper."

"No," Everett insisted. "Strictly platonic with us."

"You sure about that?"

"Hey, Everett. Abel." Macy appeared at the entrance to the stallion quarters. She had Joey in tow but no horse. At some point she'd removed her ball cap, and her blond hair hung loose around her shoulders. "Lunch is ready."

Everett couldn't move. All he could do was stare. She'd always been pretty. But three years and motherhood had given her a mature beauty.

"Come inside. We're waiting on you," she said and then was gone.

His pulse beat faster. His nerves hummed. Had she heard his and Abel's conversation? What would he say if she confronted him?

Abel took a step, using his cane for support. "We'd better skedaddle. Can't keep your strictly platonic *friend* waiting."

Everett obviously needed to work on hiding his emotions.

MACY STOPPED ALONG the fence midway back to the house. She wasn't ready to face everyone, convinced her face would reveal what she refused to admit to herself. Her heart had pinged when she saw Everett in the stallion quarters, staring at her like she'd walked straight out of his dreams. She'd needed to escape before she embarrassed herself by staring back at him in the same way.

"Hurry, Mommy. I'm hungry."

"Sorry, honey." She bounced Joey on her hip. "I had to catch my breath for a second."

That was an understatement if she'd ever heard one. What was wrong with her? Men had given her enamored glances in the years since she lost Brody. She'd ignored them, which was easy, considering no one had interested her.

And neither did Everett. Which failed to explain the ping. What was different this time? If anything, she was still mad at him for abandoning her and Joey and considering putting Pop in a nursing home. That was not the kind of man who tempted her to share long, lingering glances.

Besides, who was she kidding? After what she'd said to Brody during their fight before he died,

Macy didn't deserve happiness with *anybody*. She'd been an awful wife. A terrible person.

She'd accused him of loving rodeo more than he did her. Then, an hour later, the truck he'd been driving was struck head-on by another vehicle attempting to illegally pass. She'd never had the chance to tell him she was sorry. He'd died in the hospital before she got there.

Everett had talked to Brody in his last minutes and promised to watch over Macy and the baby. He'd told her as much, as she cried in his arms, consumed by grief and devastation. Except he'd left for good after the funeral. Far worse, he'd gotten the chance to say goodbye to Brody—a gift denied to Macy and one he'd wasted with a lie. How did he live with himself?

She'd forgiven him eventually. She'd needed to in order to move on with her life. Giving Joey the best life possible was her one and only priority now. That included growing her career by going to school and investing her money wisely, such as in the collective.

The ping from earlier turned into a stab of regret. Macy realized much of her anger at Everett was misdirected. In truth, she was mad at herself. But that didn't change the fact Everett had broken a deathbed promise to his best friend. And now he was about to disappoint his wonderful grandfather.

"Mommy." Joey dragged her name out while leaning his head way backward over her arm. Little children were so trusting. What if she dropped him? "Want down."

"Okay." She put him down, and they started walking.

One minute. That was all the time remaining to pull herself together before facing Pop, Susan and the collective. Hopefully, they'd be too busy with lunch to notice anything amiss with her.

"Where's Everett and Abel?" Kinsley asked.

She'd planted herself at the picnic table on the patio. Across from her sat Sheriff Andy, a paper plate with three sandwich halves and a massive pile of potato chips in front of him. The tall, silver-haired retiree had an appetite that belied his trim physique.

"The food will be gone if they don't get here soon," he said, taking a large bite from one of the sandwich halves.

"They're coming." Macy took Joey inside, where they filled their plates from the spread laid out on the kitchen table.

Pop gestured. "Lemonade's on the counter."

He stood beside Susan like a knight guarding his queen. She'd recovered well after her stroke several months ago, with the exception of balance issues. As a result, Pop rarely let her out of his sight whenever they were together. His devotion was sweet and, in a small way, made Macy believe in second chances.

"Got enough chips there, young man?" Pop asked Joey.

"Mmm-hmm." Joey nodded, unable to speak because of a full mouth.

The back door opened just as Macy finished pouring two lemonades. Abel entered first and then Everett. Both men removed their cowboy hats. Everett ran a hand through his wavy brown hair that he wore shorter than in years past. Macy couldn't recall ever noticing the way the ends curled at the nape of his neck.

She stifled a groan of frustration. This…whatever it was, had to stop. She had two choices. Eat inside on the family room couch—a safe but antisocial option everyone would question—or outside where Everett would likely join them.

Joey gasped. "Mommy. I spilled my potato chips."

She looked down to see half his chips on the floor. Bending, she made a cup with her hands and scooped up the mess. "It's all right. We'll get more."

Everett suddenly appeared beside him. "Here. Let me help you, partner." He took Joey's hand and led him to the table, where he lowered the bowl of chips to Joey's level. "Take what you want."

Joey gazed up at Everett with wide eyes.

"It's okay," Everett said, encouraging him.

Joey reached into the bowl and transferred three large handfuls onto his paper plate, his eyes hardly leaving Everett. Her son tended to be shy at first, though once he warmed up to someone, like Pop, for instance, he showered them with affection to the point of being a nuisance.

How would he act with Everett, should they wind

up spending time together? She didn't know how much, if any, experience Everett had with children. He had no siblings, no nieces and nephews. But he could have dated a woman with children. He might even have a current girlfriend that he hadn't mentioned to anyone. Was that the real reason he was so eager to return to competing?

Macy threw away the spilled chips, her emotions awhirl. If Brody had lived, Joey would likely be treating Everett like a favorite uncle. He might also be treating him that way had Everett kept his promise to Brody. She'd wanted that. It was, in a way, another loss. An unnecessary one.

"Let Mommy carry this." She reached for Joey's plate. "You can get the door."

He scampered off.

She nodded at Everett. "Thank you."

"He's a great kid. You've done a wonderful job with him. Brody would be proud."

"I've had a lot of help. My parents. Brody's parents. Friends."

Everett showered her with a tender smile. "I remember Brody saying almost those same words once in a TV interview he gave after a big win in Texas. That he'd had a lot of help from his family and friends. And you, too."

She also remembered that interview. They'd rewatched the recorded show a dozen times. And then, later during their fateful argument, she'd claimed that recording was the only thing she had of him sometimes.

"I… I…"

Macy hurried to the door before she burst into tears. She couldn't remember a more trying lunch. She should have gone home. Was it too late?

Outside on the patio, she sat Joey at the old wooden picnic table with Sheriff Andy and Kinsley.

"You need a phone book to prop up that boy," Sheriff Andy commented. "He's too short."

"What's a phone book?" Kinsley asked.

Sheriff Andy gawked at her. "How old are you? Fifteen?"

She lifted her chin. "I'm twenty-six."

"And you don't know what a phone book is?"

"A book of phones?" she guessed.

"Good grief, girl. It's a book with everyone's phone number in it. People. Businesses. Emergencies."

She held up her cell phone and wiggled it. "I got all that in here. And a GPS. And a search engine. And I can read the newspaper." She pressed a button and aimed the phone at him. "I'm making a video of you right now."

Sheriff Andy snorted a laugh. "You can't sit on a cell phone when you're too short for the table."

Whatever relief their amusing banter had provided Macy instantly vanished when the back door opened and Everett stepped out.

"Where's Abel?" Sheriff Andy asked.

"He stayed inside to talk to Pop and Susan. They're discussing some healthy lifestyle event at the community center. Trying to decide which one of them is worse off."

"Maybe I should get in on that. I need to change my diet. My blood pressure's been off the charts lately."

Macy could relate. Hers, too.

"There's nothing wrong with you, Sheriff Andy." Kinsley rolled her eyes.

"I'm seventy-one. There's plenty wrong with me."

"Wait till you're eighty-seven, like Pop and Susan."

"God willing, I live that long."

That elicited a laugh from everyone except Joey, who didn't understand adult humor, and Macy, whose mouth refused to work because Everett chose the seat directly across from her.

He lifted the top piece of bread on one sandwich half and arranged several potato chips on the egg salad before replacing the bread. Then he took a bite. The sandwich made an audible crunch.

She stared. She'd forgotten about this quirk of his.

He chewed, his brows raised in question.

Beside her, Joey removed the top slice of bread on his sandwich half and layered several potato chips.

"Now you're teaching my son bad habits," Macy said.

"How is putting potato chips on your sandwich a bad habit?"

"Hey, it's good." Kinsley took a crunchy bite of

her sandwich made with vegan bread and avocado spread. "I'm going to eat all my sandwiches with potato chips. Try it, Sheriff Andy."

He did. "Not bad."

Macy harrumphed. "You've corrupted everyone."

"Corrupted or inspired?" Everett grinned, the sparks in his eyes the first genuine ones since his return.

She felt a shift inside her. It had been like this once between them. Casual, comfortable joking around. Even after she went from being his girlfriend to being his best friend's wife. He'd treated her like a close friend.

The memory unnerved her. Macy hadn't believed herself capable of ever falling in love again. Brody had been her soulmate. People told her she'd meet someone, someday. But Everett? No. Impossible, despite their brief past.

He was still grinning at her.

"Try it, Mommy," Joey mumbled around another mouthful. Chip particles rained onto his lap. Thank goodness they were outside.

"You know what else is good on egg salad sandwiches, Joey?" Everett asked.

"What?"

"Dill pickle slices."

Joey turned to Macy, his eyes bright. "Mommy, I want dill pickles."

"Maybe next time, honey."

"I'll bring a jar." Everett reached across the table to give Joey a fist bump.

And then Macy's son did something completely unexpected and that caused her to suck in a breath. He returned Everett's fist bump and beamed at him in a way she'd once imagined Joey beaming at his father. It was hard to take, and she fought back tears. Yet, a part of her was touched by this charming interaction.

She contributed little to the conversation after that, hoping no one noticed. Everett chatted easily, making friends with Sheriff Andy and Kinsley, too.

When they were close to finishing their meals, he said, "Tell me more about the collective. I know Macy is in charge of the mares' health. She mentioned the Hays family provides feed at a discount."

"Also supplies," Kinsley chimed in.

"You handle the finances, right?" he asked Sheriff Andy.

"That I do. I keep the monthly books and file the annual tax returns. Though, at this point, we won't have any income until the foals are sold. I also worked with the attorney in drawing up our partnership agreements and creating the LLC."

"Partnership agreements? As in more than one?"

Sheriff Andy nodded. "There's the agreement the members of the collective have with each other and the one the collective has with Pop."

"Right." Everett nodded.

"I handle our social media accounts and website," Kinsley added. "But mostly, we're manual labor. Though, with all of us, the work gets spread out."

"Do you ever disagree?"

"Not often." Kinsley hitched a thumb at Sheriff Andy. "He's a pretty good mediator."

The older man chuckled. "It's easy when everybody's nice and wants the business to succeed."

"Business?" Everett asked.

"Yes, indeed. We all love Pop, but none of us are in this just for fun or to do a friend a favor. We expect to earn a return on our investment. A decent one, at that."

"Makes sense."

"But we won't earn that return on our investment if we have to move the mares and pay a hefty board fee to a different facility. This arrangement works, for all of us, because of our agreement with Pop."

Everett sat back, appearing to contemplate that last remark.

Macy couldn't stop herself and blurted, "Do you understand? If you force Pop to sell the ranch, you'll be causing problems for many good, kind people who helped him out when he was in trouble."

So much for his earlier grinning. Everett sobered. "I understand."

"Okay. Good."

He rose from the table. "And I hope you understand that I won't be strong-armed."

"Strong-armed?" Macy drew back.

"Look, I appreciate everything you've done for Pop. I'm glad you've told me about the collective, how it operates and its relationship with Pop. But I, *he* and I, need to decide what's best for him and his long-term health. That takes precedence. He had a recent heart attack and nearly died." When Everett next spoke, his tone had softened. "I promise you, I'll look at everything. And we can talk again."

With that, he walked back into the house.

"Hmm. That didn't go as expected." Sheriff Andy exchanged glances with Kinsley, who shrugged.

"Give him time," Macy said, realization dawning and, with it, a sympathy for Everett she hadn't felt before. "He's scared. He's already lost one person he loves. He doesn't want to lose another."

CHAPTER FIVE

EVERETT STOOD IN the kitchen with Pop and Susan, only half listening to them. His mind kept returning to his conversation outside with Macy and the other collective members. Admittedly, he hadn't considered how many others besides Pop would be affected if the ranch was sold.

He tried to concentrate on Susan, who was chatting about an upcoming community-wide garage sale. Her granddaughter and caretaker, Callie, thought Susan needed to downsize, and the garage sale would be a perfect opportunity to sell a few items.

She disliked the idea of parting with any of her treasured possessions as she referred to them, and Pop heartily agreed with her. Everett suspected the conversation was for his benefit—a subtle message that Pop didn't want to sell the ranch.

"It's not as if I use that china tea set," Susan said. "But I've always loved it. And it looks nice on the cherry side table. Not that I need a cherry side table, either." She sighed. "My bungalow isn't big, but I've already donated or gave away roomfuls of things before I moved in. I feel like I'm losing my life, piece by piece."

"I understand completely. Do what makes you happy." Pop patted Susan's hand. He'd finally sat down beside her after everyone had received their fill from the serve-yourself-style lunch. "There's no rush. You're still recovering from your stroke."

"Callie says there'd be less housework if I down-sized."

"Don't you have a cleaning service?"

"Yes, but she's worried I'll trip and fall, and she does have a point. My little bungalow is crowded. A person gathers a lot of things over the course of a lifetime."

"You could sell one or two items in the garage sale," Pop suggested. "Not too many and nothing important. Show Callie you're trying."

"A compromise." Susan cupped his wrinkled cheek with her frail fingers. "What a good idea. You're so smart, Winston."

Pop gazed at her like a besotted schoolboy.

Winston? Everett stared in astonishment. Had he ever heard anyone call Pop by his given name? Not that he remembered.

If love were the cure to poor health, these two would be fit as any twenty-year-old. But they weren't fit. The sad truth was, the older one got, the harder it was to look after a house, much less a large ranch. From what Susan said, her grand-daughter seemed to recognize this. Susan, too, though she didn't like admitting it. Abel, who'd left to join the others outside, appeared to appreciate his sister's help rather than resent it.

Why was Everett a villain for wanting to lighten his grandfather's load and see him well cared for?

Because five other individuals had invested in a business arrangement with Pop that required him to keep his ranch. That was why. If not, they'd lose their investment.

How would Macy and the rest of the collective feel if Pop had another heart attack while performing some labor-intensive task? One that resulted in his death? Would they blame themselves for pressuring Everett not to sell the ranch? He'd for sure blame *himself.*

He had a sudden urge to get out of the house and clear his head. Maybe he'd throw a saddle on Champ and go for a short ride. Since the accident, he had a tendency to blow things out of proportion. A change in scenery and a little exercise often helped him calm down and put things in perspective.

On second thought, he'd wait until later. Macy and the others were still sitting on the patio, and he wasn't ready to face them again. Not this soon.

Turned out, staying or leaving made no difference.

The back door abruptly opened, and Macy entered with Joey. She carried a bulging bag with various pockets and zippered compartments slung over her shoulder.

"Hi." She directed her greeting to Pop. "We need to use the restroom."

"You know the way."

Joey ran ahead of her down the hall. Macy followed without so much as an eye flicker in Everett's direction.

That wasn't so bad. He'd expected a fiery glare.

The instant she disappeared around the corner, he said, "Hey, Pop. I'm going to take Champ out for a bit before it gets too hot. You okay with that?"

"He'll love it."

"I'll clean the kitchen when I get back."

"Never you mind about that." Susan shooed him away. "Your grandfather and I have it covered."

Everett needed no further encouragement and hightailed it outside before Macy returned. Yes, that was cowardly. No, he didn't want to face her. They'd already had two difficult conversations today. He wasn't ready for a third.

To his relief, Kinsley and Sheriff Andy had returned to the mare barn, taking Abel with them. They looked to be wrapping up for the day. Everett waved as he walked past toward the stallion quarters. Abel lifted his cane in return. Kinsley and Sheriff Andy gave slight nods. Everett, it seemed, had alienated two more people and given them reason to worry about their investment.

Four hooves on the ground beneath him. That was what he needed to clear his head and look at the situation with Pop and the collective from a different perspective. He understood where Macy and her friends were coming from. And, in their defense, they'd entered into their agreement before Pop's heart attack when circumstances were different. But Pop's health and well-being were a priority. His life might be on the line.

At the stallion quarters, Everett grabbed a halter from where it hung on a post. Champ had trotted inside from the paddock the moment he'd spotted Everett approaching and was waiting at the stall door. The big chestnut must have sensed they were going for a ride because he snorted lustily and stomped the ground with a heavy foot.

Everett slid open the latch and squeezed into the stall, careful not to let the eager stallion escape. "You raring to go, boy? Me, too."

He led Champ to the hitching rail at the end of the aisle where the stallion investigated everything within his tethered reach, his muscles quivering in anticipation of the ride.

For all his nervous energy, the well-trained stallion behaved under the saddle. Once he let off a little steam, that was. Champ didn't have an ornery bone in his body. But he was a big horse and strong-willed, like a lot of stallions, and required the skills of an expert rider. Everett decided to ride the hills behind the ranch where the up-and-down grade would give Champ a good workout in a short amount of time.

After saddling and double-checking the girth, he put on the bridle and fastened the straps. He'd noticed the tack could use a good cleaning and added that task to his mental list. As he worked, he heard the sound of departing vehicles. With luck, everyone in the collective would soon be gone, and he could avoid another encounter.

Untying Champ from the hitching rail, he headed outside. Best to mount in the wide-open should the stallion have a little buck in him. Everett had no desire to be slammed into a stall or tossed onto the concrete floor.

His concerns were for nothing. Champ behaved like a, well, a champ.

"Let's go, boy."

They trotted the length of the long dirt driveway to the road. No holding back on the reins slowed them down, forcing Everett to focus all his attention on Champ. Thoughts of the collective retreated to a dim corner of his mind.

A quarter of a mile later, he turned onto an often-used trail that took him and Champ into the gently sloping hills. Cottontails and jackrabbits both skittered across his path then disappeared into the brush. A red-tailed hawk watched them from its perch in a paloverde tree. Everett kept a lookout for rattlesnakes. Though they were usually more active in the early morning and at dusk, they could be out anytime during the day.

Champ settled into an easy walk, climbing the slopes as if they were no higher than dirt piles. After half an hour, Everett started to head home. The temperature was rising, and he'd forgotten to bring any water.

The moment they reached the road, Champ picked up speed. He was as eager to return to his stall as he'd been to embark on the ride. Everett changed their route on the way back, and they entered the ranch from the pasture gate. Champ pulled hard on the reins, his breathing growing heavy.

"Slow and steady, boy. We're in no rush."

Everett figured he'd check on Pop when he was done and then drive into town for groceries. An inventory of the refrigerator and pantry this morning had yielded few contents. They'd be out of food in two days.

At the stallion quarters, Everett untacked Champ and cooled him down with a quick spray of the hose. Everett then removed his hat and doused his own head, soaking his hair and neck. The relief from the heat was instantaneous.

After a final rubdown, he returned Champ to his stall. The ride had done them both good. Patting the stallion's neck, he said, "I'll be back at six to feed you dinner."

He no sooner walked outside than he came face-to-face with Macy. Apparently, by returning through the pasture, he'd missed seeing her truck parked alongside the mare barn.

She stood with her hands stuffed in the front pockets of her jeans, an unreadable expression on her face.

"Hey." An awkward silence followed. "I thought you'd left."

"Joey fell asleep on the couch while I was saying

goodbye to Pop and Susan. Rather than wake him, I let him sleep and helped Pop with a few chores around the house."

"You didn't have to do that. What about your laundry and studying?"

"I'll finish tonight. And, besides, Joey would have been a grumpy bear if he missed his nap."

"Thank you." Everett shifted his weight and waited. "Was there something else?" he asked when she didn't make a move.

"Yeah, there is."

"Look, Macy." He released a long breath. "Can we give it a day before we—"

"I want to apologize," she said, interrupting him. That was unexpected.

"I came on too strong earlier."

"I did, too."

"We both care about Pop, and I hate that we're not in agreement." She hesitated. "He told me you're reluctant to turn down the youth coaching job."

"I am," Everett said. "I gave them my word."

"You gave me your word once. That didn't seem to matter."

The bite in her tone hit him squarely in the heart. "You're right. I did."

"This job matters more to you than me and Joey."

He blew out a long breath. "I'm sorry, Macy. I shouldn't have abandoned you."

"Thank you for calling it what it was. Abandonment."

He considered telling her about his part in Brody's death, only to change his mind. This wasn't the time or place. Instead, he said, "If you think the coaching job is affecting my feelings about selling the ranch, you're wrong. My first priority is Pop and his health."

"I agree."

Except it sounded as if she didn't.

"I don't know the first thing about owning and operating a horse breeding business," he said.

"You know more than you think you do. You spent a lot of time here at the ranch with Pop while you were growing up."

He didn't agree but let that go for now. "Whether or not I can run the business doesn't change the fact Pop will eventually need help with his long-term care. And I have no experience with that."

"Few people do when they assume responsibility for a loved one. I didn't automatically know how to care for Joey when he was born."

"Caring for a kid isn't the same as an eighty-seven-year-old man with a stubborn streak."

"You're right." She tossed her ponytail over her shoulder as if to vent her frustration. "There has to be a solution. One that gives Pop the help he needs and doesn't put the collective in jeopardy. Maybe we can brainstorm while you're here."

"Sure. Why not?" When she lifted her gaze to his, hope rather than irritation shone in her eyes. It breached the barriers Everett had constructed around his heart and made him regret his unkind thoughts regarding her motives. "Let's brainstorm."

"Great." She clasped his hand in hers. "I'm sure we can figure something out."

Everett froze. Her fingers wrapped around his sent a shock wave through his system. A very pleasant shock wave.

He quickly snatched his hand away. If she knew that he was the one responsible for making her a widow, she'd hate him forever.

Pain and confusion shadowed her features, and she retreated a step. "What happened, Everett? We used to be friends."

He swallowed, his throat having gone bone-dry. "Nothing."

"Tell me. Please."

Before he could answer, Pop shouted from the house.

"Everett. Macy. Hurry! We need help."

MACY BROKE INTO a run. Everett was faster and beat her to the back patio. There, she discovered him and Pop standing over Susan, who sat awkwardly on the Saltillo tiles, cradling her left ankle.

Everett knelt down beside her. "Are you all right? What happened?"

"She fell," Pop said.

"I didn't fall," Susan insisted. "I took a misstep. The tiles out here are uneven."

"She went down like a ton of bricks, and I

couldn't lift her." Pop shook his head in disgust. "Blasted heart of mine. It's useless."

Macy patted his shoulder. "Don't blame yourself. We're here. Everett, can you carry Susan inside?"

All at once, the back door opened, and Joey appeared. Judging from his sleepy expression and the lines indented on his face, he'd just awoken from his nap.

"Mommy?"

"Hey, honey. Miss Susan fell and maybe twisted her ankle. Can you be a big boy and hold the door open for us while Everett carries her inside?"

Joey ducked into the house, swinging the door wide.

"You ready to go for a ride?" Everett asked Susan.

"Really, young man." Her wrinkled cheeks flushed with embarrassment. "That's not necessary. I'm sure I can walk."

Everett didn't argue. He simply hooked one arm under her knees and the other around her waist, lifting her as he stood.

"My goodness," she exclaimed. "You'll hurt yourself."

"I'm fine."

Macy hurried ahead into the house, making sure Joey didn't get in the way.

"I'm hungry, Mommy."

Hungry? They'd just eaten an hour and a half ago. "Give us a minute, honey. Then I'll get you some juice and crackers."

Pop directed them to the couch, hovering as if

Everett was carrying priceless cargo, which, in Pop's mind, he was. Pop then gathered two throw pillows. Once Everett had arranged Susan horizontally on the couch, Pop placed one pillow behind her back and the other gingerly beneath her afflicted ankle.

When Susan moaned softly, he fretted. "What do you need, my dear?" He took her delicate hand in his. "Water? An ice pack? Should we take you to the emergency room?"

"A glass of water would be nice." She smiled up at him, and he scurried off to the kitchen.

"I'll help." Jocy ran after him.

"I'll go, too, and get an ice pack. Her ankle looks swollen." Macy paused. "I think you should call Callie."

"Nonsense." Susan waved her away. "She'll be here shortly. No need for her to rush. Besides, you'll just worry her."

"Maybe she *should* be worried."

"I'm certain after the ice pack, I'll be good as new."

Macy doubted that. Older people's bones tended to be fragile. Susan might have fractured her ankle.

She crossed paths with Pop on her way to the kitchen while he was returning with the requested glass of water. Because Joey would only continue to pester everyone, she got him juice and some vanilla wafers from a box she found in the cupboard.

"Stay here, honey." She sat him at the kitchen table. "Mommy's going to help Miss Susan." A search of the freezer yielded one of those blue ice packs, which she wrapped in a clean dish towel and took to Susan. "Here, let's put this on your ankle."

With that task accomplished, she returned to the kitchen in order to keep an eye on Joey. Everett joined them, dropping onto an empty chair beside the boy.

"I got booted out."

"Pop is very attached to Susan," Macy said, "and a little possessive."

"Tell me about it."

"You sound mad."

"Are you kidding?" A hint of humor laced his voice. "I'm jealous. My eighty-seven-year-old grandfather has better luck with the ladies than I do."

Did that mean Everett was single? Not that Macy cared. She didn't care one whit.

"Pop has swag. No doubt," she joked in return.

Everett chuckled. Their recent easy, teasing exchanges reminded her of the days when they'd gotten along.

The next moment, they heard the sound of a vehicle outside. Macy checked the window, feeling abundant relief at seeing the SUV.

"Callie's here," she announced.

"Thank goodness," Pop said from the other room.

"Oh, my." Susan sat up and wrung her hands. "I think I might be in for a scolding. Now she'll have the excuse she's been looking for to force me to use a walker." She sniffed. "I don't want to use a walker. They're for old people."

Macy hurt for Susan. No one wanted to think of themselves as getting on in years and losing their mobility.

"I'll go fetch Callie," Macy said. "Let her know we're in here and not the marc barn. Come on, Joey."

"I wanna stay." He hadn't yet finished his juice and wafers.

"We'll only be a minute."

"I'll watch him." Everett gave Joey a friendly jab with his elbow. "That okay with you, sport?"

Joey beamed and nodded.

Macy couldn't quite bring herself to walk toward the door. She was about to leave her son in Everett's care. Only for a few minutes, but in his care nonetheless. Never in a million years would she have anticipated this.

"O...kay." She supposed it was all right. Pop was right there, though he was preoccupied. "Be right back."

On the patio, she waved to Callie, who turned the SUV around and parked next to Everett's truck.

She wore the same scrubs and comfortable shoes from earlier, having come straight from work. Her chin-length hair was scraped back from her pretty oval face with a wide headband.

"Hi." She smiled brightly. "I should have figured with this heat you'd be inside."

"Listen," Macy began when the home care nurse

got closer. "Your grandmother had a tumble on the patio."

Concern instantly filled Callie's expression. "Is she hurt?"

"She definitely twisted her ankle. Maybe worse. We wanted to call you, but she refused to worry you."

Callie huffed in frustration as they entered the door. "I swear she's the most obstinate person on the face of the earth."

"Which is why she and Pop get along so well. They're two peas in a pod." Macy opened the door and went in first. A quick glance assured her Joey hadn't come to some horrible harm during his brief time in Everett's charge. "Mommy will be right over there." She pointed. "You behave."

"Mommy, look-it." He held up his hands pressed together. "I made a horse."

Macy didn't understand.

Everett moved Joey's fingers into place. She saw it then, the shape of a horse's head.

"Ah." She smiled. "That's great. Very clever."

"Everett showed me."

"Nice." Where had Everett learned that? she wondered, and then was distracted.

"Grandma," Callie exclaimed while fussing over Susan's swelling ankle. "This is serious."

"It's nothing."

"It's not nothing. You need an X-ray. We're going to the hospital ER."

"No, we're not." Susan's vehemence triggered a flurry of raised eyebrows around the room.

"Grandma, please."

"I think I'd know if I broke my ankle."

"Not necessarily," Callie said, reexamining the ankle. She gently palpated the swollen area. "Does this hurt?"

"A twinge."

"A sharp or dull twinge?"

"It's a twinge," Susan insisted, a note of impatience in her voice.

"Well, you're not yelping in pain." Callie straightened. "Can you put any weight on your foot?"

"I haven't tried."

"Then, let's do it."

Taking hold of her grandmother's arm, Callie sat her up and carefully swung her legs off the couch and onto the floor. The instant Susan's foot met the plush area rug, she let out a soft, involuntary whimper.

"That settles it," Callie said.

"No, it doesn't."

"Be reasonable," Pop interjected. "You're in pain."

All at once, Susan started to sob. "I'm an old, useless woman fraught with health problems. Why would you want to have anything to do with me?"

"My dear." He sat next to her and cradled her hand as if holding a tiny bird. "Nothing could be further from the truth. You are not fraught with health problems. If either of us is, I am. You're beautiful and strong and vibrant, and I'm crazy about you."

Macy didn't know whether to burst into tears or song. Pop and Susan were so cute together.

"Grandma," Callie pleaded. "If we don't treat your ankle, it'll only get worse and might cause permanent damage. You already have balance issues."

Susan sniffed. "I honestly don't think I broke it."

Callie scrunched her mouth, contemplating. "Let me make a phone call. I may have an idea."

While she went outside onto the patio, Macy and Pop convinced Susan to lie back down on the couch and elevate her ankle. Macy readjusted the ice pack, then checked on Joey. He and Everett were seeing which of them could make the bigger juice mustache. Boys, Macy supposed, will be boys.

A moment later, Callie returned. "I have good news."

"I'm not going to the ER," Susan reiterated.

"I called Dr. Alverez from work. You've met her. One of her specialties is geriatric orthopedics."

Susan made a noncommittal sound which Callie ignored.

"She's willing to stop by your place in the morning before her first call. She'll examine your ankle and tell us, in her professional opinion, if you sprained or broke it. Then, depending on what she says, we either go to the ER or not. I'll stay with you tonight. Make sure you're doing okay."

"I guess that would be all right," Susan relented.

"In the meantime, she recommends complete rest, over-the-counter pain relievers, if you need them, icing the ankle and stabilizing it. I have an elastic bandage in my car."

"Wait," Pop interjected. "Doesn't Dr. Alverez live right off of Juniper Lane?"

"How do you know that?" Callie asked in surprise.

"She visited me a few times after my heart attack when I first came home from the hospital. She mentioned it." He glanced down at Susan and patted her arm. "That's not far from here. A mile at most. Much closer than your place."

"What are you saying, Winston?"

"You can't walk on that ankle. Why don't you stay here? In the spare room, of course. There's an old daybed in there."

"An old daybed for an old woman."

The way Pop gazed at her said he thought she was young and beautiful. "You'll be able to rest, and then Dr. Alverez can stop by here in the morning. Which will be much more convenient for her."

"I don't know," Callie wavered.

"Everett will be here." Susan shot her granddaughter a playful glance. "If you're worried that Winston and I will get into mischief."

Macy bit the inside of her cheek to keep herself from laughing.

"It's not that, Grandma."

"I'll be perfectly fine. And didn't Dr. Alverez say I shouldn't walk on the ankle?"

Pop sprang up from the couch with more pep than he'd shown in weeks. "I'll order pizza for dinner. Everett can pick it up. Won't you, sonny?"

"Um, you bet." He probably didn't know how to refuse.

"It's settled, then."

Callie groaned. "I'm feeling outnumbered."

"I won't let a thing happen to her," Pop insisted. "You can count on me."

She smiled, half defeated, half amused. "All right. I'll call Dr. Alverez on the way home. Then I'll come by later with some clothes and your toothbrush and meds."

"Call me," Susan said. "I'll tell you what to pack."

"I have an extra pair of crutches I can bring."

Her features fell. "Crutches?"

"Nonnegotiable, Grandma. You have to keep weight off the ankle."

"All right. You've convinced me."

Everett thought it might have been the other way around. Susan had twisted Callie's arm.

Pop turned to Macy. "Will you and Joey be staying for dinner?"

Her gaze cut to Everett who kept his reaction in check.

"No. Thank you, though," Macy said. "I need to get home. Those piles of laundry waiting aren't going to wash and dry themselves. And I really need to study at some point."

"You sure?"

Again, she glanced at Everett. This time, he nodded. Was that an invitation or him agreeing that she should leave? His vague signals were confusing. She wasn't sure what to do.

Joey made up her mind. He hopped down from his chair at the table. "I gotta go, Everett."

Gosh, the way he talked to Everett, so grown-up like, couldn't be cuter.

"All right, sport." Everett stood.

He accompanied Macy and Joey to the patio after she said her goodbyes to the others. She didn't bother insisting that wasn't necessary. He wouldn't listen.

"About earlier," Macy began while Joey went in search of more caterpillars.

"Can we talk about something different? Give this a rest until tomorrow?"

"I know you're tired of me rehashing the same old thing."

"It isn't that, Macy." His tone changed, reminding her more of the sweet, considerate Everett from before. "After watching Pop and Susan, I feel good. The best I have in some time. I'd like to sit with that for a while if you don't mind."

She could have hugged him in that moment. Thrown herself at him and squeezed with all her might.

Instead, she reached out and captured his hand. "I don't mind, Everett. Not at all."

She expected him to pull away like before. He didn't, and they stood that way for several seconds before parting, their fingers linked. The contented feeling lingered until long after Macy and Joey arrived home. She didn't fool herself, however. She imagined she and Everett were going to butt heads again over Pop and the ranch and the collective. But for this one afternoon, they were of like minds.

CHAPTER SIX

TWO DAYS LATER, Everett awoke to the sound of rain outside his bedroom window. Finally, they'd have a break from the oppressive heat, although, according to the weather app on his phone, a short one. Clear skies were in tomorrow's forecast, which meant the added agony of humidity.

For once, he beat Pop to the kitchen and started preparing breakfast. The old man insisted on playing the role of host, which included preparing all their meals. Everett needed to put a stop to that; Pop was wearing himself out.

Everett had spent the previous morning on chores and repairs around the ranch before running to town. He'd stocked up at both the hardware and grocery stores. Now, in addition to having the necessary material to start work on his long list of projects, the kitchen pantry was fully stocked. Good thing, as Pop had extended Susan's invitation to stay at the ranch with them after Doctor Alverez's visit yesterday morning, and Susan had required very little convincing.

After a thorough examination, the cheerful MD

determined Susan had suffered a sprain, not a fracture. She needed icing and rest. If she didn't respond to over-the-counter remedies and her pain continued or worsened, then she absolutely must see an orthopedic specialist and get X-rays. Susan promised, otherwise Callie would never have allowed her grandmother to remain at the ranch.

The home care nurse wasn't crazy about the idea to begin with, but Susan had insisted. She didn't want to put any weight on her ankle. Better she should stay.

They all knew she could have gone home. The ankle was an excuse for Susan and Pop to spend time together. He doted on her, and she let him, enjoying the attention. Everett just chuckled to himself.

"What smells so good?" Pop asked.

"Pancakes."

He ambled over to the stove to inspect Everett's culinary efforts and frowned. "They look funny."

"These are oatmeal pancakes. Very healthy for the heart."

"Sounds terrible."

"You'll like them. Especially when you add the organic maple syrup and fresh strawberries."

"I'd rather add sausage links."

"Sorry, Pop. That's not on the menu."

He grunted. "Last time I send you to the grocery store." The next moment, he broke into a besotted grin. "Good morning, Sleeping Beauty."

Everett didn't have to look behind him to know

Susan had entered the kitchen. The soft scuffling sound alerted him that she was using the crutches Callie had brought for her.

"Here. Let me help." Pop hurried to the table, where he pulled out a chair and relieved her of her crutches, leaning them against the counter. "Would you like some coffee?"

"Thank you, dear."

While Pop fussed over his lady friend, Everett finished preparing breakfast. Unlike Pop, Susan complemented Everett when he placed a large platter of pancakes and a bowl of sliced strawberries in front of them.

She clapped with delight. "This looks marvelous."

"Can I at least have margarine on my pancakes?" Pop asked.

"You can have unsalted butter." Everett set a dish on the table. "I tossed that big tub of yellow oil you had in the fridge. Unsalted butter is better for you."

"Says who? I like my margarine," Pop grumbled.

"He's right, dear," Susan concurred. "And, besides, with syrup, you can't tell the difference."

"Well, if you say so." Pop sliced off a generous pat of butter with his knife.

Everett sat across from them and waited until they'd both filled their plates, amused his grandfather had resisted when Everett suggested unsalted butter but changed his mind when Susan endorsed it. Whatever it took to get Pop to improve his eating habits was fine by Everett.

That wasn't all. Pop, Everett noticed, had shaved the last two mornings and wore his best everyday shirts. Susan also took care with her appearance. The evening of her fall, Callie had dropped off a small suitcase containing clothes and toiletries to Susan's exact specifications, along with her medications.

Some people might call Susan fussy. Everett, however, thought of her as a woman who knew her own mind, and there was nothing wrong with that.

Kind of like Macy, who was the definition of independence.

She hadn't really needed him to check on her and Joey these past three years. They'd managed just fine, especially with her parents nearby and Brody's, too. But that wasn't the point. There were things Everett could have done to make her life simpler. More importantly, he'd promised.

"Who from the collective is coming today?" Susan asked, taking a dainty bite of her pancakes.

"Macy, of course," Pop said. "She'll be by on her lunch hour with Joey."

She hadn't come by yesterday. Perhaps she'd taken a day off.

"And Sheriff Andy," Pop continued. "He's hauling a load of manure to the high school. Their landscapers use it for fertilizer."

"What a grand idea," Susan exclaimed. "All natural. And saves the school money."

"Sheriff Andy says it's a tax deduction for the collective. He would know, being the money guy."

Everett had learned that not a single day went by without someone from the collective appearing at the ranch. He'd offered to feed and tend the brood-mares while he was here. Macy wouldn't hear of it. The mares were the collective's responsibility. Specifically, *her* responsibility. When he'd countered that the collective helped with Champ, she claimed it wasn't the same thing.

At the end of breakfast, Pop and Susan insisted on cleaning the kitchen. Well, Pop cleaned. Susan sat and kept him company. The arrangement suited them both.

Everett excused himself to tackle more items on his list of projects. The rain had let up, and he wanted to replace the roof tiles on the mare barn and stallion quarters while it was cooler. Plus, this may be his only chance during his stay.

A short time later, he left the mare barn carrying an extension ladder and whistling a tune. Hearing an approaching vehicle, he stopped. Sheriff Andy must be here.

Except it wasn't the retiree's vehicle that pulled up, but rather a small, ancient motor home. The brakes squealed as it came to a stop, and the body rocked. New shocks were in order. A new fender and bumper wouldn't hurt, either. Dents and rust spots peppered the old ones.

Everett set down the ladder and walked over to see about this new arrival. As he neared, he recognized Glynnis Pottinger at the wheel and her older brother Abel in the passenger seat. A moment later, the side door opened and Glynnis stepped out.

"Morning, Everett." She bent and lowered the single metal step.

Abel appeared in the doorway. "How are you this fine morning?" His sister extended her hand, but he waved it away. "Gotta learn to manage on my own."

His descent was a slow process, hampered by his Parkinson's. Everett and Glynnis watched, ready to jump in and help. When Abel had two feet planted firmly on the ground, Glynnis accompanied him to the rocking chairs, which had been moved into the mare barn to keep them out of the recent rain.

"Have a seat, Abel."

He leaned on his cane. "I'd rather stand a bit. Been sitting all morning."

It wasn't even eight thirty.

"Don't tire yourself out," she cautioned.

"You fuss too much."

"You'll get wet if it starts raining again."

Their back-and-forth squabbling held an affectionate note. Glynnis clearly worried about her older brother, and he took her worry as she intended it: evidence of her love.

"Is Pop around?" Glynnis asked.

"He's inside with Susan. They should be out shortly."

She fidgeted, reminding Everett of her brother's involuntary muscle movements.

"I can go inside and get him, if you want."

She sighed. "I should have called first."

At that moment, a car drove onto the ranch, one Everett didn't recognize.

"That's my husband," Glynnis said. "Our daughter went into labor late last night, two weeks early. This is her first baby, and she's nervous. She wants me and her dad there. She lives in Casa Grande."

"Okay." Everett didn't understand anything about having babies, but a daughter wanting her parents there sounded reasonable to him.

"Our son, her brother, was supposed to keep an eye on Abel while we were gone. But he's on a business trip and won't be home until late Friday."

"I don't need a babysitter," Abel grumbled from where he stood.

"Abel, you can't stay alone." Glynnis addressed Everett, "The last time we tried, it was a disaster. He woke up disoriented from a nap and rolled off the couch. He couldn't get up and lay there for almost six hours until we arrived home."

"You're exaggerating," Abel grumbled.

"I'm not." She told Everett, "I know it's last minute, but we were hoping he could stay here until Saturday morning. He'll be okay in the motor home with someone peeking in now and then. It's self-contained. Water and propane tanks. Just need to run a heavy-duty extension cord to an outlet for power. We brought one. He has plenty of food and won't be any trouble. Since he and Pop are friends—"

"It's not a problem." Everett held up a hand. "I'm sure Pop won't mind."

"Really?"

"Really. What's one more houseguest?" Everett winked at Glynnis, then looked over at Abel. "You'll have to help me with my work around here."

Abel, who'd been frowning, brightened. "I can do that. Used to be pretty handy with a hammer and wrench back before I became such a butterfingers."

"Sounds great, sir. Now, let's figure out where to park this beast. I'm thinking behind the stallion quarters. The ground is level, you'll have shade from the overhang, and there's a motion activated security light on the outside wall."

By then, Glynnis's husband had joined them. "How's it going?"

Her relief was palpable as she filled him in on what Everett had said.

Next, her husband moved the motor home, parking it where Everett indicated. The car was just leaving when Pop and Susan emerged from the house.

"What's going on?" Pop hollered from the patio.

Everett and Abel started walking their way.

"Abel's going to be staying here until Saturday morning," Everett said. "If that's all right with you."

Pop helped Susan to sit at the picnic table. "The more, the merrier."

His grandfather meant it, Everett realized. Pop liked having people around. That was new. He'd led a mostly solitary life since becoming a widower ten years ago. Maybe it had something to do with his heart attack. Nothing like nearly dying to change one's perspective about spending any remaining years in the company of friends and loved ones.

Perhaps Everett could learn something from his grandfather. After the accident with Brody, he'd closed himself off to everyone. In hindsight, that may not have been the best move.

MACY PLASTERED A tired smile on her face. It had been a long day at Red Hills Veterinary Clinic, and she had a long evening ahead studying.

At times, she considered taking a break from school. She was juggling a lot, and she couldn't help but feel guilty about leaving Joey at her parents' so often. Not that he didn't receive the best possible care there. But she spent too many restless nights worrying about neglecting him when she should be sleeping.

Then, she'd recall her vow to give Joey the best life possible. As a vet tech, she could increase her earning potential. And with the money from the sale of the foals next year, she'd be able to start a college fund for him.

"Your total for today will be four hundred and eighty-five dollars."

"What!" The pet parent's mouth fell open in astonishment. "That much?"

"Actually, the final bill came to fifteen dollars less than the estimate of services you signed this morning when you dropped off Taco Bella." Macy slid the document across the counter to remind the young woman.

She huffed. "Are you sure? I don't remember."

"We wouldn't have proceeded with blood work and treatment without your consent," Macy calmly explained.

The woman squinted at the signature on the bottom of the paper as if questioning its authenticity. Macy waited patiently. A lot of people were distressed or panicked when they came into the clinic, especially during an emergency. Then, once the crisis had passed, they were suddenly upset about the money.

Owning pets was a commitment and, often, a costly undertaking. This woman's five-month-old shepherd mix had instigated a tussle with another pup at doggy day care—resulting in a nasty bite on her ear requiring ten stitches and her immediate expulsion from the facility—which might be the real cause of the woman's annoyance.

"Fine." She huffed again and produced the payment app on her phone, which Macy scanned. "I don't know what I'm going to do with her now while I have appointments."

Macy didn't bother suggesting puppy obedience classes, believing the owner wouldn't listen. Taco Bella was a sweet dog but also big and rambunctious. Not her fault her owner saw no need to enforce socialization skills.

As much as Macy loved dogs, she didn't currently own any. Too much responsibility when her plate was already so full.

One of these days, when Joey was older, she'd get him a dog. And maybe a pony. That was if Everett didn't force Pop to sell the ranch. She'd need an inexpensive place to board a pony. Anywhere else would charge a small fortune.

After processing the woman's payment, a tech led her back to an exam room where she'd be reunited with Taco Bella and receive discharge instructions from Dr. Beck.

Macy sighed and rubbed her temples.

"Hard day?" Jasmine asked. She was another of the clinic's vet techs and always wore a sweater over her animal paw–print smock regardless of the season.

"Yeah. I can't wait until Adam returns."

Their lone male tech was away on vacation for his brother's destination wedding, and he was expected to return on Monday. Macy had been handling both her office manager duties and filling in for the vacationing vet tech whenever a third pair of hands was needed.

"I can't wait for six o'clock," Jasmine said around a yawn. "Quitting time can't come soon enough."

Macy got off an hour earlier. She was the only one at the clinic with regular hours that didn't change from week to week. For that reason, she could stop at the ranch most days for a look at the mares.

She'd skipped going today at lunch. They'd just

been too busy at the clinic. According to Kinsley, who'd handled the morning feeding and chores, everyone was doing well. Everett had said he'd watch the mares, as well. She could trust him, right? Just because he'd bailed on her before was no reason to think he would again.

Still, she hadn't been to the ranch for two full days. That was too long for her comfort level. After work, she'd grab Joey from her parents' house and head to the ranch. The half hour she spent there would go a long way toward restoring her peace of mind.

The woman burst from the exam room, Taco Bella dancing alongside her and chewing on the leash.

"Come on," she said in a baby voice. "Let's go to the pet shop and buy you a doggy doughnut. You deserve a treat for being such a good girl and letting the doctor fix your boo-boo."

They tumbled out the door, enamored with each other.

Ah, thought Macy. How quickly pet owners forgive and forget. As do moms and dads, too.

An image of Everett rushing to grab Joey after he'd cut his finger on the old rocking chair surfaced. A dad would do that. Everett may not have much experience with children, but he seemed to have the instincts. Why, then, had he ignored her and Joey after the funeral?

Never getting a straight answer from him only increased her frustration and caused old resentments to resurface. She decided to find a time to raise the subject with him. It's true she and Joey had survived without his help, but that wasn't the point.

She pushed the question away as her cell phone rang. Retrieving it from the front pocket of her smock, she checked the display. Seeing Everett's number, she drew in a sharp breath. He wouldn't be calling unless something was wrong!

"Hello."

"Sorry to bother you at work, Macy."

"What is it?" At his serious tone, her apprehension skyrocketed.

"It's Roxie. I think she might have colic again."

"What are her signs?" Macy was already charging down the hall toward the office where she kept her purse.

"I found her lying down in her stall about fifteen minutes ago. I got her up, but she went right back down and tried to roll. I got her up again and have been walking her ever since. She keeps biting her side, and I think her gums might be tacky, but she won't let me get a good look."

"I'll be there as soon as I can. I have to pick up Joey first." If not for her parents participating in a pickleball tournament this evening, she'd have asked her mom to keep Joey longer.

"Don't worry. I won't let anything happen to Roxie."

She started to hang up, only to pause. "Thank you, Everett."

"Drive careful. No speeding."

"See you soon."

Before she left, she spoke with Dr. Beck. They discussed colic treatments and Roxie's history. He agreed to come out to the ranch and treat Roxie if necessary.

"Call me anytime, day or night," the perpetually cheery vet told her on her way out the door.

En route to her parents' house, she phoned her mom and explained the emergency. As a result, when she arrived, her mom had packed healthy snacks for her and Joey in case they needed to stay late at the ranch. It was already after five, and he'd get hungry soon. Macy was too upset to eat.

At the ranch, she drove straight to the mare barn. Everett was walking Roxie in the pasture. The mare kept stopping and required encouragement before continuing.

"Come on, honey." Macy unloaded Joey and gave him a box of raisins.

"Where's Pop?"

"I don't know. He must be in the house."

"I'll find him."

"No, Joey. Stay with me."

She briefly wondered if Susan was still here, but then her concerns for Roxie took over. Everett had led the mare to the pasture gate. Macy waved and motioned that she'd meet him in the barn. Next, she removed her medical bag from the truck and carried it over to the barn's front entrance.

"Stay close to Mommy, honey." As much as she

hated imposing on Pop, for once, she wished he was here to watch her son. "How's she doing?" Macy asked Everett the second he approached.

"The same."

"Can you hold her for me?"

"Sure."

"Joey, honey, get back here."

He'd started running toward the house. "Wanna find Pop."

"Hey, sport." Everett beckoned Joey with his free hand. "Would you like to go for a ride?"

Joey stopped in his tracks. "I ride a horsie?"

"Well, not a horse. Here. I'll show you. Come on."

The boy tentatively approached. Macy watched, a tad nervous. When Joey was close enough, Everett lifted him in the air and deposited him onto his shoulder.

"Hold tight."

Joey squealed, first with alarm and then with glee as he settled into place.

Macy almost squealed herself. A young boy riding a man's shoulders. Such a natural, normal activity. It was something she'd expected to see Joey do with his father. Not Everett. And, yet, there they were. Both of them wearing smiles, and Macy not at all sure how she felt about it.

Wait, that wasn't right. She was unsure how she felt about *not* being upset at the sight of them together. She was mad at Everett and still didn't trust him entirely. But he was good with her son, and he'd called her about Roxie.

"Okay," she said. "Let's get started."

The first thing Macy did was take the mare's vitals and check for laminitis, as it could mimic colic. She and Everett then discussed Roxie's eating and elimination habits during the day, which Everett reported as being off.

"We shouldn't let her eat or drink, for now," Macy said.

"Right."

Joey had removed Everett's cowboy hat and plopped it down on his own head. "Look-it, Mommy. I'm a cowboy."

"Yes, you are." Macy forced her gaze away from the brown hair curling attractively at the nape of Everett's neck to study the mare, who shifted restlessly from foot to foot. "I'm going to wait before administrating any flunixin meglumine. If she gets worse, I'll consult with Dr. Beck." The anti-inflammatory could sometimes mask colic symptoms. "For now, let's continue walking her and letting her rest every twenty minutes."

"If you want to take over, Joey and I can feed the rest of the horses."

"He can come with me," Macy said.

"I'll go with Everett, Mommy."

"All…right. But, I think you should take him off your shoulders."

"You heard your mom, sport."

Everett passed Macy the horse's lead rope and lifted Joey down. He didn't release Joey's hand.

Macy couldn't quite make herself leave. "Don't let him out of your sight. Joey is a magnet for trouble."

"I'll be good."

Everett winked. "You heard him. He'll be good."

She sighed. Never, ever had she pictured this day. Her relinquishing temporary care of her son to Everett, and her being mostly okay with it.

Twenty minutes later, Macy met up with Everett and Joey in front of the mare barn. They were sitting in a rocking chair, Joey on Everett's lap. Somehow, he'd located the snacks and had given Joey a fruit bar.

"How's she doing?" he asked.

"No change."

"But no worse?"

"Doesn't appear so."

"Ready for a break?"

"I am." Macy tied Roxie to the fence where they could watch her. She then returned to Everett and Joey and plopped into the empty rocking chair.

"Rough day?" Everett asked.

"Very. And it's going to be a rough night. I can't leave Roxie until I know she's out of danger."

"You're not thinking of staying all night."

"I am." Macy pushed with her feet, setting the chair into motion. "Roxie is too valuable and too important to the collective to risk. Colic can be very dangerous for a pregnant mare and her foal."

"What about Joey?"

"I'll take him over to my parents when they get home from their pickleball tournament. He can spend the night there. Then I'll come back."

"What about you?" Everett asked. "You can't stay up all night."

"I have a two-and-a-half-year-old. It won't be the first time. Besides, I have a bunch of reading to do for class."

"No." He shook his head.

"No?" Macy drew back to gaze at him.

"You and Joey stay here. Have dinner with Pop and I and Susan. Then you can bunk on the couch."

"I can't. My reading."

"You can, Macy. Use my laptop to log in to your class account."

"You already have a full house," she insisted. "I heard Abel's staying in his motor home behind the stallion quarters."

"My point exactly. What's two more?"

She hesitated.

"Let us help," Everett said. "Let *me* help."

She almost asked why he hadn't offered before, after Brody died, but she didn't.

And what he did next surprised her more than anything else he had done today. He reached for her hand and held it in his.

The familiar sensation took her momentarily aback, and she almost snatched her hand away. Only she didn't. She liked it too much, and that also took her aback.

They stayed like that for several minutes before she reluctantly withdrew. She shouldn't encourage him when she didn't know how she felt.

CHAPTER SEVEN

EVERETT STOOD AT Roxie's stall, watching the mare stomp her foot and shake her head in an angry demand for water and food.

"Sorry, girl. I get that you're feeling better, but nothing for you until Macy gives the okay."

Roxie wasn't appeased and lashed out with her front foot, kicking the wall. The loud bang startled her neighbor, and the palomino squealed in surprise.

"Enough already of your bad temper, Roxie. Why don't I take you outside where you can't get into trouble?"

Everett and Macy had alternated shifts during the night to watch and walk the mare. Pop, who was delighted at having two more houseguests, had prepared a simple dinner of spaghetti and salad—which Joey loved. Abel had joined them, too, and they all ate on the patio at the picnic table. Joey had loved that, too.

After dinner, Everett took the first shift with Roxie while Susan helped Macy make up the family room couch into a bed for her and Joey. Macy had relieved Everett around eight o'clock after giving Joey a bath and putting him down for the night.

The plan had been for Everett to catch five hours of sleep and then relieve Macy for the rest of the night so that she could then get some sleep. There was only one problem. Eight o'clock was too early for Everett. When he had finally lain down at nine thirty, all he could think about was the moment he spent with Macy, holding hands.

He'd expected Macy to instantly withdraw. Only, she hadn't, eventually letting go to search for Joey. Neither of them had mentioned the hand-holding or what, if anything, it meant.

Everett dozed off after a while. Too soon, his phone alarm played an obnoxious melody that never failed to rouse him. He'd dressed and dragged himself into the kitchen, careful to be quiet. After making himself a large mug of coffee, he'd headed outside to the marc barn. He and Macy had exchanged information on Roxie's no worsening and possibly improving colic before she went inside.

Now, at five thirty, the sun was peeking over the hilltops and turning the reddish-brown ground a glorious bronze.

Everett opened the stall door. "Going to be another beautiful day, Roxie. And hot."

He removed the lead rope from where he'd draped it over the stall door and fastened it to the halter. Because he'd been walking her forty minutes out of every hour, he hadn't removed her halter in between.

Rather than follow him, Roxie banged her nose against the metal waterer, making it clang.

"I know you're thirsty." Everett had turned off the water to her stall the previous evening. Horses with colic sometimes still ate and drank even when they were in pain, which could aggravate their condition. "My guess is it won't be long now." He patted the mare's neck.

The other eleven barn occupants nickered and circled restlessly in their stalls.

"I'll feed the rest of you in a few minutes." He wanted Roxie out of sight when he did. She was already agitated. Seeing her stablemates eat when she had to go hungry would be miserable for her.

Everett finally coaxed the mare out of her stall and into the early morning sunshine. They didn't get far before she jerked on the lead rope, lowering her head and trying to take a bite from a small cluster of dried grass.

"That's not good for you." Everett pulled her head up.

His cell phone promptly rang, and he checked the display before answering, grinning upon seeing his roping partner Rusty's number.

"Hey, buddy, how you doing?"

Rusty's booming voice with its strong Texas drawl filled his ear. "Tell me I didn't wake you."

"Nah, I've been up since one. Got a pregnant mare with colic."

"One of your grandfather's?"

"A friend's." He wasn't about to explain the collective to Rusty. Not now. "She's doing better."

"That's good. Anyway, I just called to find out when you're arriving in Tucson for Big Timber. We need to get some practice time in."

They did. Rusty wasn't wrong.

"I'm not sure. I have to look at my calendar."

His friend must have heard something in Everett's voice, for he asked, "You haven't changed your mind, have you?"

"No."

"Cuz if you have, I need to know now while there's still time to replace you."

"My plan is to leave here by the eighteenth. That'll give us at least three practice days before the rodeo."

"I'm calling you again on Friday," Rusty said, a note of irritation in his tone. "Just to make sure."

Everett must have sounded as unconvinced as he felt, and he grumbled to himself. Rusty had always been a good friend, and he owed him complete honesty.

"I plan to be there, pal. But, there is a chance something might come up. Things are more…complicated here than I anticipated."

"Your grandpa doing all right?"

"The heart attack took a toll on him. And the ranch isn't in great shape. On the chance I get stuck, you may want to ask Chet Lindon or Junior Abrahams to be your backup partner. If I can make Big Timber, I will. But I don't want to leave you in the lurch."

"Okay, okay. I just talked to Junior yesterday. He's interested. So, I'll just give him a jingle."

Everett heard his friend's relief, making him glad he'd been up front. Missing one rodeo wouldn't hurt Everett's ranking much. No worse than if he went to the rodeo and lost in all of his events, which could happen if he had a bad streak.

And he did still have every intention of making the rodeo. What had Macy said? He could go and come back? That did make sense. And it gave him flexibility.

"I hope you're not mad at me, buddy," he said.

"You kidding? Junior's twice the roper you are."

They both laughed at the joke. Everett liked to think of himself as better, but Junior was talented in his own right. And he was available.

"I'll still call you Friday," Rusty said.

"You got it."

By then, Roxie was tugging on the lead rope. She wanted to eat. Everett said goodbye to his friend and started to walk back toward the mare barn. Seeing a flash of movement, he glanced in the direction of the stallion barn. He thought Abel might be up and puttering around. He had a habit of sneaking Champ apple cores and carrot stubs when no one was looking. The thing was, everyone noticed. But they said nothing, letting Abel think he got away with it.

When did Macy normally rise in the morning? Everett checked his phone again and glanced at the house. The kitchen window remained dark, giving him reason to believe everyone inside was asleep. Maybe he'd tie up Roxie, go inside and get another cup of coffee. After the night he'd had, he could use a boost.

"What the—"

He stopped in his tracks as he caught sight of Joey running across the open area between the house and the garage where his and Macy's trucks were parked. A quick visual sweep told him Macy wasn't nearby.

"Come on, girl."

Everett walked briskly toward the garage, Roxie trotting to keep up. He may not know much about kids, but he figured the boy shouldn't be outside by himself, especially this early in the morning. He must have escaped Macy's watch.

"Joey. Hey, sport. Where you off to?"

The little boy stopped and pivoted. "Hi, Everett. Can I ride a horse?"

"You can pet her."

Everett wasn't going to put the boy on a horse, not without his mom there. And he wasn't sure about Roxie. Though normally docile, she had just come through a bout of colic and was understandably testy.

As Joey reached him, Everett bent and opened one arm. The boy held both his out, and Everett scooped him up, holding him close.

"Go slow," he said. "Be careful of her eyes."

Joey did neither. He patted Roxie on the hard

ridge just above her left eye and then tugged on her forelock. "Good horsie."

Roxie proved to be extremely tolerant, a trait that would come in handy when she had a rambunctious foal to contend with.

"Easy, sport." Everett moved to Roxie's neck where Joey's affection would be less bothersome to the mare. "What are you doing outside?"

"I don't know."

"Hmm." Everett wasn't sure if Joey misunderstood the question or really didn't know why he'd come outside, other than to explore. "I should probably have taken you back. How about we tie up the horse and go inside."

"Can I tie the horse?"

"You can help me." Everett looked around. "We'll use that tree over there."

They walked to the paloverde tree. Everett managed to keep hold of Joey and tether the horse to a low branch without anyone getting scratched.

"Pull this as hard as you can." He passed the end of the lead rope to Joey who tugged. The rope didn't need any tightening, but Joey was thrilled with the task, given his huge smile.

Yet again, Everett was struck by how much the boy resembled his late father. A renewed tightness formed in his chest. Yes, he felt guilty that this small boy had lost his father, and Everett should have been the one driving that day. But Pop was right. No one could have predicted what would happen. And the man who'd struck them was driving recklessly, crossing the double yellow line and passing when no passing was allowed.

He, more than Everett, bore the blame. He, more than Everett, had to live with the guilt that his actions had cost someone their life.

This tightness in Everett's chest was also the result of an unfamiliar feeling: protectiveness toward a child. And deep regret. He shouldn't have stayed away.

"I'm sorry, Brody," he murmured to himself.

"My name is Joey."

"Yeah, I know, sport."

They started toward the house, Everett still carrying Joey. At the same moment, the back door burst open, and Macy ran outside, shouting as her frantic eyes searched the area.

"Joey, Joey! Where are you? Joey, please answer me." She raced through the patio gate.

"Here we are," Everett called out. "I found him outside and was just bringing him back."

She came to a grinding halt. A sob escaped as her shoulders slumped, and she pressed her hands to her heart. After a moment, she raised her head, visibly more composed.

"You scared Mommy. I woke up, and you were gone."

Everett put Joey down. The boy ran the remaining twenty feet to his mother. "I helped Everett tie the horse."

"You did?" She lifted him into her arms and squeezed the stuffing out of him. Tears glistened in her eyes. "Next time, wait for Mommy." She buried her face in his neck.

Everett stood there. The protectiveness he'd felt for Joey a moment ago expanded to encompass Macy, too. He was suddenly very glad he'd told Rusty to line up a substitute roping partner. Everett didn't want to leave the ranch. Not now. Not yet.

"ENOUGH, MOMMY. No more hugs." Joey squirmed to get down.

Macy wasn't ready to let go. The panic she'd felt when she'd wakened on Pop's family room couch, disorientated and finding her young son missing, had yet to wane. Joey was her world. She'd lost his father. She couldn't bear it if she lost him, too.

"Okay." Releasing a long sigh, she lowered him to the ground. "But you stay right here."

"Can I ride a horse?"

"After breakfast." Macy glanced at Everett, and his tender expression tugged on her heartstrings. "Thank you."

"He was only outside for a few minutes, from what I could tell."

"A lot can happen to a small child in a few minutes. I'm grateful you were here to find him."

Everett nodded. "Me, too."

"I'm hungry, Mommy." Joey pulled on the hem of her shirt, wrinkled from sleeping in her clothes.

"All right." Macy looked around, noticing Roxie tied to the tree. "We need to feed the horses first."

"I'll do that," Everett said. "I was just going to

when I spotted this escapee here." He bent and patted Joey's head.

The little boy beamed up at him.

Macy wanted to cry and almost did. Her emotions were all over the place. "How is Roxie?"

"Much better in my opinion. But you're the expert."

"My medical case is still in the mare barn."

"I'm hungry." Joey's voice had taken on a whiny quality.

"I know, but Mommy has some work."

"No." He pouted and crossed his arms over his cute little protruding belly. "No work."

"I have an idea," Everett said. "I can really use some coffee. Why don't I take Joey inside with me. He can have a bowl of cereal while I put on a pot. Meanwhile, you take Roxie to the mare barn and give her a once-over. When Joey and I are done, we'll join you and feed the horses."

"Um…"

It was a decent plan with one exception. She worried that Everett spending time with her son was becoming a habit. Her little boy became quickly attached to people he liked, and Everett may be leaving soon.

Roxie whinnied, reminding Macy of her reason for being here.

"All right," she conceded. "Joey, you be good for Everett. You mind him, you hear?"

"I'll be good." He reached up for Everett's hand, grabbing on to his first two fingers.

"Okey dokey, sport. Let's go."

"Okey dokey," Joey repeated.

They walked off together toward the house, taking a piece of Macy's heart with them.

At the tree, she untied Roxie. By the time they reached the mare barn, Macy felt more like herself. The horse, too, apparently. She instantly buried her nose in the feed trough when Macy returned her to her stall, then came up quickly, a disdainful expression on her face, when she discovered there was no hay or grain.

"I'm going to take that as a good sign." Macy ran her hand along Roxie's flank, observing only a pregnancy curve and no digestive bloating.

The other mares nickered and stomped their feet. No one wanted to wait for Roxie's exam to be over before eating.

"Give us a minute, girls. Let's see if Roxie can have breakfast, too."

Macy found her medical bag where she'd left it by the rocking chairs and conducted a speedy exam. She tried to keep her mind on Roxie, listening to the mare's gut with the stethoscope and checking her gums, but images of Everett and Joey kept distracting her.

What kind of cereal did Pop have? Joey could be a picky eater and would probably consider heart-healthy cereal boring and tasteless. Maybe she should text Everett and tell him to fix Joey a peanut butter and jelly sandwich instead. Did Pop keep fruit on hand? Of course, he did. She should tell Everett to give Joey a banana or apple slices.

Roxie snorted and banged the feed trough with her nose, returning Macy's attention to the exam.

"You're definitely hungry." Macy patted the mare's generous hind end. "Let's try a light breakfast. See how you do with that."

Closing the stall door behind her, she pushed the wheelbarrow outside and across the open area to the hay shed. There, she loaded up with enough feed for all the mares and Champ. She then walked a thick flake over to the stallion quarters. Champ pranced in place with excitement at the prospect of a meal. Finishing with him, she returned to the mare barn where she fed all twelve mares. Roxie got half her usual amount. If she tolerated that well, Macy would give her more in a few hours. Lastly, she turned on the water.

She was just emerging from the mare barn, intending to head to the house and see how Joey was faring, when the back door to the house opened. Her little boy charged outside. Behind him came Pop and then Susan on her crutches. He held what appeared to be two cups of coffee. Giving Macy a good morning wave, they sat at the picnic table where, she assumed, they intended to enjoy the sunrise and each other's company.

Nice, but where, she wondered, was Everett?

"Mommy, I had oatmeal for breakfast." Joey bounded toward her, all smiles and bursting with energy.

"Oatmeal?"

"It was yummy. Everett cooked. I helped."

"Good. Where, um, is Everett?"

"In the house. Can I ride a horse now?"

"Maybe. Let me see. Mommy has to work today."

In truth, there was no need to rush. Macy had called Dr. Beck early last evening to report on Roxie. He'd told her to come in late if necessary. She was grateful, as she really wanted to see how Roxie responded to her light breakfast before leaving. She had to fill the time with something. Might as well be giving Joey a horse ride.

Her heart gave a sudden start at seeing Everett emerge from the house and start toward the barn. He also carried a mug of coffee. No, two. She suspected one was for her.

"Extra cream, right?" He held out a steaming mug.

"Thanks. And yes."

By mutual silent agreement, they strolled into the mare barn. Macy gave Joey an old empty coffee can so he could find more rocks for his collection. That way, he'd stay busy and not find trouble.

"Don't go far," she warned him. "Stay right here where Mommy can see you."

Joey skipped off.

"How's Roxie?" Everett asked.

They stopped in front of the mare's stall. Macy marveled at how their relationship had evolved over the last few days from strained to easy camaraderie. Then again, they hadn't discussed selling the ranch or finding Pop a good nursing home or why Everett had abandoned her after Brody's death. Plus, he'd been a real help with Roxie and intercepted her wandering son this morning. How could Macy not soften toward him?

"She's doing better. Her vitals were good. I gave her breakfast, half her usual amount."

Macy propped her forearms on the stall's half door, studying the mare. Everett stood beside her, right at the edge of her personal space. She didn't mind. If anything, she liked his proximity. That was unexpected.

Or was it? There'd been moments during that long-ago summer when they hadn't known what to do with the myriad new feelings they were experiencing. She'd purposely maneuvered herself as close to Everett as possible just to incite a spark. Then he and his family had moved away, and her teenage world had crumbled.

Later, when he'd returned to Wickenburg and she was with Brody, Everett had retreated to the friend zone. He'd made a point of keeping his distance, she now realized, in order to ensure things were comfortable for the three of them. Those were the actions of a decent and caring individual. Why hadn't she noticed before instead of taking him for granted?

"The feed trough's already empty," Everett said. "She was hungry."

Macy was going to give him the rundown on

Roxie, then changed her mind and instead said what was in her heart.

"You know, I was heartbroken when you and your family moved away."

His brows rose. "What made you say that?"

"I was just remembering."

He nodded. "The move was hard for me, too. Having to leave my girlfriend behind, my best friend, my football teammates, and finish my senior year at a new high school where I didn't know anyone."

"But you met people."

"Some. I couldn't wait to come back here after I turned eighteen and graduated."

Except, by then, Macy had fallen head over heels for Brody.

"It's too bad you couldn't have stayed with Pop," she said.

"Believe me, I begged my parents. They refused to budge."

"They would have missed you. I can't imagine being okay leaving Joey behind, even for just eight months."

"That wasn't the only reason. They didn't trust Pop to be a reliable guardian."

"Seriously?"

"He was a wreck in those days. Grandma had died less than a year earlier. He was…not himself for a while. Drinking too much. Staying out with his cronies at the bar or playing poker. Leaving every weekend for some horse sale. Mom was sure he'd lead me to ruin."

"He missed your grandmother. Her death was pretty sudden, as I recall."

"Very sudden. She was fine one minute and then the next, she fell and died from a brain hemorrhage."

His voice held a mixture of anger, grief and sorrow. He missed his grandmother, too. She understood what it was like, losing someone you loved with no warning. They both did.

"I'm sorry, Everett."

"Pop pulled himself together not long after that. But by then, I only had another month or two of school. It made no sense for me to transfer at that point. Not when I was planning on returning, anyway."

Had he hoped to pick up where they left off? She doubted it. By Christmas that year, distance and separation had impacted their relationship, and they'd drifted apart, no longer calling or texting or chatting online.

Macy swallowed a painful lump. They couldn't help what had happened; their lives went in different directions. And she'd gone on to have a wonderful marriage to Brody and become mom to an amazing little boy. But she probably could have handled things better with Everett. Warned him before he arrived back in Wickenburg that she and Brody were together.

"Macy?"

"Yeah." She shook her head, rousing herself.

"You looked sad for a second there."

"I was just thinking. Thank you, Everett. Seriously. For earlier. When I woke up to find Joey missing, I nearly had a breakdown." Her voice started to tremble as the emotions from that terrifying moment returned. "I'm probably overprotective, but after losing Brody…"

"Are you okay? You're shaking."

"Am I?" To her shock, she started to cry. A delayed reaction, apparently. "I'm s-sorry. Some days, it's hard." Her glance cut to Joey, who was playing quietly by the rocking chairs. "I didn't sleep much last night." That must be the reason for her high emotional state.

Before she quite knew what was happening, Everett's arm went around her shoulders, and he pulled her close.

"You have a lot going on. And I…" He paused. "I haven't made things any easier for you."

"No, you haven't." She sniffed, on the verge of crying again. "What went wrong, Everett? We used to be friends."

"I want to still be friends."

"Can we find a way?"

"I think so. Maybe."

She turned into him, resting her cheek on his chest. His arm tightened, and Macy sighed. It had been so long since someone held her, and she'd missed it.

Raising her face to his, she said, "I'd like that."

His answer was both unexpected and, Macy realized, may have been what she was secretly longing for: Everett lowered his mouth and pressed his lips to hers. She sighed and melted into the kiss. His arm went around her, drawing her closer. She stood on her tiptoes, giving herself over to the moment.

This wasn't their first kiss, but it might as well have been. It didn't compare to the awkward, innocent ones they'd shared as teenagers. She reveled in his confidence and his maturity and the changes the years had brought in him.

When she moved her hands to cup his cheeks, he suddenly broke off the kiss and stepped away as if she'd kicked him in the shin.

"I shouldn't have..." He faltered. "I'm sorry."

"Don't, Everett." An apology would turn the lovely moment they'd shared into something tawdry. "There's no need. I wanted you to kiss me."

"That's not it." He swallowed. "I—I've been lying to you, Macy. And I can't keep doing it. I care about you too much. And Joey, too."

Macy felt a chill course through her. "Lying about what?"

"The accident. Brody didn't have to die."

She straightened and stumbled backward, needing to distance herself from Everett more than she'd craved his closeness minutes ago. "I think you'd better tell me everything."

CHAPTER EIGHT

"LET'S SIT DOWN," Everett said, his stomach churning. He'd dreaded this conversation and hoped to never have it.

Macy sent him a worrisome look. "What do you mean, Brody didn't have to die? What are you saying?"

"Please." He gestured to the rocking chairs. No way would he tell her about the accident standing there in the middle of the mare barn. Her knee joints might not be giving out, but his were.

Nearby, Joey played with his rocks, lining them up in a long and crooked row. Everett worried the boy could overhear them, but he appeared focused on his activity, paying no attention to them.

"Does this have something to do with our kiss?" Macy strode to the rocking chairs and claimed one. "Because we did nothing wrong."

"*You* did nothing wrong." Everett lowered himself into the empty chair beside her.

"I understand if you feel like we betrayed Brody, but we didn't. I loved him. I still do. A part of me always will. But it's been three years. I don't believe he'd want me to spend the rest of my life alone. Not that there's anything between you and I," she hastily added. "We had a moment. That's all it needs to be and doesn't have to happen again. Not if we'd, *you'd*, rather it didn't."

"This has nothing to do with our kiss. At least…" Everett drew a breath. "Not *just* the kiss."

"What then?" Exasperation had crept into her voice.

"I like you. I always have. When I first came back after high school and you and Brody were dating, I admit I was jealous."

"I like you, too. When we're not disagreeing." She paused. "Is that what this is about? Are you still trying to convince Pop to sell the ranch and move to a nursing home—"

"No." How could he tell her? Revealing a three-year-old secret was no easy feat.

She began rocking the chair with extra force, his stalling clearly getting to her.

"You said you lied about the accident. I don't understand. I read the police report. The other driver was in the wrong and caused the collision. He was found guilty of vehicular manslaughter and served time, then released early for good behavior. But you know that."

"I was notified by the court."

Everett often wondered how the driver lived with himself. Did he, like Everett, have regrets and play the what-if game? *What if my wife had been killed by someone disobeying a traffic law? What if my three kids had been in the car with her and died, too? What if I hadn't been in such a hurry that day and been five minutes late to my appointment instead?*

"Okay. Tell me about this supposed lie."

Everett closed his eyes. Maybe this would be easier if he didn't have to look at her and Joey over there playing with his rocks.

"Brody wasn't supposed to be driving that day. It was my turn."

The rocking slowed.

"But I was tired and, to be honest, a little hungover. I'd been out late the night before celebrating our roping championship and wasn't in the best shape to drive. Brody volunteered. He told me to nap in the back seat and take over later. He said he had some things on his mind, anyway, and driving would give him a chance to think."

Her face took on a stricken expression, and a small whimper escaped her lips.

"I am so sorry, Macy. It's all my fault." Fresh guilt tore at Everett. "Brody would be alive today if not for me."

"You don't know that." She spoke in a voice barely above a whisper.

"I do. I should have been the one driving. If I hadn't gone to the bar the night before—"

"What, Everett?" she snapped and twisted sideways in her seat to face him. "You'd be dead instead of Brody?"

He waited a beat. "Yes."

"Maybe. Maybe not. You might have left twenty

minutes earlier if you weren't hungover and missed the man who hit you altogether. I mean, did you? Leave late because you had a slow start?"

"We, um…" They had left late. Everett remembered Brody shaking him awake multiple times in the hotel room bed and lingering in the hot shower.

"Maybe, if you were the one driving," she continued, "you wouldn't have been distracted by things on your mind, seen the other vehicle coming at you and swerved out of the way in time." Her face distorted into a mask of pain, and a bitter sob broke free. "I can do this all day. I've had plenty of practice over the last three years."

"Macy."

"You're not to blame for Brody's death. I am." The sobs came in force then, making speech difficult for her. Sharp intakes of breath punctuated every third word. "We argued on the phone the night before and again that morning. I was so angry at him. I wanted him to quit rodeoing, stay home and find a regular job. We had a baby on the way. And he was gone all the time. I was sick of having a part-time husband. I accused him of loving rodeo more than me and the baby. Those were the last words I said to him. I hung up on him after that. Hung up on him," she repeated and burst into gut-wrenching tears.

"Macy. Don't cry. Please." Everett scooted closer and rested a hand on top of hers. Rather than pull away, she clutched at his fingers in a desperate need for reassurance.

"He died before I had the chance to apologize or tell him that I loved him."

"He knew you did. Trust me on that."

"I'm a terrible person."

"No, you're not. We were on the road a lot. You were stuck at home dealing with a pregnancy all on your own. That had to be hard."

"I was selfish. He was winning that year and trying to earn enough money for when Joey came along. All I cared about was myself."

"He didn't think you were selfish. He understood."

"Did he tell you that? At the end? In the hospital?" Her voice broke. "You said he made you promise to look after me and Joey, but what else did he say? Did he mention our argument?"

"No. Not a word about that. Before or after the accident. I swear, Macy."

"Was he planning on leaving me?" Pain filled her eyes.

"Absolutely not."

"I don't believe you." She stiffened and tried to draw her hand away. "You two were best friends. You're trying to protect me. Or him."

Everett squeezed her fingers harder. "I would tell you. I swear. Brody never said a single negative word about you or your marriage. Ever. He loved you. More than anything in the world and was fully committed. He couldn't wait to be a father and talked about it all the time."

She sniffed, her composure slowly returning. Everett gave her a moment before continuing.

"He was unconscious right after the crash. I was able to kick open the rear passenger door open and crawl out of the truck. People had stopped to help. Someone called 911. I wanted to get Brody out, but two guys held me back. He was in bad shape, and they were afraid moving him would cause more injury. I tried talking to him through the window. He didn't answer. But we could see he was breathing. Then help arrived."

"You didn't tell me this before," Macy said.

"I probably shouldn't now. It's hard to hear."

"No, go on."

Everett cleared his throat as old memories assaulted him. Three years hadn't softened the blows. "The paramedics took me to the other side of the fire truck to examine me. They wouldn't let me watch. I kept asking about Brody, how he was, and they'd give some generic answer like the firefighters and EMTs were doing everything in their power to save him. We were taken to the hospital in separate ambulances. By the time they let me in to see him…" An intense pressure compressed Everett's chest. Breathing became a struggle. "He was alive but drifting in and out of consciousness. It was during one of his lucid moments when he made me promise to watch over you and Joey."

She nodded but said nothing.

"He asked me to tell you how much he loved you and the baby. I got my phone out and started to call you so he could tell you himself. But he… he lost consciousness again and didn't… It wasn't long after that he…he passed." Everett didn't tell Macy how he'd held Brody's lifeless body and refused to let go, having to be pulled off by a pair of nurses. "The doctor said the trauma he sustained was just too great."

It was the same explanation he'd given Macy when she arrived at the hospital and Brody's parents on the phone.

"God, I would give anything to relive that last day." Macy's tears started anew.

Everett's, too. He'd imagined a dozen different scenarios in his head, but all that had ever gotten him was more guilt and more frustration.

"We can't change the past, Macy. Dwelling on it does no good. Pop recently told me as much, and he's right. Brody's last words were of his love for you and Joey. That's proof enough his feelings for you didn't change because of an argument."

Sniffling, she wiped her tears with her free hand. She had a distant look in her eyes that Everett recognized all too well. He'd seen the same struggle to accept what couldn't be changed reflected back at him in the mirror many times. It had only been since this past week, and since coming home, that this had started to change.

Confessing to Macy and hearing her angst from that final day of Brody's life had lightened some of Everett's emotional burden. He hoped it was the same for her.

Their quiet moment didn't last long.

"Mommy, Mommy." Joey ran over, concern pinching his small features. "Do you have an owie?"

Everett released Macy, instantly missing her touch.

"I do, honey," she said and scooped her son into her lap.

"Where?"

She patted the area over her heart. "Here."

Joey leaned forward and touched his forehead to where she'd indicated. "Better?"

"Much better." She smiled and kissed the top of his head. "I love you, honey."

"I love you, too, Mommy. Can I ride a horse now?"

"In a few minutes, okay? I promise."

"Okay." He dragged the word out as he crawled off her lap and returned to his rocks.

"Brody would be proud of Joey." Everett watched the boy playing. "And of you for doing such a good job raising him."

"Is that why you stayed away?" Macy asked. "Because you think you should have been the one driving and died instead of Brody?"

"I figured you'd hate me if you knew the truth and deservedly so."

She started rocking again, albeit much slower. "I have no clue what I would have felt at the time. I might have been angry at you, it's true. But that's because you'd have become an innocent target for my grief and the rage I felt at myself. And that wouldn't have been fair."

"Not sure I agree with you," Everett said. "I made a big mistake."

She studied him then, her expression empathetic and without a trace of the anger she had every right to direct at him. "How hard it must have been for you, surviving an automobile accident when the other person died."

This was the second time since Everett's return that someone mentioned survivor's guilt. Was he that transparent? Or were people more understanding than he'd given them credit for?

He almost brushed off her comment. But Macy didn't need a reason to feel worse than she already did. Instead, he chose to level with her. She'd see right through him otherwise. "I've had some bad days."

"I'm so sorry, Everett." Her eyes misted again. "I should have realized what you were going through. Looking at me must remind you of Brody and the accident."

It did. That wasn't her fault.

"Stop." He held up his hand. "Do not pile on yourself. You hear me? You couldn't have known what I was going through."

"Well, no one could have known." She sent him a very mild chiding smile. "You avoided us."

"I regret that now for a lot of reasons. Including Pop. I should have been here for him. Kept an eye on him. Maybe he wouldn't have gotten so ill."

"You couldn't have prevented his heart attack," Macy insisted.

"But I might have realized he was in financial trouble before his debt became overwhelming."

"What did you say about being unable to change the past and not dwelling on it?"

"You're right." He might have chuckled if their moods weren't so somber.

"I know there are things about Pop's agreement with the collective you don't like," Macy said. "But it's not a bad deal for him. If the mares produce healthy foals, we all stand to make some money. He'll have enough to pay the ranch taxes and insurance for two years at least."

Pop wouldn't need that if he sold the ranch. The money could go toward his current and long-term health care. On the other hand, if Everett stayed and took over the horse breeding business, he could contribute to those expenses. However, that plan would rely on Everett succeeding at the business, which he'd have to learn almost from scratch. It would also still put Pop in a nursing home, since he'd eventually need more assistance than Everett could provide.

Could there be another solution? His gaze traveled to the two seniors sitting at the picnic table on the patio. They were having a great time. Neither of them was in the best of health, but they were enjoying life to the fullest.

Everett had been that happy, too, before the accident. Macy seemed to be recovering. Mostly. He imagined she had bad days.

"We'd be happy to show you the collective's

books and our business plan," she said, bringing him back to the present. "You can see for yourself how solid our plan is."

She wanted to convince him not to sell and let Pop continue to live here. If only things were that simple. But, maybe they weren't as complicated as Everett had been making them.

He didn't want to get into that now. Too risky. Their conversation could go quickly sideways. But now that he and Macy were back on somewhat level ground, he wanted to spend more time with her.

"All right," he relented. "What could it hurt to have a look?" What *could* it hurt?

"Maybe we could get to that brainstorming afterward." She smiled.

He returned it. "I'd like that."

"Good morning!"

At the greeting, they both glanced up to see Abel hobbling toward them from his motor home behind the stallion quarters.

"Hey, Abel." Everett raised his mug. "Can I get you some coffee?"

"Already had a cup with my breakfast, thank you." When Everett started to rise, he shook his head. "You stay put. I see Pop and Susan on the patio. Going to head over and say good morning." He shuffled on, his cane scraping in the dirt. "Morning, young man."

"Hello." Joey swiveled on his bottom and waved.

Everett watched Abel go. Interested in how, in a short amount of time, Pop had acquired three houseguests, two of them elderly like himself.

He marveled again at how happy they seemed as Pop gestured for his old friend to sit with him and Susan.

When you counted the collective members' daily comings and goings, the ranch was like grand central station. And Pop loved it. All Everett had to do was look at the old man to see the joy on his wrinkled face.

Macy rose from the chair. "I'm going to take Joey for a short ride. Then check on Roxie and leave for work."

"All right." Everett also stood.

She paused as if she was uncertain. Finally, she asked, "Do you want to come with us? It's fine if you don't. You're probably busy."

The tightness in Everett's chest had eased. Having a real conversation with Macy, more than their kiss, was responsible. Perhaps the two of them could work through some of their grief and guilt together while he was here.

"I'm not busy. And I'd like nothing better."

Her brown eyes shone. "Okay. Good."

While she fetched Joey, Everett went into the barn and got Butterscotch, the sorrel mare he'd seen Joey riding before. Five minutes later, the little boy was sitting on a bareback pad atop Butterscotch's back, kicking ineffectually with his short legs. The mare cranked her big head around and gave him a withering look, which made no difference.

Everett and Macy walked side by side, their hands occasionally brushing. Neither of them commented on the contact or made an effort to avoid it from happening.

"Look-it, Mommy. I'm galloping."

"Yes, you are, honey."

Macy showered Everett with a warm glance. He was glad his grandfather had summoned him home. Very glad.

A FEW DAYS LATER, Macy sat at the kitchen table with Everett, Pop and Sheriff Andy. Joey played in the family room with a hugely overweight but gentle dachshund that Sheriff Andy was fostering for the local animal shelter. The retired real estate broker had a real knack with animals and had volunteered at the shelter for years. Macy knew this well, as the clinic where she worked often provided pro bono, or very low-cost, vet services to the shelter.

This dachshund, recently homeless when her owner fell and broke a hip, was in Sheriff Andy's care until she lost weight through diet and exercise. After that, a suitable forever home would be found for her. In order to socialize the dog, ironically named Peanut, he took her everywhere with him.

Having met the dog first at the vet clinic and again today, Macy was considering being that home. She still thought a pet of any kind was too much for her busy schedule. But, if Peanut turned out to be as affable and obedient as she seemed, Macy's mom might be willing to watch Peanut, along with Joey, while Macy worked. Might. Time would tell.

Seeing Joey as he rolled around on the family room floor with the dog, the pair of them playing scratch-my-fat-belly-and-I'll-lick-your-face, her resolve was weakening.

"So, as you can see," Sheriff Andy said, pointing to the screen on his laptop, "we're projecting a twenty to twenty-five percent return on our investment."

Everett studied the screen. "That's assuming all the mares carry to term and their foals are born healthy."

"Even if we were to lose one foal, which would be tragic, we'd still see a ten to fifteen percent profit. And as long as the mare remained healthy, we could try again the following year."

"The bottom could fall out of the horse market. That's happened before when the economy soured."

"There are risks in any investment."

"Seems there are a lot of risks in this one." Everett sat back and sipped his root beer. "Pregnancy complications. Birth defects. Disease. Genetic disorders. The economy."

"The mares and Champ have all been tested," Pop interjected. "I have their health certificates."

Macy had to bite her tongue. She knew the meeting would go better if she let Sheriff Andy take the lead.

Everett had accepted her earlier offer to review the collective's books and business plan. To that end, they'd agreed to meet today at four. Macy had arranged to leave work early and brought a bucket of fried chicken along with all the fixings for dinner after the meeting. She didn't want anyone distracted by thoughts of dinner preparations.

Pop was already having trouble concentrating. Susan had returned home yesterday. Her ankle was much improved, and there was no real reason for her to stay. Her granddaughter had come by and collected her.

Macy hadn't been here at the time. She'd heard from Everett that Pop had been down in the dumps ever since. Of course, he'd see Susan again soon. They already had future lunch plans. But he missed her terribly. His gait had slowed in the last two days, and frown lines creased his brow.

Yet another reason why Macy wanted this meeting with Everett to go well. If he felt confident in the collective's agreement with his grandfather, once he learned of the income potential, he would hopefully be more open to remaining in Wickenburg and taking over the horse breeding business.

And then Macy could broach the subject of Pop remaining on the ranch with Everett and receiving home care rather than going to a nursing home. She and Everett had made tremendous strides in their relationship this past week. However, she wasn't ready to test it by tackling a touchy subject too soon.

What if she scared him off? Macy hadn't forgotten his broken promise. She wanted to believe he'd changed or *was* changing. But her trust in him had yet to be fully restored.

"We've tried to cover every contingency," Sheriff Andy continued. "And you can see from our bank account balance, we have plenty of funds to support the mares and their foals for two years."

"Are you taking advance deposits on the foals?" Everett asked.

"We're discussing that. We'd have to get our attorney involved. Have him draw up an agreement."

That remark launched a discussion about the collective's LLC and how it worked. Macy almost objected. That part wasn't any of Everett's business, only their agreement with Pop. But, again, she kept quiet, opting for complete transparency. That was the only way to earn Everett's trust.

"Mommy." Joey appeared at her side. "Peanut wants to see the horses."

"Are you sure?" Macy suspected Joey wanted to take the dog outside to play, and this was an excuse.

"I'm sure."

The meeting wasn't over. "In a little while, okay?"

"Please."

A whine had infiltrated his voice. If Macy continued refusing him, he'd have a meltdown. That wouldn't help the meeting.

"Just for a few minutes." How much could she miss?

"Yay! Come on, Peanut."

Joey returned to the family room and tugged the dachshund along by the bright red collar she wore. For a dog that supposedly wanted to go outside and see the horses, she moved rather reluctantly.

"We won't be gone long," Macy told Everett, Pop and Sheriff Andy.

They hardly glanced up from the laptop screen.

"Take your time," Everett said.

What had them so riveted? She'd been preoccupied with Joey and lost track of the conversation.

Outside, Joey ran ahead toward the mare barn. Macy lagged behind with Peanut. The overweight dog waddled along, her tongue lolling, her tail wagging.

She had a sweet face, Macy decided, and her sable coat glistened in the late afternoon sun. She certainly had the right temperament for a young child, and small dogs were easier to care for, too.

"You think you could develop a bad habit or two so I'd have a reason not to adopt you?" Macy asked.

Peanut raised her head and gave Macy a silly dog smile.

Macy's resolve softened with the beginnings of affection. "I think I'm in trouble."

The dog wasn't the only one growing on her. Everett was slowly worming his way into that soft spot she'd carefully guarded since Brody's death.

She hated the idea of that meeting going on without her. What were they discussing? Everett had impressed Macy with the intelligent questions he asked. Why did he not think he'd be good at taking over Pop's horse breeding business?

In the barn, Joey showed Peanut the mares, which consisted of him running up one side of the aisle and down the other, banging a hand on each stall door with an occupant and saying, "Here's a horse," and, "Here's a horse," over and over. Once the mares realized they weren't going to be fed yet or get a treat, they ignored him.

Everett had let them all out into the pasture for most of the day, giving them a bit of exercise. Macy wished she'd been there. She always liked seeing the entire small herd milling peacefully.

Peanut also ignored Joey. She'd waddled to a corner near the door and was sniffing in earnest. A bug or mouse must have caught her attention. Well, dachshunds were small hound dogs and good hunters. Though, with twice the girth of a normal dachshund, Peanut might not be good at anything beyond sniffing.

Joey joined the dog, dropping to his knees to investigate the corner.

"Be careful, honey. Get back," Macy said. What if Peanut had discovered a snake or a black widow spider? She should see for herself. "What did Peanut find?"

Before she could get there, Joey withdrew his hand and raised it high in the air. "Look-it."

He held an old, decayed chicken bone. Peanut tried to jump up and grab the discovery from his hand but was unable to achieve enough height.

"Joey!" Macy hurried over. "Put that down." The moment the words were out of her mouth, she changed her mind. "No, wait. Give it to me. Don't let Peanut have it." The filthy thing was not only a choking hazard, it was likely riddled with germs and would make the poor pup sick.

She took the bone and walked over to the trash barrel. Peanut danced after her. At this rate, she'd lose half a pound.

"Sorry, girl. When we go back inside, I'll give you a healthy snack, like carrot or apple pieces."

Peanut sent her a pitiful look that Macy was certain had weakened her former owner's resolve and accounted for all the extra pounds.

"I think you're going to be trouble, young lady."

Peanut barked. Joey came over, his hands and jeans from the knees down covered in dirt.

How was the meeting going? Macy really wanted to return to the house.

"Time to go inside, honey."

"Aw, Mommy. Do I have to?"

"What if we take Peanut for a walk?" Five minutes, and she could circle back around to the house.

"Sounds like fun."

Hearing Everett, Macy spun. He looked tall and rugged, his broad shoulders filling the doorway. "Oh. You're here."

"Everett." Joey raced over to him. "Peanut found a bone."

"Really?"

"Mommy threw it away."

"Was it a dinosaur bone?"

Joey burst into giggles. His idea of dinosaurs came from the picture books Macy read to him.

"We're walking Peanut. You want to come?"

"Sure." He smiled at Joey, and then Macy. "If your mom's okay with that."

"What about the meeting?" she asked.

"We're done."

"You are?"

"Sheriff Andy's just leaving. He said to tell you thanks, but he has other plans for dinner."

"Um, okay." Macy hedged. "How'd it go?"

"Good. I'm actually impressed. You and the other members have quite the operation." His handsome smile widened.

Macy experienced the now familiar little ping in her heart. Was it attraction or something deeper? She was afraid of the answer. She didn't feel ready for a relationship, not yet, and Everett didn't seem willing to settle down. If he was willing, taking over for Pop wouldn't be an issue. He'd have agreed in the beginning to stay.

She had to protect herself, and Joey, until he made his intentions clear. Better to squash that ping before it turned into something bigger, like real feelings. The last thing Macy wanted was to get hurt. She was still healing from losing Brody.

"Has your mind been put at ease?" she asked.

"About some things, yes."

"Not others?"

"Let's walk Peanut," he said and gestured. "We have a few minutes before the horses need to be fed and dinner's ready." He chuckled. "And she can't go more than a hundred yards without dropping from exhaustion."

He was right about that.

Like before, Joey led the way. When he wasn't skipping, he extended his arms as far out to the sides as they would go and pretended to be a plane, even providing engine sounds. Peanut lagged behind with the adults.

"I'm thinking of maybe adopting her," Macy said.

Everett did more than chuckle this time. He laughed out loud. "Macy Sommers, you are a pushover."

"She's a good dog."

He just shook his head.

Their interaction was so very reminiscent of days gone by when they were friends. The sensation increased with Everett's next remark.

"Hey, Joey," he called and waited for her son to turn around. "Did anyone ever tell you about the time your dad and I were riding our horses in the desert, and we came across a mountain lion?"

"A lion?" Joey ran back to join them.

Macy expected him to take hold of her hand. Instead, he placed his small one in Everett's.

"Yep. I was scared and wanted to get out of there. Your dad, he was brave and rode his horse right up on that big old cat."

Joey gasped. "What happened?"

"Your dad and that mountain lion stared at each other for a full two minutes. And then, all of a sudden, the mountain lion took off running licketysplit into the brush."

"Lickety-split," Joey repeated.

"It was something else."

Macy had never seen anything like this. Her son completely enraptured with a man other than his grandfathers. And Everett? He couldn't be more charming.

She'd done her best to bring Brody to life for Joey. She'd told many of her own stories, shown him pictures of Brody and videos and magazine articles. Having never had a father, she wasn't sure Joey, at two and a half, understood. Maybe this interaction with Everett would help.

"Tell me another story," Joey pleaded.

"Okay," Everett said. "Might take a while. I have a lot of them. But first. A riding lesson."

"I'm gonna ride a horse?"

"Not quite." He lifted Joey into his arms, and they returned to the mare barn. There, he sat Joey in a saddle on a freestanding rack where it awaited cleaning. "I'm going to teach you how to ride."

Joey gasped with excitement.

"First, hold on to this." He patted the saddle horn.

Joey gripped it tight with both his hands. He was much too small for the saddle, but that didn't seem to matter.

He then moved Joey's legs into position. "Keep these straight, okay? Not all bunched up. That's how cowboys do it."

"I'm a cowboy."

"Just like your dad." He patted Joey's shoulder, keeping his hand there to steady the boy.

Joey gazed up at Everett with undisguised hero worship. The ping Macy had felt earlier sharpened into a stab of pain. She suddenly realized more was at stake here than just her renewed attraction to Everett. Her son was also becoming attached to him. And if Everett left, which he well might, he'd break Joey's small heart. That would hurt worse than Macy's own disappointment.

Tears stung her eyes, unbidden.

Everett turned, and when he saw her, his expression filled with concern. "What's wrong?"

Macy composed herself, deciding to be straight with him. "I just hope you'll be around for a while to tell Joey a lot more stories. You're one of the few connections he has to his dad."

For a second, she thought she might have scared Everett off and that he'd leave them and go into the house. Instead, he continued speaking, a pleasant rumble in his voice.

"When your dad and I were fifteen, we rode our first bulls. And we both got thrown. I lasted two seconds longer than your dad, and I didn't break my arm, either."

They spent the next fifteen minutes with Everett interjecting tips on horseback riding in between feeding the horses and stories of him and Brody during their errant youth. Nearby, Peanut snoozed. When Pop called them for dinner and they sat around the table eating, it felt a little like a family gathering.

Macy didn't want the evening to end.

CHAPTER NINE

EVERETT WENT IN search of the footstool, finding it in the storeroom. He then wandered over to where Pop and Abel sat in the rocking chairs. They'd scooted the chairs inside the mare barn in order to watch the most recent downpour without getting wet. After an overcast, gloomy day, the rain finally made an appearance around four o'clock.

The instant twenty degree drop in temperature was a welcome relief from the sweltering heat and humidity. Everett had gotten Champ in from the pasture only moments before the first fat drops fell and turned the red-brown dirt a deep, muddy rust.

Sitting on the footstool, Everett removed his cowboy hat and shook off the water before replacing it on his head.

"We sure do need this rain," Abel commented.

Pop nodded as he rocked. "That sprinkle the other day wasn't near enough."

Everett's pocket vibrated. He removed his phone and read Macy's text. A small spark of anticipation flashed. He'd been thinking of her nonstop since yesterday and the riding lesson with Joey.

He should have told her he was no longer averse to the idea of staying. The two of them were getting along better. Well, in fact, their brief kiss aside. And after their talk when he'd confessed his part in the accident and she told him about her last gut-wrenching argument with Brody, him being unable to live in the same town with her had ceased being an obstacle.

There were still problems to resolve, and Everett didn't want to get ahead of himself. For one, his uncertainty about his ability to take over the horse breeding business remained. He had no experience—either with running a business or with breeding horses. There had to be more to it than throwing two horses together and hoping for the best.

If they didn't sell the ranch, Pop would be able to advise Everett. Macy could be a help, too, assuming she was agreeable. But what about Pop's medical care? His needs were growing daily. And what if he got worse? As little as Everett knew about the horse breeding business, he knew less about taking care of an ailing octogenarian.

What if he failed to notice that Pop was having another heart attack? Or he grew dizzy and fell while Everett was away from the ranch on business? He supposed he could insist Pop wear one of those medical alert devices, though that would be an uphill battle.

Everett's biggest concern was generating immediate income. If he had to foot all the ranch bills, his savings wouldn't last past the first quarter of the year. Could he accomplish that with the breeding business? To attract new customers, they needed to make repairs to the ranch. He may be a rookie when it came to running a business, but he knew that it took money to make money.

The rodeo coaching job did pay well, and part of him hated the idea of turning it down. Everett believed he'd be good at working with teens and preteens. Too bad he couldn't give lessons here on the ranch. That would require an arena, however.

Though, on second thought, there were other small arenas in town. Maybe he could work with the owners. Give them a percentage of the registration fees in exchange for use of their facility.

Wait a minute. Him giving rodeo lessons in town? He hadn't even figured out his next move when it came to Pop and the ranch.

Rereading the text from Macy, he told Pop and Abel what it said. "Because of the rain, the collective won't be here today."

"I'll miss seeing them," Pop said.

"She's still coming." Everett typed a reply. "She asked if I can help her clean the stalls. I'm telling her she can skip a night. I'll feed the mares and clean the stalls."

"Good idea. She should stay home." Abel squinted at the distant hills. "Roads are dangerous in this kind of weather. Gotta watch out for flash floods."

Everett's phone vibrated again. He read Macy's

message out loud. "She insists on coming. Says she needs to put a fresh dressing on Beauty's injury."

The large black had cut her foreleg on a piece of wire in the pasture yesterday. While not serious enough for stitches, the wound did require a daily cleaning and a fresh dose of antibiotic ointment.

"Can't you do that?" Pop asked.

Everett typed into his phone. "I'm telling her now."

"She fusses over those mares as much as she does her own boy."

"What she needs is to find someone new." Abel tapped his cane on the barn floor. "A shame for a pretty young girl like her to spend her life alone."

Everett wasn't sure Macy would appreciate Abel's remark. If she decided to have a relationship with a man, it would be because she wanted to or had fallen in love, not because she was spending her life alone. But Abel meant well. He liked Macy and wanted to see her happy.

Once again, Everett's phone vibrated. "She insists. But she's leaving Joey at her parents'."

"That's smart," Pop agreed.

Everett typed a response.

See you when you get here.

While Pop and Abel chatted, Everett pulled up the rodeo schedule on his phone. He then checked his current ranking, which hadn't changed significantly over the weekend. If he stretched his week-to-ten-day stay to, say, three weeks, he could return to the circuit and, as long as he did well, still qualify for Nationals in December.

The extra time would give him a chance to explore more options, like taking over the business from Pop and arrangements for his care. Perhaps Pop would agree to let Everett speak with his doctors and get the full scoop on his condition, giving Everett a better picture of the situation. Pop could be capable of more than Everett was giving him credit for. Or less. At the end of three weeks, Everett could decide— on that and a lot of things.

He closed the schedule on his phone and texted his buddy Rusty, letting him know he should definitely partner up with Junior for the Big Timber Rodeo. As he hit send, a thought occurred to him. Rusty might make a good coach, too. Would he possibly be interested? Would the Oklahoma Twisters be interested in him?

A short while later, Macy arrived. Standing, Everett motioned for her to park in front of the barn rather than alongside it. Too much runoff water accumulating back there. Her tires might get stuck. And while he wouldn't mind an unplanned stay, she no doubt wanted to return home to her son.

She darted from the truck to the barn, her plastic rain poncho flapping in the breeze. Inside the barn, she came to a stop and pushed back the hood, revealing a head of damp hair and face glistening with rainwater.

For just a second, she looked like the teenager

who, at seventeen, had stolen Everett's heart. He was instantly smitten, like he'd been ten years ago. He also felt some of the same awkwardness he had in those days and struggled for words.

"Do you, ah, need your medical bag?"

"Oh." She glanced at her truck and sighed. "I forgot to grab it in my rush."

"I'll go."

Before she could protest, he dashed out into the rain and retrieved the bag from the back seat of her truck. When he returned, he, too, was soaked.

"You didn't have to do that." She beamed at him.

"No problem." He nodded at the bag in his hand. "Where do you want this? Beauty's stall?"

"Thank you."

Ignoring Pop's and Abel's amused chuckles, he accompanied Macy. They stopped in front of the stall holding a sleek black half-Arabian and half-quarter horse with a long, thick mane and tail. Beauty had been aptly named, and her breeding would produce an interesting foal, especially when crossed with Champ's dark chestnut coloring and heavily muscled body.

From her Arabian ancestors, she'd inherited an often fiery temperament, which explained how she'd gotten into a fix with the pasture fence and injured her leg.

"Hiya, girl." Macy opened the stall door and squeezed inside.

Everett passed her a halter, and a moment later, she led the mare out and into the aisle where there would be more room to maneuver. She tethered Beauty to the hitching rail and then removed the old dressing from her lower front leg. The angry-looking wound didn't appear infected.

It would, however, leave a scar. When the rain stopped, possibly tomorrow, Everett would walk the pasture fence and search for any other sharp pieces of metal or protruding wires.

"If you don't need me," he said, "I'm going to feed the horses."

The rest of the mares were making a ruckus.

"You want to borrow my poncho?" Macy had removed it and hung it from a nearby hook.

"I'll be fine. I won't melt."

She smiled. "I would have disagreed with you five days ago."

"I wouldn't have made that claim five days ago."

She laughed before redirecting her attention to Beauty's injury.

Everett retrieved the wheelbarrow, which had been left outside, and, dumping the accumulated water, pushed it to the hay shed. After feeding Champ first, he maneuvered the full wheelbarrow into the mare barn where the hungry occupants greeted him with eager nickers and restless pacing.

"You're drenched." Macy stood with her hands on her hips. Beauty's leg sported a fresh bandage, and she strained the lead rope, more than ready to eat.

"Proof positive I won't melt."

Macy rolled her eyes, and he went about tossing

flakes of hay over stall walls and into feed troughs. Heads dived in, then popped up, jaws working as sprigs of hay stuck out of the sides of mouths.

Macy untied Beauty, and the half-Arabian muscled her way into her stall, unwilling to wait even for her halter to be removed.

"Okay, Miss Piggy," Macy chided, refastening the latch. "Excuse me for getting in the way."

"She's willful, that one." Everett much preferred the generally more docile quarter horses.

"I'm going to give Roxie a quick once-over while I'm here. Can't be too careful with colic."

At some point while they'd been busy, Pop had gone inside the house and Abel had returned to his motor home. Everett had no reason to stick around. Macy, either. He anticipated her heading to leave in order to pick up her son. Only she didn't.

Together, they meandered to the barn opening and watched the rainfall. It had lessened somewhat. Though only about six o'clock, the sun made an appearance, the rays hidden behind a heavy blanket of clouds that gave the impression of it being much later.

Everett decided to tell Macy about his recent decision. "I changed my mind."

She faced him, her expression expectant. "About what?"

"I'm extending my stay in Wickenburg. At least for a few more weeks."

"At least?"

He lifted one shoulder in a shrug. His wet shirt

clung to his skin. "We'll see. I'm giving myself some time to explore options."

"What kind of options?" Hope lit her expression.

"I don't know the first thing about the horse breeding business."

"You're smart. You can learn."

"I can," he agreed. "My biggest concern is Pop and his care. Present and future. You know how stubborn he can be and independent."

"I thought your plan was to put him in a nursing home."

"He'd be miserable. And if I were to stay—"

"Oh, Everett." Macy went limp with relief. "I'm so glad to hear you say that. He *would* be miserable. And depressed."

"I'm just not sure what else to do. I searched online earlier. I guess there are caregivers you can hire."

"What about Callie?" Macy said excitedly. "She's great at her job."

Everett shook his head. "I don't know if Pop would agree to that. A young woman... He's a private person. He'd be embarrassed and resist, which would defeat the purpose."

"Total Home Nursing Services has male caregivers."

"Hmm. That might work. I'm hoping Pop will let me talk to his doctors and get an idea of his needs."

"That's a really good idea. Will he?"

"Maybe. If I tell him that me staying is contingent on it."

She grinned. "You'd blackmail him?"

"Not blackmail. Encourage. He wants me to stay. I think he'll be willing."

"I think he will, too. If you want, I can ask Callie for some advice on how to approach Pop with the idea of accepting home care."

"Thanks, but I'll talk to her. After Pop and I have a chat. I'm not going behind his back."

"What if he refuses?"

Everett let out a breath. "I'll cross that bridge when I come to it. But I'd like to think he'll be co-operative if it means me staying."

"You could involve Susan," Macy suggested. "I'm sure she'd have some sway with him."

"We'll see. There's a lot to think about and to research. Guess I need to bone up on horse breeding, too."

"I have a thought." Her eyes sparkled.

Everett tried not to get lost in them—which was easier said than done. She was getting to him. And the feeling was both the same and different than when they were younger.

"I'm listening," he said.

"The collective has enough money to purchase another mare. Me and Kinsley and Sheriff Andy are attending a horse sale in Cave Creek on Saturday. You could come with us. You'd learn a lot."

"Are you taking Joey?"

"Of course." Macy grinned. "He'll have a blast."

Everett wanted to go, but he hedged. "I'm not sure about leaving Pop alone."

"Abel is here. Won't the two of them be all right for the day?"

"I suppose. And Susan's coming by for lunch."

"Which means Callie can check on everyone."

That was true. And Everett was only a phone call away. He could also let the neighbors know he'd be away and ask them to drop by in the afternoon.

"I would like to go," he admitted.

"We can feed the mares and Champ before we leave." Macy spoke quickly, her excitement contagious. "And either Glynnis or one of the Hays can come by and feed at six if we're running late. But the sale should be over by three or four at the latest. We might have to stop for dinner on the way home, though. Joey gets hungry."

How could he say no? Then again, he didn't want to say no. Nothing appealed to him more than spending the day with Macy and Joey, and not just because he'd learn about breeding horses.

"Sure. Why not? Sounds great."

"Oh, Everett. I'm so happy."

He wasn't prepared for what happened next. Macy threw herself at him and wrapped her arms around his neck.

His, naturally, circled her waist. And then he pulled her close as his lips sought hers. She didn't pull away and, instead, leaned into him, giving herself over to the kiss—which lasted and lasted.

"Macy," he said during a pause to take a breath.

"Shh. Don't talk. We can figure this out later.

For now, let's just enjoy." She brought his mouth down to meet hers for yet another amazing kiss.

And they remained that way until Pop came looking for them five minutes later.

MACY HADN'T BEEN to the rodeo grounds in Cave Creek for years. She used to frequent it in those days to watch Brody compete. Everett, too. He and Brody had been inseparable as friends and roping partners.

"See all the horses, Mommy," Joey chimed from the back seat and pointed with his chubby finger.

"Yes. There are lots of them."

She shifted in the truck's front passenger seat to check on her son. He'd handled the ninety-minute drive from Wickenburg well. She'd expected him to nap, as they'd risen earlier than usual. But no. Joey had been a chatterbox the entire drive, washing down his bites of dry cereal with a sippy cup of milk.

Everett maneuvered the truck and empty horse trailer through the crowded parking lot. Macy didn't bother telling him where to park. He was more familiar with the grounds than her.

"How are we doing on time?" he asked, studying the side mirrors as he eased into a space, reversed, adjusted and then pulled forward.

"Great. It's only seven forty-five."

Their goal had been to arrive well before the sale started at nine, affording them plenty of opportunity to walk the holding pens and inspect the hundred-plus horses being offered for sale.

Sheriff Andy parked his sedan alongside them, and he and Kinsley emerged. They'd taken two vehicles rather than cram the five of them together in Everett's truck. Sheriff Andy carried a travel cup of coffee, which had been filled at the start of their trip at the gas station on the outskirts of town. Knowing him, thought Macy, he'd be refilling the cup at the concession stand.

"At least we have beautiful weather," the older man commented as he skirted the truck to join Macy.

"The rain the other day helped. It's not quite so hot."

She opened the rear passenger door and removed Joey's portable stroller before lifting him from his car seat. He preferred to walk, but in case he grew tired, she'd have the lightweight stroller available for him to doze in. Her little boy had grown too big for her to carry around for long periods of time.

"Where to first?" Everett asked. He'd locked the truck after making sure Macy had everything she needed.

"The registration booth." She slung her backpack onto her shoulders. It contained Joey's emergency necessities, including snacks and drinks, boredom buster toys, disposable underpants and a clean shirt, along with her wallet and keys. She shoved her phone in her zippered shirt pocket. She needed her hands free and without having to worry about losing anything. "First, we get our bidder number."

They started out. Macy pushed the empty stroller, already having trouble with Joey who refused to listen.

"Don't run ahead, honey. Here, hold on to the stroller. No, don't touch that. Come back, Joey. Right now. I mean it."

She worried she'd lose her voice by the end of the day.

"Hey, sport." Everett motioned to Joey. "Why don't you walk with me. I need someone to point out all the good horses."

Joey didn't hesitate. He ran to Everett and grabbed his hand.

"I'll go with you, Everett."

"Okay, but we're both sticking with your mom. She gets lost easily."

"I do not," Macy protested, but her smile stretched wide. That was until she noticed Sheriff Andy and Kinsley watching them. Kinsley waggled her eyebrows.

Was her and Everett's mutual attraction obvious to onlookers? She imagined so. They hadn't kissed again since the other day when Pop interrupted them. There had been lingering looks, however, and frequent, not-so-accidental brushing of fingers.

They'd spent the drive here this morning talking about Everett's research on home nursing care and his chats with Pop. The older man had been receptive to Everett accompanying him to his follow-up doctor appointment next week. He'd been less receptive about home nursing care, insisting he didn't need any help. That was no surprise.

At her suggestion, Everett had spoken to Callie and learned from her a better way to approach this sensitive subject with Pop. As a result, Pop had agreed to sessions with a physical therapist and an occupational therapist who would teach him ways to make everyday tasks easier. Both would prolong Pop's independence.

Whether Everett stayed or left Wickenburg, these were good steps for Pop to take. Macy was pleased for him and Everett, who'd expressed a sense of relief. And she was pleased for herself. Forward progress meant a better chance of Everett staying and the collective's agreement with Pop continuing.

They hadn't discussed what the future held for them. It was too soon. But Macy had already begun picturing what having a relationship with him might look like. As she watched him and Joey walking hand in hand, that picture came more into focus.

Beneath a large canvas canopy marked Registration, they approached a folding table set up in front of the rodeo grounds office. Later in the day, the office staff would process payments for the successful bidders. Macy presented her ID and the collective's credit card. With the paperwork complete, she received her card stock bidder's number.

Assuming they were heading to the horse pens, she was surprised to see Everett registering.

"You thinking of buying a horse?"

"I might." He grinned.

"For yourself?"

"For the business."

"Really?" She suppressed her excitement. He must be considering staying if he was buying a horse.

"I don't know. Just thought I'd be prepared should I see something that strikes my fancy. Maybe I'm just caught up in the excitement."

He glanced around. Macy, too. People were everywhere and from all corners of the horse world. Many wore cowboy hats and ball caps with their jeans. Some sported dress slacks and button-down shirts. Others, overalls or shorts with Hawaiian shirts.

Most of the sellers appeared to be reputable breeders—such as the collective—and horse traders who made their living trading in livestock. Some of them represented stables specializing in cutting, roping or dressage horses. One hailed from the Prescott Valley racetrack. Macy recognized a seller who bought wild mustangs from the Bureau of Land Management and rehabilitated them.

There were also less scrupulous buyers and sellers in attendance. Those looking to make either a quick buck or unload a sick or injured animal on an unsuspecting bidder. Which was why Macy and the others had come early. A wise bidder inspected the horses up close before they were put in the ring where flaws could be disguised by a clever handler.

Sheriff Andy met them outside the canopy. He carried his freshly filled travel mug of coffee. "Where do we start, boss?"

She blushed slightly at his nickname for her. Macy was the official head of the collective, but she really considered them a team comprised of equal partners.

"That way, I guess." She indicated the pens and set out with the stroller.

"Come on, sport." Everett took Joey's hand. The boy had yet to leave his side. "Where's Kinsley?"

"At the vendor tents." Sheriff Andy walked along beside them, sipping on his mug.

"Buying new tack?"

"Checking out the competition. There's another metal artisan here."

"She should look into renting a tent herself at the next sale," Everett said.

"I bet she's doing that very thing right now."

They reached the first long row of connected pens, each one only large enough to hold a single horse, a mare and her foal, or a pair of yearlings. There were even a few ponies, donkeys and mules.

Attached to each pen, dangling by a cord, was a plastic document protector containing information on the occupant that could include registration papers, health certificates, photos, medical history and information on the seller. Displays sat in front of a few pens with ribbons and awards to show off the occupant's winning potential.

They walked down the first row. Macy only examined the documentation if she was seriously interested in the horse. She was only interested in purchasing a mare, preferably a registered quarter horse. Color and conformation caught her eyes. Temperament mattered. A proven breeder was a plus.

A veterinarian was on-site and could be hired for a consultation if there was a concern. Macy was grateful for her equine knowledge. In addition, Dr. Beck had instructed her to call if she needed advice.

"Look-it," Joey said, his face all smile. "There's Champ."

They all turned to see a horse of similar chestnut color to Pop's beloved stallion that stood in a pen near the end of the row. Only this horse was a mare.

"Let's head over there." Macy took the lead.

The others followed. At the pen, she removed her backpack and placed it in the stroller. She didn't want to be encumbered in any way.

"Hey, pretty girl." She leaned her forearms on the pen's top railing. The horse met her gaze but remained rooted in place. Not a concern. This was a strange place with a lot of strange people. Exhibiting wary behavior was expected.

"You want to go for a ride, sport?" Everett swung Joey up onto his shoulders, probably to keep him busy and out of Macy's way—something she much appreciated.

The mare continued to assess Macy from the center of the pen. Another bidder was also looking at her, a tall, skinny cowboy with a silver belt buckle the size of a saucer.

It was no wonder the mare garnered attention. She was striking. There were other slight differences between her and Champ. The mare's mane and tail were threaded with strands of gold that reflected the sun's light. Smaller and more finely boned, she had a sweet face accented by large dark eyes.

The seller hovered nearby. An old-timer with bowed legs and a full beard, he appeared to have several horses here today for sale and was going from pen to pen, answering questions for interested bidders.

"What's her bloodlines?" the cowboy asked.

Macy's ears pricked up. Nearby, Everett and Sheriff Andy chatted, though she noticed Everett glancing her way, as if also paying attention. Like before, Joey had removed Everett's cowboy hat and put it on his head, something that greatly amused him and strummed Macy's heartstrings.

"Her sire is out of Double Dun Down," the seller said and removed a sheet of paper from the document protector, which he passed to the man. "Here's a copy of her registration."

Macy knew the name. Most people in the horse business did. She really wanted to see that registration but waited. There was an unspoken rule at horse sales. If the seller was currently engaged in conversation with a bidder, anyone else interested had to wait until the bidder walked away.

While Macy cooled her heels, she gnawed the inside of her lip. After a moment, the mare sidled over and sniffed her arms and gently nipped her skin.

"Hi, girlie."

She reached up and scratched the mare's ears. The seller and the bidder were still engaged in conversation. From what she could gather, the bidder was in the market for a cutting horse. This mare had the right conformation and disposition. Did she have a born instinct for cows? That was less easy to determine in a sale pen.

Some sellers put a saddle on their horses and let potential bidders take them for a short ride. Generally, it was a good sign. This seller offered the option to the bidder.

"Let me have a closer look first," he said.

Macy thought she noticed a shadow of concern cross the seller's face, but it quickly disappeared. He opened the pen door, and the two of them entered. As they neared the mare, she moved away from Macy, presenting her previously hidden right side.

The reason for the seller's concern became immediately apparent. A prominent scar eight inches long ran along her back leg from her stifle to her gaskin.

"What happened?" the bidder asked.

"She was kicked," the seller explained. "Couple years ago. But she's sound. Everything's in her medical records. I had her vet checked just last week."

"How does it affect her performance?"

"Not at all." The seller motioned with his hand. "What have you been using her for?"

"Mostly, my daughter's been barrel racing on her."

The bidder dipped his head and then retreated toward the pen door. "Sorry, man. She's a dandy, but I can't take a chance. An old injury like that could come back on her out of the blue, and a lame horse doesn't make me any money."

Macy saw her chance. As soon as the bidder walked away, she approached the seller before anyone else. "Can I see her?"

"She's not lame," the old-timer insisted, his expression determined. He hadn't liked the cowboy's insinuation. "I have a good reputation. Just ask the auction company."

"I'm not concerned about the injury, sir. At least, I'm not overly concerned," Macy added. "The mare's breeding and health matter more to me."

"Yeah?" He studied her with a mixture of curiosity and doubt. "And why's that?"

She straightened, wanting, *needing*, to be taken seriously. "Because I'm looking for a broodmare."

CHAPTER TEN

EVERETT HAD KNOWN Macy since they were freshmen in high school and in the same algebra class. They'd been friends much of that time, save for the last three years, and sweet on each other for a short while. But he'd never seen this side of her and, he had to admit, she impressed the heck out of him.

He and Sheriff Andy had stopped talking in order to move closer and observe her in action, conversing with the seller. There was a reason the collective looked to her as their leader, and it was on full display now. She handled herself with confidence and poise. Her expertise was evident in the intelligent questions she asked and thoughtful observations she made. More than once, the seller's brow rose with surprise and admiration.

"I'm thirsty." Joey swayed frontward and backward atop Everett's shoulders. "I want juice."

Everett gripped the boy's legs tightly. "In a bit, sport. Your mom's busy."

"I'm thirsty now," Joey repeated.

Sheriff Andy hitched his thumb at the stroller.

"Macy probably has some of those pouch things in her backpack. I'll get one."

"Thanks," Everett said.

Probably a good idea to placate the kid. He didn't need to be out of sorts while his mom was impressing the socks off everyone.

The seller flashed Macy a gap-toothed smile. "Lady Moon Dust here would make a fine broodmare. She's had one foal already. It's right here in her paperwork."

Macy leaned closer. "Is that so?"

She went through the documents with the meticulousness of a police detective reviewing evidence. When she finished, she returned the packet to its place hanging from the railing. Then she entered the pen.

Lady Moon Dust showed no hesitation and came over to greet Macy. The seller extolled, in his opinion, the mare's many fine qualities while Macy conducted a thorough once-over. From what Everett could tell, the horse appeared healthy and well cared for and no more than eight or nine years old.

More interested buyers gathered at the sidelines to watch Macy, awaiting their turn and listening intently. This seller would have no trouble finding an interested buyer today. But would he get the price he wanted? Auction companies that operated the horse sales took a commission, cutting into profits.

"I'd like nothing better than to see her get a good home," Lady Moon Dust's seller said, giving her a pat. "She's a sweetheart."

Macy straightened from inspecting the mare's hooves. "Can I take her out and see how she walks?"

"Absolutely."

That was a good sign. If he'd objected, Everett would have wondered why. Macy spent another twenty minutes with the mare, even riding her bareback around the grounds with no more than a halter. The mare behaved impeccably. Another good sign. When Macy finished, she had one last question.

"How much to you want for her?"

"You offering to buy her outright?" the seller asked.

"Yes, I am. If my partners agree."

Sheriff Andy nodded at her and immediately got on his phone, presumably to contact the other collective members.

Sometimes, at horse sales, transactions were conducted at the pens. It was an accepted practice, as long as the commission was still paid to the auction company. There were benefits and drawbacks to both. A seller might get more in the ring. Or less. No way to tell. And a sale at the pens was guaranteed money.

Five minutes later, Macy and the seller shook hands. Each wore a wide smile. Everett, too. He liked watching her in action and had developed a newfound respect for her. He'd always believed she had potential, even back in high school, and was pleased to see her proving him right.

"Mommy."

Joey would have run to Macy if not for Everett holding him back. The kid had grown tired and bored in the last several minutes, given his pout. This was the point where Everett's lack of experience showed.

"She's almost done, sport."

"Mommy. Hurry, please."

Macy finally rejoined them, beaming from ear to ear.

"Congratulations," Everett said.

"She's a looker." Sheriff Andy hitched a thumb at the pen. "I'm going to take some pictures."

"I missed you, Mommy."

"Sorry, honey." Macy lifted him into her arms and hugged him tight. He laid his head on her shoulder. "Thank you for being so good."

"Can I ride the horse?"

"No. Not here. We don't have your special saddle."

"I wanna go home."

Macy sent Everett an apologetic smile. "He's tired. We were up early."

"I understand. I get cranky when I'm tired, too."

"I appreciate you watching him."

"No problem." Everett reached out and ruffled Joey's hair. He'd reclaimed his cowboy hat earlier after Joey had dropped it twice. "I suppose we could leave. We got what we came for."

"Yes." Macy hedged. "Except it's barely past nine. The sale just started in the ring. It's kind of fun to watch."

"What about Joey?"

"Let's walk around a bit. Find Kinsley. See what she wants to do."

"I vote for breakfast," Sheriff Andy said, returning from the pen.

They'd grabbed stale pastries from the gas station early this morning. Everett wouldn't mind something more substantial.

Macy coaxed Joey into the stroller, bribing him with a toy from the dollar store she'd hidden in the backpack in case of an emergency—an emergency being preventing Joey from having a meltdown.

Her ploy worked. Sort of. They started out walking along the last row of pens. By the time they reached the end, Joey had started to nod off.

And that was when Everett saw him. A tall gray horse with prominent dapple markings that caused him to stop in his tracks.

"Wait a second," he said.

"What is it?" Macy peered past him.

"See that young stallion over there? Next row over."

"He wasn't there before. Must be a latecomer."

Everett's feet were already in motion. Something about the horse drew him. It wasn't just his unusual color and markings or the regal shape of his head. He had an air about him that commanded attention. And he had Everett's.

"Wow, he's something else," Macy said as they reached the pen.

"Pop would call this kind of horse a showpiece."

"He's a little standoffish."

"A lot of stallions are, if they haven't been handled much or handled wrong."

Macy smiled. "And you said you knew little about the horse breeding business."

"I've been around bucking broncs enough to tell this guy isn't mean. He's just had very little human contact. Probably left in a pasture with his dam until someone weaned him and threw him in with a bunch of yearlings."

"And now he's here."

Fortunately, no one else was at the pen. Everett went right to the railing. Unlike Lady Moon Dust who'd immediately approached Macy, the young gray stayed back, staring at Everett with the same intensity as Everett stared at him. He liked that about the horse, despite his wariness of people.

After a few moments, a woman in her mid to late forties approached. With her tailored business attire and expensively styled hair, she looked nothing like the usual horse traders in attendance today. Then again, the rich populated the horse world every bit as much as those hanging by a thread.

"Morning," the woman said.

Everett nodded and touched the brim of his cowboy hat. "What can you tell me about him?" He and the young stallion continued their visual standoff.

"This is Gran Hombre Gris. The hands at my ranch call him Hombre."

Big Gray Man in Spanish. The name fit.

"He was foaled in February of last year," the

woman continued, mindless of the dirt on her expensive suede shoes. "Registered quarter horse but, like a lot of them, he has some thoroughbred blood in him going back a couple generations."

Everett could see that in the set of Hombre's eyes, his bone structure and his height, which would only increase during the next year.

The seller removed the paperwork from the packet and handed it to Everett. According to the logo, the woman's ranch was located in northern Texas. Why had she come this far for a horse sale? Everett's curiosity was admittedly piqued.

"Take a look for yourself," she said. "If you're in the market for a stud, he'd be a fine addition to any breeding program."

Everett studied each page before passing them to Macy for her to inspect. By now, Joey was sound asleep. Sheriff Andy had wandered off in search of Kinsley and food, not necessarily in that order.

"Why are you selling him?" Macy asked.

It was a good question.

The woman sighed. "I'll be honest with you. I need the cash. I have two kids in college, and tuition is very expensive."

In Everett's opinion, she didn't look like someone who needed money. Then again, she may have recently encountered financial difficulties. Or her assets could be temporarily tied up—like the collective, which was waiting on the birth of the mares' foals.

"Why *this* sale?" Macy asked. "You're a long way from Texas."

"I had to deliver three horses to a buyer in Phoenix yesterday. Unfortunately for me, the buyer changed his mind about Hombre. Or I should say his wife changed his mind for him. She apparently controls the purse strings. On a whim, I brought him here rather than taking him all the way home."

"Why wasn't he trained?"

More good questions. Everett could learn a lot from Macy.

"He's young still," the woman said. "Plenty of time for training."

Except training should start as early as possible. If not, bad habits developed. Still, Everett liked the horse and thought he had potential.

"I don't see any genetic testing in the paperwork." Macy riffled through the pages.

A really great question this time. Everett should have paid better attention when Macy was buying Lady Moon Dust.

"My secretary forgot to include those." The seller pulled out her phone. "I had her take a picture and send it to me." She opened the photo and enlarged it for Everett and Macy to read. "He passed. Negatives across the board. I can have my secretary email the result to you. That is, if you buy Hombre."

Here was the moment of truth. Money wasn't an issue. Everett had enough of his own saved up. But did he have the time and willingness to commit to training a young, exceedingly green stallion? That wasn't anything he could accomplish on the road or if he convinced Pop to sell the ranch. Was he ready?

To be brutally honest, his grandfather's business didn't need another stallion. Champ was more than enough. If Everett bought Hombre and then decided not to stay, he'd have two horses to sell.

Macy must have been reading his mind, for she gazed at him expectantly. What if he bought Hombre, decided to stay, and then Pop took a turn for the worst, forcing them to sell the ranch? Everett would then have to add disappointing Macy to his long list of mistakes.

He stepped away from the pen. "I need to think about it."

"You can take Hombre out," the seller said. "He's not broke to ride yet, obviously. But he's good under halter."

"No." Everett shook his head. He was afraid if he got close to the horse, his resolve would weaken. Buying a stallion was a step he wasn't ready to take. Not yet.

"All right." The woman retreated. "We'll be here if you change your mind."

Everett avoided looking at Macy. He didn't have to see her face to know he'd let her down. She'd wanted him to buy Hombre, seeing it as a commitment on his part to stay.

"How about we find Sheriff Andy and Kinsley and get something to eat?" he said.

By general consensus, the four of them agreed to stay for a while before heading home. Kinsley had never been to a horse sale before and was quickly caught up in the excitement. She tried to guess the final sale price for each horse that came into the ring and missed the mark each time.

All around them, bidders called out and raised their numbers in the air. Spotters in the ring kept a lookout, making sure no one was missed. The announcer described each horse as it entered the ring, listing its attributes and giving a bit of history. There were plenty of bargains to be had and a few horses that went for way too much money, in Everett's opinion.

Joey woke up soon after they'd entered the sale area, where they found seats on the bleachers. Like Kinsley, he was swept up in the newness and the excitement. Unlike her, he lost interest quickly. Every distraction Macy presented him with lasted only five minutes at most.

After a while, containing him on the bleacher seat became a challenge.

"What do you say we head home?" Everett said.

"Is that okay with everyone?" Macy looked around.

Sheriff Andy and Kinsley were in agreement. As they were organizing and preparing to leave, Hombre came into the sale ring, led by one of the ring hands. Everett went still, watching. Everyone else did, too.

"I just want to see what he sells for," he said and sat.

"Sure." Macy settled Joey in the stroller.

And then the bidding started. It began slowly. What others saw as misbehaving on Hombre's part, Everett saw as high spirits. A trademark of stallions. The auctioneer tried his best to excite the crowd and get the people to bid. Action picked up a little, but not much.

A seller had the right to refuse if the price didn't reach what they wanted. They'd still have to pay a fee to the auction house. The decision to sell or not was often made in a split second.

"Going once," the auctioneer said. "Going twice."

The price was ridiculously low. Hombre was worth five times that for his breeding alone.

"One thousand dollars."

Macy turned to stare at Everett. Only then did he realize he'd bid and that his hand was raised in the air, the one holding his number.

Bidding resumed with interest renewed. The price went up. Everett didn't think. He just bid.

"Twenty-two hundred," he hollered.

"Over here," a spotter shouted.

A young woman entered the action but fell out quickly when Everett outbid her.

"Going once," the auctioneer said. "Going twice." He paused for several seconds before banging his gavel. "Sold to number 344."

Everett turned to Macy and felt his mouth break into a wide grin. "I think I just bought a horse."

She grinned back at him. "I think you did, too. What happened?"

"I don't know." He shrugged. "I suddenly realized I wanted him."

He also wanted everything that owning Hombre represented. But he didn't want to think about that now. Not yet.

MACY AND EVERETT headed to the auction office while Sheriff Andy and Kinsley made a final run to the concession stand. Joey wanted to walk, but Macy insisted he stay in the stroller. The crowd had increased in size. Too easy for a small child to get lost.

She bit her tongue as they went along, hoping Everett would mention his future plans for Hombre and, beyond that, his intentions to stay in Wickenburg. He did neither, his only comment wondering if he'd lost his mind for a moment.

"I'm not sure what got into me."

"It can be like that when bidding," she said as they stood in line. "In fact, auction companies count on the electric excitement running through the crowd and your natural competitive spirit to drive prices higher."

"I got a smoking deal on Hombre."

"I think his lack of training scared people off. I'd be surprised if he's ever seen a saddle, much less had one on his back."

What she thought but didn't say aloud was, if Hombre's behavior didn't improve, he'd be of no use, and Everett would have wasted his money. His claims of not being qualified to take over for Pop would have merit. She still believed he could learn the breeding business, but this could be a setback.

Was Everett always this impulsive? She tried to remember and thought yes. It hadn't bothered her before when they were just friends. Now, she had a son and future career at stake. Impulsivity could be a red flag.

After finalizing his transaction at the auction office, they met up with Sheriff Andy and Kinsley at the horse pens. Kinsley took over pushing Joey in the stroller so that Macy was free to lead Lady Moon Dust. The mare came willingly, following Macy as if she couldn't wait to get to her new home.

Hombre was a different story. He charged through the gate and would have escaped if Everett didn't have a strong hold on the lead rope. Once out, he pranced alongside Everett to the parking area, his erect head swiveling in every direction. With the sun reflecting off his sleek coat, Macy had to admit the horse was indeed a looker who would only grow more striking as he matured.

Lady Moon Dust loaded into the trailer with no problem. Everett and Hombre waited a short distance away just in case. When Hombre's turn came, he initially balked. Digging in his heels and snorting angrily, he put his weight on his back end and lowered his head.

After several failed attempts, Everett recruited help from Sheriff Andy and two other cowboys who'd stopped to watch. Between the four of them, they were able to convince Hombre that loading was in his best interest. Hating the cowboy hats they waved at him, the young stallion leaped into the trailer as if clearing a three-foot fence, landing awkwardly with a clatter of hooves.

"Look-it, Mommy." Joey pointed from their safe vantage point well away from the action. "The horse jumped."

"Yes, he did."

"Not the most graceful thing," Kinsley commented. "Everett's going to have his work cut out for him."

Macy almost asked Kinsley if she thought he intended to stay in Wickenburg, then decided against it.

Lady Moon Dust wasn't thrilled at the prospect of a ninety-minute drive home beside Hombre and nipped him several times to let him know. Mares typically disliked the company of stallions except during the time in their cycles when they were ready to breed. Only then did they welcome any attention, and sometimes that was touch and go.

Hombre wasn't deterred and kept reaching over to her side of the trailer, trying to make friends. Weary, she rebuked him with a swift kick that landed on the metal panel separating the two of them. Had Everett anticipated buying a stallion, they would have brought two trailers. With only one, the horses had no choice but to make peace.

"They'll settle down once we're on the road," Everett said, latching the trailer gate and engaging the safety chain. "The motion will distract them."

Soon after that, they left the rodeo grounds behind. Again, Macy silently willed Everett to raise the subject of Hombre or Pop's care or anything having to do with him staying. Instead, he talked about the last time he'd competed at the Cave Creek rodeo arena, the latest family news from his mom and gathering his courage to call Brody's parents.

"They'd love to hear from you, I'm sure," Macy said, reaching into the back seat to retrieve Joey's dropped toy.

"You don't think they'll be mad at me? For not coming around?"

"Absolutely not. They probably think you avoided them because they remind you of Brody and the accident."

"I'm sorry to say, they're not entirely wrong."

Eventually, they reached the outskirts of Wickenburg. Just as she'd given up all hope, Everett finally raised the subject of Hombre. Sort of.

"Are you planning on breeding Lady Moon Dust now or wait until after the first of the year?" he asked.

"I have to check with the collective first. But I'm going to recommend we give her a month or two to get used to the ranch and her surroundings, make sure no health or behavioral problems arise, then breed her. We can't afford to keep a mare who isn't earning her keep."

"Makes sense." He turned at the next intersection, executing the corner with care so as not to unbalance their passengers in the trailer.

"What about you?" she asked, daring to probe. "Are you going to give Hombre time to get used to the ranch and his surroundings before starting training?"

"Not much time. I need to start working with him right away. He's gone too long without training as it is. With luck, I should be able to tell within a week if I made a good investment. If I can't use him for stud, I'd probably turn him into a gelding, train him and sell him. Hopefully for a profit."

"What about rodeoing and your coaching job?"

"I'm not sure, Macy. I don't have all the answers yet."

What she heard was he had no intentions of staying longer than his original time frame. "You can't procrastinate forever."

"I know that." A pronounced V appeared between his eyebrows.

How could he be impulsive one minute and stall the next?

The answer hit her even before she'd fully formed the question. Because he didn't like confrontations and dealing with unpleasantries. Like coming home after Brody's death. Macy faced her problems head-on and needed someone who did the same.

At the ranch, they drove past the house to the mare barn. Both Sheriff Andy and Kinsley were already gone. Able to drive faster, they'd reached the ranch well ahead of Everett and Macy.

"I can unload and feed the mares," he offered,

"if you and Joey want to head home. You must be tired."

"I'll stay." She was tired, but she refused to leave without first making sure Lady Moon Dust was tucked in safe and sound for the night.

By the time he parked the trailer and unlatched the rear gate, Pop and Susan were strolling hand in hand from the house. Apparently, she'd stayed after lunch. Macy noticed the elderly woman still sported a slight limp from her sprained ankle and used a sparkly red cane.

Before long, Abel meandered over to observe the happenings. He'd probably be returning home tomorrow or the next day. His sister Glynnis was due to return from her trip. Too bad, really. Pop would miss the company, and Abel would miss his reprieve from his mother hen sister.

The three seniors stood in the shade of the mare barn to watch Everett unload the horses from the trailer. By now, Joey was refreshed from his long nap and bursting with energy. Macy couldn't take her eyes off him or he'd find trouble.

"Mommy, I'm hungry."

She'd begun to truly wonder if her son had a hole in his stomach. He never seemed to have enough to satisfy him.

"Okay. Okay. You wait over there with Pop while I get something from the truck."

Good thing she'd loaded up on snacks before they left. Glancing over at Everett, she quickly grabbed a package of peanut butter crackers from her backpack.

"Who are you unloading first?" she called out, giving Joey the opened package.

Her answer was a loud banging. Hombre was making his presence known as he shot backward out of the trailer, showing as little grace and agility as when he'd loaded back at the rodeo grounds.

From the paddock, Champ whinnied and raised a ruckus. He'd no doubt smelled the new horses and was ready to challenge Hombre while making Lady Moon Dust's acquaintance. He would get the opportunity to do neither today.

Everett tied Hombre to the side of the trailer, where he alternated between pawing the ground, prancing in place and whinnying.

"I want to give him a few minutes to calm down before I take him over to the stallion quarters. He's young, but I guarantee you he'll act up around Champ."

"Will they be all right together in the stallion quarters?" Macy asked.

"The two stalls are across from each other. That should put enough distance between them. If not, Hombre can stay in the round pen for a few days until they get used to each other."

Macy couldn't help saying, "I always thought stallions couldn't live together. That they fought."

"Some of the bigger horse breeding operations have more than one stallion. Pop did, too, for a while years ago. I remember him telling me they have to be introduced slowly and carefully managed. Hombre's immature enough Champ may not view him as a threat to his position."

"Yet."

"Right. I'm definitely going to have to research stallion management."

"Aren't a lot of racehorses stallions?" Macy asked. "And they race side by side on the track."

"They are. And an agent from the Bureau of Land Management once came to a rodeo. He talked about groups of bachelor stallions banding together in the wild."

"What if Champ and Hombre don't ever get along?"

Everett mulled that over before answering, his brow furrowing. "I suppose I'd have to sell Hombre."

Macy could tell he didn't like that option. Not only had he already developed a fondness for the horse, he wanted to prove himself as a capable successor to Pop's business.

"Your girl is next," he said. "Time to see if she likes her new digs."

Like before at the rodeo grounds, Lady Moon Dust exited the trailer with grace and composure. Macy immediately collected her from Everett and led her inside. She created quite a stir. Her new barn mates reached their heads out over the stall doors in an attempt to catch a whiff or nuzzle noses.

There were plenty of empty stalls to choose from. Macy picked the one next to Butterscotch, confident the older broodmare's sweet temperate would made her a good neighbor.

Dusty, as Macy was already beginning to think of Lady Moon Dust, immediately quenched her thirst with a long pull at the waterer. After that, she explored every corner of the stall, sniffing and digging with her front foot. To the dismay of the other mares, Macy gave Dusty a half bucket of grain. Food went a long way in aiding a horse's acclimation.

She stood at the stall watching the mare. "You're a good girl, aren't you?" She knew she should get back to Joey and start for home. But he was fine with Pop and the others, and Macy wanted a moment to herself.

This day trip with Everett had gone far different that she'd expected. Then again, so had her relationship with him since his return. She really needed to get her head on straight. They'd kissed, more than once, and she'd enjoyed it. There'd been no declarations from Everett afterward, however. Any expectations she had, including those she'd come to after he bought Hombre today, were entirely her own.

"Hi."

She started at the sound of his voice and spun. There he stood alone at the entrance to the mare barn.

"Admiring your new purchase?" he asked.

"Yeah." She collected herself. "I thought you were with Hombre."

"He's fine for the moment."

"Getting along with Champ?"

"I wouldn't say getting along." Everett joined her at Dusty's stall. "The two of them are squaring off from across the aisle. Whether they decide to fight or get along remains to be seen."

Suddenly, Macy was tired of tiptoeing around the subject. "You bought a stallion, one who needs training, without any forethought."

"Yeah?"

"You can't return to the rodeo circuit or head off to Oklahoma and leave Hombre here for Pop to deal with."

"No, I can't." He paused and inhaled deeply, his gaze connecting with hers. "I'm starting to think I can't leave here under any circumstances."

"What are you saying?" Hope flared anew.

"Nationals may have to wait another year. Or, if I show any promise at this horse breeding business, I just might retire."

"Oh, Everett."

"I'm recommending Rusty take my place with the Twisters. He was already on their short list, and I know he's interested."

"That's a great idea!"

"There's still the matter of Pop's care."

"We can figure that out."

"We?" His lopsided smile melted her heart.

"Yes." She went out on a ledge. "We."

"What are *you* saying, Macy?"

"You're not in this alone. I'm here to help in any way I can."

He inched closer. "And if I want more than just your help?"

The moment had come for her to decide. She either took a leap and told Everett how she really felt, or she put a stop to whatever was happening between them in no uncertain terms.

"Like I said." She also inched closer. "You're not in this alone."

And just in case she hadn't made herself clear, she wrapped her arms around his neck and planted her lips on his in a kiss that spoke way more than words could convey.

CHAPTER ELEVEN

EVERETT DROVE HIS truck into town on Monday afternoon, his destination Hayloft Feed and Tack. In addition to vitamin supplements, salt blocks and a training halter for Hombre, he wanted to introduce himself to the Hays, the only members of the collective he'd yet to meet.

He told himself he was simply being neighborly. The fact was, he thought it wise to establish a good relationship with all the collective members in light of him taking over the business from Pop.

Glynnis and her husband had returned from their trip yesterday. However, rather than take Abel home, everyone agreed he'd remain at the ranch a while longer. Pop liked the company, and enjoying a semi-independent lifestyle, it seemed, had a positive effect on Abel. His Parkinson's disease may not have improved, but his mood had flourished.

Plus, leaving Pop with someone else there rather than alone eased Everett's mind. Abel could at least call Everett or dial 911, should anything happen. Same could be said for Pop if Abel had a mishap. The two looked after each other. Everett knew the arrangement wasn't permanent. But in the meantime, everyone benefited.

Was that also true for him and Macy, that their arrangement, for what it was, benefited them both? He'd never forget their spontaneous kiss on Saturday and hoped not to disappoint her. He intended to stay in Wickenburg. And while they hadn't spoken about any kind of future, he wanted a commitment more than a one day at a time kind of relationship. What that would look like, he wasn't sure.

Often, during his and Brody's heyday, they'd visited Scottsdale, Arizona, a place self-dubbed the West's most Western town. Everett considered the name a misnomer. Wickenburg, with its old-time storefronts and boardwalks, cowboy museums, multitude of cantinas and bars, dude ranches and Vulture City Ghost Town just outside the city limits, was far more Western than the highly commercialized Scottsdale.

He'd loved growing up here as a kid and hated having to move. Returning wouldn't be so bad. It might actually be great.

On the corner of West Wickenburg Way and North Mariposa Drive sat a small strip center. Everett pulled in and parked outside the feed store, easily identifiable by the large sign above the shingled awning and life-size fiberglass palomino horse on display in front.

A buzzer announced his arrival when he pushed open the front door, and a chorus of tiny cheeps greeted him. There, immediately to his right, sat a brooder with chicks and ducklings for sale. They bunched together under the light bulb, keeping warm against the store's air-conditioned interior.

Pop used to keep a few laying hens around the ranch years ago. That might be something to consider. Everett would need to build a pen for them. Without a safe place to roost, chickens were vulnerable to hawks, coyotes and other predators.

"Hi. Can I help you?" A jeans-clad middle-aged woman with the upbeat demeanor of a salesperson sauntered over to Everett.

"Are you by chance Brenda Hays?"

"Oh!" Her mouth dropped open and then curved into a bright smile. "You must be Pop's grandson Everett. I recognize you now. I've seen your picture in the house at the ranch."

"Nice to meet you, ma'am."

"Please, call me Brenda."

When he went to shake her hand, she pulled him into an embrace. "I hope you don't mind. I'm a hugger."

Everett didn't mind.

"Besides," Brenda said, releasing him, "we're practically family. My husband and I belong to the collective, and you're Pop's kin. Which reminds me." She grabbed his arm and escorted him deeper into the store. All around them, customers perused shelves and displays. The store contained everything from equine medications to pet food to Western clothing to gift items. "You have to meet Larry, my husband and partner in crime."

They found Larry in the rear bay, overseeing the loading of a large order of hay and grain into the delivery truck.

"Larry," she hollered to be heard above the din. "Come here. You'll never guess who this is. Everett. Pop's grandson."

Her husband motioned to the young man operating the Bobcat and wearing a Hayloft Feed and Tack T-shirt and then jogged across the bay to join them.

"Everett. Welcome." He didn't insist on hugging Everett when they shook hands. "We've heard a lot about you."

"I want to thank you both for all you've done and continue to do for Pop."

"He's been a good customer since we opened the store," Brenda said.

"And a better friend," Larry added.

They chatted for some time. Everett liked the couple, same as he did all the collective members. He didn't remember such camaraderie when he lived in Wickenburg. Then again, he'd been young, just seventeen, when he moved away. And from the time he graduated high school, he'd lived mostly on the road.

It reminded him a lot of the community of professional rodeo competitors. There were many similarities. Some people were as close as siblings. Like him and Brody had been.

With the loading finished and the truck dispatched to the customer's address, the three of them returned to the main part of the store, where Brenda gave Everett a tour while Larry waited on customers. Everett's compliments were sincere. He'd been in plenty of feed and tack stores during his life. This one compared favorably.

"You know, we're the ones who brought the collective members together." Brenda beamed.

"No fooling."

They stood near the front door. Everett held a bag containing the supplements and his new training halter. Larry had used a handcart to transport the salt blocks outside, where he placed them in the bed of Everett's truck.

"Well, credit where credit is due. Macy had the original idea. Since we're acquainted with just about everyone in town who owns horses, she asked us if anyone might be interested in purchasing Pop's mares. We were, naturally. Larry's always had a hankering to raise foals, but the commitment was more than we could take on, with the store and two kids active in sports. We put her in touch with Glynnis first. She's one of our best customers. Raises and shows miniature horses."

"Abel mentioned it. He talks about her little critters a lot."

"Kinsley, of course, sells some of her metal art creations here. We take a small commission."

"She's very talented." He'd noticed several of her items on display during the tour. "Does Sheriff Andy also have horses?"

"Him? No." Brenda laughed. "Just those dogs he

fosters for the shelter. He joined the collective strictly as an investment. That man is smart as a whip."

"Rumor is he was pretty successful in real estate."

"That was his main livelihood. He also dabbles in stocks and bonds and insurance. All kinds of stuff that goes way over my head." She gestured with her hand. "He advises a lot of us on our retirement and investment portfolios. Made Larry and I a tidy profit on our nest egg."

Everett would have to ask Pop if Sheriff Andy advised him, too. "And he doesn't charge?"

"We've tried to pay him. He refuses. Money, that is. We give the shelter a deal on dog kibble and donate ripped bags that we can't sell. Which we take as a tax deduction. He told us to. Said it's considered a donation to the shelter."

Everett recalled Pop mentioning donating horse manure to the high school and taking a tax deduction was also Sheriff Andy's idea. He was clearly savvy when it came to managing the collective's books. Everett had seen that firsthand.

"He's been a true asset to the townspeople," Brenda continued. "And to the collective. Man has a heart the size of the Grand Canyon."

Everett nodded, storing this new information away. Maybe he could hit Sheriff Andy up with a few of his own questions about the horse breeding business. What could it hurt?

On a whim, he asked Brenda, "You have your finger on the pulse of horse people in this town.

Do you think there'd be any interest in youth rodeo classes?"

"Without a doubt. Why? You thinking of giving classes?"

"Tossing the idea around." He'd spoken to the head of the Oklahoma Twisters last evening. She'd taken the news better than he'd expected and felt confident if Randy didn't accept, another candidate from her short list would take the position.

At the door to the feed store, Everett shook hands with Brenda. "Thanks again for showing me around. I'm glad we finally got to meet."

"You're staying on then?" she asked.

"I think so. For now."

"That's great. Pop must be thrilled."

"He is." The memory prompted a grin. Everett and his grandfather had celebrated with root beers on the back patio. Pop had gotten tears in his eyes he'd failed to hide. "There's still a few details to work out."

"How do you feel about giving up rodeoing?"

He'd lie if he said he didn't suffer a small pang of regret when he thought about it. "I may not have to give it up entirely. We'll see."

"You can always enter one of Wickenburg's rodeos."

"I could." The town also hosted various roping events.

Brenda walked him outside to his truck. Everett waved as he reversed and drove away. He made two additional stops before returning to the ranch:

the first was filling up at the gas station, and the second was picking up Pop's prescriptions at the drugstore.

When he arrived at the ranch shortly before dinnertime, it was to find Sheriff Andy's sedan parked at the mare barn and not Macy's truck. She didn't come to the ranch every evening. He had no reason to expect her. Only he had.

Maybe he should send a text? Unless that would be misconstrued. Too pushy? Too needy? Too impersonal? He was seriously overthinking this, the result of being out of practice.

The thing was, he and Macy weren't an official couple. Heck, they hadn't even gone on a date yet. Maybe he should rectify that and ask her out.

Were they ready for that step? What did she want from their relationship? Dating, even causal dating, implied a commitment. He could always suggest a trail ride one morning. There wouldn't be much pressure with that, especially if they took Joey along.

"Howdy, Everett." Sheriff Andy waved as he emerged from the mare barn. He still had Peanut, the fat foster dachshund, and she waddled after him. "I fed Champ and Hombre already."

"Appreciate that. I was running late." Everett met him halfway. "How are they getting along?"

"Seemed like they were more tolerant of each other than the other day." He whistled low. "That Hombre is one fine looker."

"Yes, he is."

The remark reminded Everett to check his phone for any new emails. He'd texted the seller earlier in the day about Hombre's genetic testing results. She'd forwarded the screenshot she'd shown him at the sale on Saturday, but Macy had told him to ask for the actual paperwork. He'd need it for when he began breeding Hombre.

"Pop invited me to dinner," Sheriff Andy continued. "Wish I could accept, but I got a call right before you showed. Something came up."

"Maybe next time, then. We're having turkey meat loaf. It's not bad, but it's not the same as regular ol' meat loaf."

"Better for one's health, though." The older man chuckled. At his feet, Peanut sat and panted, her heavy sides heaving.

Everett put his phone away, disappointed there was no response from Hombre's seller.

"Tell Abel I'll have those CD brochures he was asking about next time." Sheriff Andy paused. "How long is he staying on, if I can ask?"

"Honestly, I'm not sure."

"He seems to like it here. And Pop likes having him."

"True on both accounts."

Sheriff Andy squinted at the house. "It's none of my business, and you can take what I say or leave it." He hesitated. "Would Pop consider letting Abel rent from him?"

"What do you mean?"

"I'm suggesting Abel permanently parks his

motor home here and pay Pop a monthly rent. It would be extra income for Pop, and a solution for Glynnis. Abel, too. He doesn't need constant supervision. Not right now. But he can't live entirely alone. I wouldn't have mentioned it if you weren't staying on. Someone physically fit needs to be here to oversee everything."

"I...don't know."

"Might be more than you can take on right now. Your first priority is the business, which has come to a standstill this last year."

He was right. Everett needed to hang out Champ's shingle again. Maybe Kinsley could lend him a hand. Set up social media accounts for him and a website. Pop had always operated by word of mouth. That didn't work as well these days.

"Going to take some time," Sheriff Andy said, echoing Everett's thoughts. "Meanwhile, money's not rolling in. Charging Abel monthly rent could cover some ranch expenses."

"Too bad we can't rent out space to more people. There's a lot of land on this ranch going to waste."

"You probably can. The Conroys down the road rent to his brother-in-law. I'm sure a phone call to the city will better answer that."

"I wouldn't know what to ask."

"I can help you," Sheriff Andy offered. "I used to manage rental properties back in my real estate broker days."

Hadn't Brenda said Sheriff Andy was smart

when it came to business and investments? Clearly, he knew something about rental properties, too.

"I'd have to talk to Pop first." Having a renter could solve more than one problem for him. "You sure you're not free for dinner?"

"Not tonight." Sheriff Andy flashed an apologetic smile.

"What about breakfast tomorrow morning? I'd like to discuss this with you. If you're willing, and I'm not imposing. My treat."

"No imposition. I'm working at the shelter tomorrow. Can we meet beforehand?"

"Absolutely. What about the Roadside Café? Seven thirty?"

"One of my favorite places. See you then." Sheriff Andy whistled to Peanut, and the two of them headed to his sedan. Everett checked the time. He had a few spare minutes and wanted to try out Hombre's new training halter.

He also wanted to dwell a little on this potential new venture. If Pop was agreeable, having Abel live on the ranch would mean no backing out for Everett. He couldn't leave two old men alone, much less just one.

Suddenly, he wanted to talk to Macy, too. Get her input.

Digging his phone from his pocket, he gave her a call. She answered on the second ring.

"Hi. Joey and I are just leaving the folks' house."

"You free for dinner tomorrow?"

She gave a nervous laugh. "Dinner?"

"Not what you think. Sheriff Andy has an interesting potential moneymaking venture for Pop, and I'd love your input."

"I'd have to bring Joey. And I can't stay long. I'm observing surgeries early tomorrow morning for my class. Going to be a full day."

"I promise not to keep you late."

"Then sure. I was going to be there, anyway."

"Great. Thanks, Macy."

She paused a moment. "Maybe next time you call about dinner, you'll ask me out."

Any doubts he had about them dating vanished. She was definitely willing to consider taking a step forward with him. And he couldn't be happier.

"Count on it. And you pick the place."

EVERETT MADE A special trip to the grocery store. Macy was coming to dinner, and he wanted to fix something a little more special than the usual broiled chicken breast or turkey meat loaf. Not that he'd veer too far from Pop's healthy diet.

There were also Joey's likes and dislikes to consider. Everett knew the kid liked egg salad sandwiches with potato chips. That was about the extent of his knowledge, however.

Perusing the store aisles and meat cases, he ultimately decided on grilled salmon for the adults—him, Macy and Pop—and hot dogs on buns for Joey. What kid didn't like hot dogs? In the deli section he chose premade heat-and-serve twice-baked potatoes. Lastly, he grabbed a bunch of asparagus in the produce department only because they were easy to grill alongside the salmon.

He was about to hit the checkout line when he remembered dessert. Since there were few things he could get that were on Pop's diet, he settled for a carton of orange sherbet and fresh raspberries. Once, when a bunch of them had gone out to celebrate at a fancy restaurant after a big rodeo win, one of the barrel racers had ordered sherbet and raspberries for dessert. If it was good enough for a fancy restaurant, Everett figured it would be fine for dinner tonight. And Joey would probably like it.

Breakfast that morning with Sheriff Andy had been informative and interesting. Everett had taken Pop along, and the three men had tossed ideas around about how to use the ranch's available acres to make the business even more profitable: from renting some lots to more RVs, to a small arena where Everett could give rodeoing lessons, to turning a far corner of the property into an equipment storage yard. They were just brainstorming at this point, but several of the ideas appealed to Everett, and he couldn't wait to tell Macy.

In the truck, he checked his phone again for an email from Hombre's seller. She'd responded to his phone call earlier, apologized profusely and then promised again to email the test results. So far, she'd failed to keep that promise. Maybe Everett would ask Macy about it tonight.

When he arrived home with the groceries, Pop was waiting for him, a noticeable spring in his step.

At first, Everett didn't think too much of it as he put the food away. Pop's mood had been jovial for days, the result of Everett's decision to stay.

Except Pop was acting especially peppy and practically two-stepped around the kitchen. Though, for him, it was more like shuffling. He hummed as he opened two root beers, one for each of them.

"What's gotten into you?" Everett asked.

"I have some news."

He shut the refrigerator door and joined his grandfather at the kitchen table. Pop had quite liked the idea of Abel staying on and paying a modest rent when Everett suggested it. They'd talked with Abel, who couldn't have been more enthused, and planned on running the idea by Glynnis tomorrow morning when she arrived to take him home.

Everett assumed Pop's news had something to do with that. He couldn't have been further off base.

"I was talking to Susan right before you got home." Pop cleared his throat. "We're going to the movies on Thursday afternoon."

"Nice. You need a ride? I can drop you off. I won't horn in on your date."

"Nope. Got it handled. We're going to take one of those car ride services."

"Seriously, Pop? I can drive you."

"We're going out to eat afterward. We might be late."

Everett tried not to laugh. If Pop and Susan stayed out past eight o'clock, he'd be shocked.

"Besides, it might turn into a special dinner."

Pop broke into a wide smile. "I'm thinking of proposing."

Everett almost fell out of his chair. "You're what?"

"I'm going to marry her, if she'll have an old geezer like me. She'd be smart to refuse." Pop's expression turned wistful. "At first, I thought I'd wait until I bought a ring. Give her flowers. The whole nine yards. But then I decided she might want to pick out her own ring. And that way, she can help me pick out mine, too."

"Pop." Everett searched for the right words. "Have you given this serious consideration?"

"I have. She's a wonderful woman."

"I couldn't agree more. But this feels fast."

Pop's grin waned. "We've been seeing each other more'n six months now. You just haven't been around to see."

That part was true.

"I love her, sonny. And she loves me back. She told me." His voice cracked. "The fact is, neither she nor I are getting any younger. Waiting seems like a waste of time that we could be spending together."

Everett wanted to feel about someone special like his grandfather did about Susan. Was that someone Macy? "I'm happy for you, Pop. Really."

"She'd be moving in here. You okay with that?"

"This is your home," he insisted, wondering if he should find another place to live. But then who would care for Pop when the time came? Susan couldn't.

"It's your home, too. Or half yours. As soon as I make an appointment with my attorney. I won't ask you to leave."

"Then I guess the better question is, are you okay living with a third person underfoot?"

Pop chuckled. "We'll try not to disturb you."

Everett didn't want to think about that and tried to wipe the image from his mind.

"I reckon I could move into that bungalow of hers," Pop said, his tone dejected. "If that was our only choice."

"What's wrong with her bungalow?"

"For starters, it's smaller than a matchbox. And there isn't ten feet between her and her neighbor."

"That would be a change for you." His grandfather had lived over fifty years on the ranch.

"Besides, I need to be here to help you run the business."

"You talk like she's already accepted your proposal."

"I'll be lower than an ant's ear if she says no." Pop's grin returned. "But I don't think she will."

"Me, either."

"It won't mean any more work for you. Callie will come by and give Susan a hand, just like when she sprained her ankle."

That was encouraging and a relief to Everett. If Pop accepted Callie's help with Susan, he might be more willing to accept help for himself.

"I do have a favor to ask." Pop looked hopeful. "Any chance you'd be my best man?"

Everett couldn't remember being more touched. "I'd be honored."

"You think your folks and Aunt Laurel would make the trip out?"

"Of course, they will. Uncle Kenny, too," he said, referring to his aunt's husband.

A moment later, they heard the sound of a vehicle. Everett pushed back from the kitchen table. "Macy's here."

"You go say hello. I'll start on this special dinner you planned."

"You sure? I can do it."

Pop shooed him away. "She's waiting on you."

He clapped his grandfather on the shoulder. "Susan's a lucky woman."

"Thank you, sonny, but I'm the lucky one."

Turned out, Macy wasn't waiting on him. Joey had escaped the second she lifted him from his car seat and set him on the ground. It seemed he wasn't alone. A short, fat dachshund waddled after him. The pair made straight for the mare barn.

"Is that Peanut?" Everett asked when he approached Macy.

She blew out a long, weary breath. "It is."

"You adopted her?"

"No. Well, yes." Macy sighed. "We agreed to a week's trial."

"And the dog's not behaving well?"

"The dog is a dream. Housebroken. No bad habits. Sweet as can be. So patient with Joey."

"What's the problem, then?"

"It's Joey. He's incorrigible when it comes to Peanut. Won't listen to a word I say."

"He'll get better once the newness wears off."

"Let's hope you're right." She smiled. "I do like the little scamp. And every kid should have a pet, right?"

"You'll get no argument from me. Remember Pogo?"

Her face brightened. "Your border collie? She was a great dog. So pretty and smart."

"Except she wouldn't leave the horses alone and wore herself out herding them for hours on end."

They strolled into the mare barn where Joey was telling Peanut the occupants' names, making up ones for those he didn't know.

Everett barely paid attention. He had trouble keeping his eyes off Macy. She'd worn her blond hair loose, and he imagined himself running his fingers through it.

In need of a distraction, he said the first thing to pop into his head. "Pop is going to propose to Susan."

CHAPTER TWELVE

MACY SHOULDN'T HAVE been surprised to learn Everett's grandfather intended to propose to his lady love. Especially since Everett had decided to remain and take over the business.

"He told you he's going to propose?" she asked.

"He did."

"When?"

"Right before you got here."

"No, no. When is he *planning* on proposing?"

"They're going to the movies and dinner on Thursday. He's thinking of doing it then. He's in a hurry."

Macy got misty-eyed at the thought of the two octogenarians walking down the aisle. "I'm so happy for them."

"She hasn't accepted yet," Everett cautioned.

"She will. They're in love. It's obvious."

"That's what Pop said."

A thought occurred to Macy. "Where will they live? Or is it too soon to ask?"

"Here, according to Pop. He's not crazy about moving into her bungalow."

"Wow. That's…interesting." She thought a moment. "You know, this could be the answer to your worries about Pop's future care."

"You mean Callie? I've already thought of that. Pop mentioned she'd still come to look after Susan. And, who knows? He might eventually be okay with the idea of having someone looking after him, too."

"That could solve a lot of problems."

"Yeah." Everett hesitated.

"What's wrong?"

"Don't think me selfish because I'm really happy for Pop and Susan. But what if things don't go as planned, their health takes a turn, and I wind up having to look after two elderly people? My skills are limited, and I have the ranch and a business to run. They may need more assistance than I can give them."

"Callie won't let that happen."

"I'd hate to be the reason Pop and Susan don't get married. I can see the positive effect she's had on his health."

Macy liked that Everett's perspective had changed since his return.

"There are some downsides, however," he said. "To be honest, I'm not sure how I feel about living with them. Newlyweds need their privacy, even if they are in their eighties, and I need mine."

She laughed. She couldn't help herself. "I get that."

"I doubt Susan wants to look at my ugly mug every morning and evening."

"I can think of worse things."

"Yeah?" Everett leaned in and traced his knuckles along her jawline.

A small, pleasant shiver skittered up Macy's spine, reminding her of their kiss the other day. Their many kisses, actually. Would there be a repeat today? Once could be blamed on getting lost in the moment. Twice, harder to call it an impulse. Three times? That was something serious and warranted a discussion.

"Mommy, look-it. I'm cleaning."

They turned to see Joey and Peanut. Unable to keep up with a rambunctious child, the overweight dog had plopped down in a patch of shade near the door and proceeded to pant. Joey had found the push broom and was moving dirt around the barn aisle in an attempt to sweep.

"Thank you, honey," Macy said. "You're a good helper."

With the romantic mood ruined—for the moment, anyway—Macy mentioned something else on her mind. "I heard from Brody's mom yesterday. She said you called."

"I finally worked up my nerve."

"She sounded really glad to have heard from you."

"She invited me to dinner."

"Really?" Macy smiled. "That's nice."

"We have no definite plans." Everett let out a long breath. "It'll be hard facing her and Brody's dad."

"You don't have to tell them about Brody taking your turn to drive on the day of the accident."

"If I'm going to see them again, I think I should. I won't lie to them. They deserve more than that from me."

Macy felt for him. Telling Brody's parents would be every bit as hard for Everett as it had been for him to tell her. And while she believed Brody's parents, like her, wouldn't hold him responsible, she couldn't say for certain.

"If you do have dinner with them, would you like me to go with you?" she asked.

He drew back to study her. "You'd do that?"

"I would."

"Okay. I'll give it some thought."

She could see in his expression that he didn't want to talk about this anymore, and she wouldn't force him. Instead, she changed the subject.

"What's this idea you wanted to run by me?"

Everett instantly relaxed. "I may have a way to bring in extra income."

"Tell me about it while we feed the mares and I give Roxie and Beauty a quick once-over."

Macy listened intently to Everett as they worked side by side. He told her about Abel staying and paying rent rather than leaving, possibly leasing spaces to more RVs and the other ideas under consideration. She concurred they all had potential and were worth exploring.

"I'm impressed, Everett."

"Well, it hasn't happened yet."

"You don't think you'd be taking on too much?

You were worried about two elderly people, and now it seems there might be three."

"You're right," he conceded. "That's why I need to do my homework first. And convince Pop to accept home care help from Callie."

To her satisfaction, Beauty's leg was healing well, and Roxie showed no signs of colic. It was just five thirty when they finished. Still a little early for dinner. Rather than go inside, they sat in the rocking chairs. Nearby, Joey entertained himself and Peanut with an old stick and a game of fetch. Only he did more fetching than the dog.

Everett chuckled at the pair. "There's a good chance Joey'll take a few pounds off that dog with all his energy."

"That's actually the goal." Macy rocked slowly. "I spoke to Kinsley today about a website for the horse breeding business. She's willing to set that up and refused to let me pay her."

"She's a good kid."

"I've also started calling Pop's previous customers and letting them know that we're open for business again. I already have two meetings scheduled for next week."

Macy gave him an admiring look. "I'm impressed."

"I don't want to have to ask the collective for any more funds to cover ranch expenses."

"That won't happen, Everett. You're going to do well taking over for Pop."

"I'd feel better if Hombre lives up to his potential." He sat back, a frown on his face. "The seller still hasn't forwarded the test results. I'm getting annoyed."

"Give it another day."

"Then what? Can I call the auction company? If she fails to supply the results, wouldn't that void our sale contract?"

"I doubt it." Macy shook her head. "Read over the auction contract you signed. I'm pretty sure you'll find a clause in there that basically says all sales are final and buyer beware."

"I was afraid of that." He turned to face her. "Did I make a mistake, Macy?"

"Not necessarily. Don't panic. Give the woman another couple of days. Sellers tend to place sold horses low on their priority lists. Out of sight, out of mind kind of thing. And she mentioned having some financial woes."

"I hope you're right."

She hoped so, too. Not having the testing results would affect Everett's ability to breed Hombre one day. Any customers would want to be assured he was free of genetic disorders.

"How is Abel doing, by the way?" she asked, wishing she could erase the frown from Everett's face. "His legs were bothering him the other day."

"Better. The pain seems to come and go."

"You know, you won't be the only one encroaching on the newlyweds."

"Abel's room isn't right down the hall."

Macy couldn't say what prompted her to suddenly blurt, "Why don't you build a place for yourself?"

"Like an apartment in the barn?"

"Or add a suite onto the house."

"That's a good idea. Except I'd want Pop and Susan to have the suite. Assuming she accepts his proposal."

"You might have to get a permit."

"That's the least of my problems," Everett said. "Changes to the ranch are going to cost money. Money we don't have."

Abel wandered by at that moment on his way to the house. "No worries. I'm not crashing your dinner."

"You'd be welcome," Everett told him.

"I'm just returning the newspaper Pop lent me." He motioned to the paper tucked under his arm. "Got a pot of stew on the stove for me."

With that, he wandered off, but not before stopping to give both Joey and Peanut pats on the head.

"Maybe I should build two bungalows," Everett said with a laugh. "One for me and one for Abel. He can't stay in that motor home forever."

"Or three."

"What would we do with a third bungalow?"

"Rent it out," Macy answered with all seriousness. "Like Sheriff Andy said."

Everett laughed at first, only to sober. "That's either a crazy idea or a really good one."

"You're clever, Everett. You can make this place

pay for itself again. You just need to think outside the box."

"You have more faith in me than I do myself."

"I have enough faith for the both of us."

She reached for his hand and squeezed his fingers before going in for a kiss that made her heart sing and give her a whole new outlook on life. Everett didn't hesitate and returned her affection, measure for measure.

When they drew apart a short time later, she couldn't help asking, "What does the future hold for us?"

She thought he might hedge or dodge her question entirely. He didn't.

"I care about you. A lot." He cradled her cheek and skimmed his thumb along her lower lip. "Things with me, with Pop, are a little up in the air right now."

"I get that."

"I don't want to make a promise I can't keep. Not again. You don't deserve that, from me or anyone."

"Which means?"

"I'd say let's take things one day at a time. But that sounds trite, and this, what you and I have, is too important to me to treat it lightly."

"I'm glad to hear you say that."

"This is serious for me, Macy. More serious than any previous relationship I've been in. I don't want to screw up. We need to go slow, however. Pop, the business and the ranch are my priorities."

"And I have mine. I've been building a life for

myself and Joey since before he was born. That won't change just because I bring someone new into our lives."

"I wouldn't expect it to. I want nothing more than to see you succeed at your career and will support you however you need. Joey, too."

"You never said, do you want children? Can you see yourself raising someone else's child?"

"I'm new at this. You'd have to be patient with me. But the answer to both is yes. I want a family, whatever shape that family takes."

She leaned her cheek into his palm. "I'm okay with slow, as long as we're moving forward."

He pulled her to him for another kiss. "Count on it."

"MOMMY, MOMMY!" Joey ran across his grandmother's living room and threw himself at Macy. "I missed you."

"I missed you, too, honey." She lifted him into her arms, receiving a big hug and kiss on the cheek. "Did you have fun today?"

"Lots of fun."

As they strolled into the kitchen, Joey told her about his day with Macy's mom. They'd run an errand to the drugstore, where Joey got to pick out a coloring book and crayons, watched Thomas the Tank Engine videos and had Popsicles. Grandpa had called on the picture phone—Joey's word for FaceTiming on Grandma's tablet.

Macy found her mom at the counter, slicing vegetables for a salad. "How goes the grind?" She set Joey down and gave her mom a one-armed hug.

"Hey, sweetheart. Not bad. Joey's tired. He didn't nap long. But otherwise, we've had a nice day."

Most people commented on her resemblance to her mother, and Macy supposed they did look alike. Sometimes she caught herself making the same gestures as her mother and using the same expressions.

"Was work busy?"

She let out a tired sigh. "We had three emergencies today. A tiny Chihuahua needed a C-section and delivered five puppies."

"Five! Isn't that a lot for a Chihuahua?"

"It is for a first litter. Then we had a dog who almost choked to death on a rawhide chew toy and a cat someone shot with a pellet gun."

"Shot? Who would do such a thing?" Macy's mother stopped slicing to stare in astonishment.

"Hard to say."

"Was it a stray?"

"No." Macy shook her head. "The owners found the cat hiding in a bush in their backyard."

"How awful."

From her spot on the back door rug, Peanut waddled over to Macy, tail wagging. Macy picked her up and received another kiss on the cheek. This one wet and sloppy.

"You spoil that dog?" Macy's mom said.

"Me?"

"She is a dear little thing. No trouble at all."

"Maybe you and Dad should keep her."

"No way. But we'll dog sit anytime." Macy's mom cut off a small piece of carrot and gave it to Peanut, who chomped noisily.

"You're not sneaking her any unapproved treats, are you?" Macy put the dog on the floor with Joey.

"Me? No!" Her mom feigned shock at the suggestion. "Only things off the list you gave me. Carrots, apples, green beans and blueberries. We also went on a walk this morning. Joey was excited, but she tuckered out after fifteen minutes."

"Thank you, Mom." Macy gazed fondly at the dog who was nosing around the floor at her mom's feet for a fallen vegetable slice. "I think she may have lost a half a pound since I've had her."

"Well, I could stand to lose some weight, too." Macy's mom patted her round hip.

"You look fantastic."

"Chasing after Joey does burn calories." She returned to her dinner preparations. "You heading to the ranch? I'm making plenty if you want to stay for dinner."

Her mom always referred to Pop's place as "the ranch."

"Yeah. Dr. Beck is meeting me there in…" Macy checked her phone. "Yikes! Twenty minutes. I need to hurry."

"Something wrong with one of the mares?"

"It's their monthly well check. He's seeing another patient right down the road, so it's not out of his way."

"Okay, good. I'll pack dinner for you and Joey."

"I can stop for fast-food chicken nuggets on the way."

"Don't be ridiculous. I have a fridge filled with food."

"You're the best, Mom." Macy felt a surge of love. "What would I do without you?"

"Let's hope you'll never have to find out."

She understood the deeper meaning to her mom's words. She and Macy's dad were there for Macy because she'd lost Brody. But she would have given anything for things to have been different and Macy not to be a widow and a single mother.

While her mom filled some to-go plastic containers, Jocy and Macy gave Peanut a bowl of reduced-calorie kibbles, then Macy gathered his things.

"Give Grandma a hug," Macy said at the door. "Tell Dad I'm sorry we missed him and that we'll see him this weekend."

"Before you go…" Macy's mom hesitated. "I talked to Fran today. She called me."

"Oh?"

Fran Sommers was Brody's mom. She and Macy's mom, former mothers-in-law and both grandmothers to Joey, were on friendly terms. A phone call wasn't uncommon.

"They had Everett over for dinner last night."

Macy nodded. "I know. I offered to go with him. He decided he wanted their first meeting to be just the three of them. Less awkward, and no one would feel put on the spot."

"He told her about the accident. That he should have been the one driving. Not Brody."

Macy's heart constricted at the memory of her conversation with Everett on the same subject. "He blames himself."

"He shouldn't."

"I agree."

"Fran was surprised. She had no idea. But she doesn't hold him responsible and told him that."

"I'm glad to hear that. Though Fran has always struck me as the forgiving type. Brody's dad, too. They were always fond of Everett."

Concern filled Macy's mother's eyes. "What about you? How do you feel about Everett's confession?"

"It doesn't change anything for me. I don't blame him anymore."

"Good. That would be a heavy burden to bear. For both of you. Perhaps Everett exercised poor judgment by celebrating too much the night before. But he loved Brody like a brother and must have suffered, thinking he was responsible. No wonder he stayed away. Seeing you and Joey had to have been torture for him."

"I hadn't thought of it that way."

"Well, why *did* you think he stayed away?"

"I don't know. I was just so angry at him for doing it. I never examined his reasons. That was very wrong of me. I see that now, and I should have reached out to him."

"What's the old saying?" her mom asked. "Anger

does us more harm than the things we're angry about."

"I'm sad to say that's true. For me, anyway."

"Things are better between you and him, though. Right?"

"Yes." Macy nodded.

"A lot better? You have been spending a lot of time together lately."

Something in her mom's tone put her on the alert. "It's work, Mom. Mostly, anyway."

"Is it?" She touched Macy's arm. "Because if you and he were to start seeing each other, that would be okay."

Her first impulse was to deny whatever her mom seemed to be insinuating. Only she didn't.

"Is this something you and Fran talked about?"

"No. I wouldn't never discuss your dating life with her or anyone without your consent."

"I'd appreciate that."

"So, there is something between you and Everett? I hear the way your voice changes when you say his name."

"A lot has happened since he returned." Macy hesitated, unsure how much to admit. "He's changing. Trying."

"I'm certainly happy for Pop. Everett staying is good for him."

"He's doing much better than before." She hadn't told her mom about Pop's plan to propose to Susan. That was his personal business.

"And I'm happy for you, too, sweetheart. Whatever you and Everett decide." Her mom reached up to cup her cheek, much like she had when Macy was a child. "Brody would want you to be happy and not be alone for the rest of your life."

Macy nodded, a lump forming in her throat and preventing her from speaking. Her mom knew about the argument with Brody mere hours before he died. She'd been Macy's one and only confidante. She'd insisted Macy was too hard on herself and that Brody had loved her body and soul. Something Everett had recently confirmed.

More than that, Everett and Macy had shared the secret guilts they'd been carrying for three years, and it had freed them from their invisible shackles.

Was trauma bonding responsible for their growing attraction? Macy wanted to believe no, that their feelings stemmed from a genuine, positive connection. Nonetheless, she cautioned herself to be careful and not get carried away. She'd worked too hard these past three years building a good life for her and Joey to risk losing it over a miscalculation of the heart.

"Mommy, I wanna go," Joey whined impatiently.

"Okay, honey." Macy hugged her mom. "Thanks for everything."

She loaded Joey in the truck and gave him a cheese sandwich. Peanut rode on the seat beside him, staring at the food with puppy dog eyes in the hopes of receiving a handout.

"I wanna go home, Mommy."

"Sorry, honey. We have to go to the ranch first.

Dr. Beck is probably already there. Mommy can't be late." She glanced at the clock on the truck's dashboard. "Later than Mommy already is."

Joey proceeded to sulk, even losing his appetite, which bode well for Peanut who wolfed down the sandwich half he dropped onto the seat. So much for her diet.

Did Macy really need to go to the ranch? Yes, Dr. Beck was checking on the mares, and their health was her responsibility.

But she'd see the vet tomorrow at the clinic and could always get a report from him. If Macy was honest with herself, she wanted to see Everett.

Was her mom right? Would dating him be okay for everyone involved? Macy had never gotten that far in her thinking.

But the fact was, more people than just her would be affected if she and Everett's relationship grew serious. There was Joey to consider, of course. Everett had said all the right things the other night, and she wanted to believe him. But he'd failed her before in a big way. And he did seem to avoid confrontations rather than face them. She needed someone she trusted implicitly. For Joey's sake more than hers.

She had much to think about and had found no answers by the time she reached the ranch.

CHAPTER THIRTEEN

MACY PARKED NEXT to Dr. Beck's truck that had its side compartments open, displaying various veterinarian equipment and supplies. After unloading boy and dog, she remembered her tablet. She'd need that to update the mares' health records.

In the nearby distance, the sun slowly dropped behind the mountaintops, turning the warm golden glow of late afternoon into the soft gray of early evening. The sight never failed to inspire or soothe Macy, depending on her mood. Today, after reflecting on her relationship with Everett, it was the latter.

She cared for Everett. Not the youthful infatuation she'd experience as a teenager. This was… different. Unlike anything she'd felt before. And it gave her reason to believe that finding happiness again with someone was possible for her. Everett knew her terrible shame, yet he still returned her feelings. He gave her confidence that she wasn't a bad person.

Was he here? She glanced around. This time of day, he might be inside with Pop, preparing or eating dinner.

"Stay with Mommy, honey."

Joey dragged his feet, stirring up small clouds of red dust. She didn't blame the boy. He'd had a long day. Her, too. With luck, Dr. Beck would find no concerns with the mares, and they could all leave soon.

"Hi, Doc. Sorry I'm late." She entered the mare barn and took in the scene. The mares were finishing their evening meal, which meant that Everett had recently been there. He could be as close as the stallion quarters.

"Not a problem," Dr. Beck said from inside Dusty's stall.

"Hope I didn't miss anything important."

The hardworking and caring vet straightened, his round face flushed. "Nothing noteworthy."

"How's Dusty?"

"Perfectly healthy. You can breed her whenever you and she are ready."

"That's good news."

"She's a fine addition to your breeding program."

Exiting the stall, he disinfected his hands with sanitizer, then summarized his exam of the first three mares in the barn. Macy entered the updates into her tablet while Joey attempted to fasten a piece of twine to Peanut's collar, constructing a makeshift leash. The little dog endured this latest torture with her usual patience.

After that, Macy accompanied Dr. Beck as he examined the remaining mares.

"Next month, I'm planning on bringing the portable ultrasound machine," he said with a happy grin. "We can get some more baby pictures."

"That'll be exciting." Knowing for certain the foals were healthy would relieve a great deal of worry for the collective.

They were just finishing with the last mare when Everett's broad-shouldered form filled the barn entrance. Macy saw at once by the shadows darkening his features that something was bothering him.

"Everett." She stepped away from the stall and moved toward him. "Is Pop okay?"

"He's fine. Why?"

"You look… Are you all right?"

"Yeah."

Except he wasn't. She could tell.

"Hello, Dr. Beck." Everett nodded at the vet in greeting.

"Everett." He closed the stall door behind him and once again sanitized his hands. "How's your new young stallion doing?"

"He's fine."

"Do I hear a *but*?"

Everett's gaze found Macy's. "I still haven't heard back from Hombre's seller."

"You're kidding!"

"It's been nearly a week. I think she's ghosting me."

"How can I help?"

"Is there any other way I can get the test results? What if I contact the testing company? Will they send them to me if I show them my bill of sale?"

"I doubt it." She turned to Dr. Beck. "What do you think?"

The vet moved closer. "What happened?"

Everett explained about buying the young stallion at the sale and the seller promising to forward the original genetic test results.

"Can I see what she sent you?" Dr. Beck asked.

Everett scrolled through his phone, then held it out to the other man.

"May I look closer?" Dr. Beck took Everett's phone, enlarged the testing results document and studied it with squinted eyes. "Hmm."

"I don't like the sound of that," Everett said.

Macy concurred.

Dr. Beck tilted his head in question. "Didn't Macy tell me the stallion was around eighteen months old?"

"He is." Everett nodded.

"See this?" Dr. Beck turned the phone and showed Everett. "These results are for a two-year-old."

"What?" Everett grabbed the phone from the vet. "How's that possible?"

"Is the other information correct?"

Everett's jaw worked as he enlarged other areas of the document. "The name's not quite right. Hombre's registered name is Gran Hombre Gris. This says Hombre Gris Gordo."

"I'd say this is a different horse. Compare the document against his registration papers. See if the sire and dam match up."

"I can't believe I missed this."

"The names are similar," Macy said.

"I just zeroed in on the word negative and ignored the rest of the document." Anger hardened his stare. "Have I been swindled?"

"Everett." Macy's stomach knotted. She feared he was right. "I'm so sorry."

"Don't jump to conclusions," Dr. Beck warned. "It could be an honest mistake, and the seller gave you the wrong test results."

"Yeah, then why isn't she answering my calls and texts?" Everett shoved his phone into his shirt pocket. "I'm going to call the auction company. I may have no recourse with them, but they should know one of their sellers is not on the up-and-up."

"Again," Dr. Beck said, "don't get ahead of yourself. Let's assume this was just an oversight, and the seller has kept poor records."

"That doesn't solve my problem. I've invested in a stallion I can't use for stud unless I'm able to guarantee he's genetically sound."

"It's an easy enough problem to solve. Just re-test him. It will cost you some money and take a little time. But I have a kit in the truck and can do it now if you want. The results will take a couple of weeks. I'll try to expedite them."

Everett nodded. "Thank you, Doc."

He retreated to a corner of the barn while the vet went to his truck for a testing kit. Macy joined him, grateful for Peanut and that she kept Joey occupied.

"This is a minor setback," she told Everett.

Doubt shadowed his expression. "The seller lied

to me. I know it. Probably because Hombre failed. What will I do if he's a carrier for a condition that makes him unsuitable for breeding?"

"You said before you could turn him into a gelding and sell him. Maybe even make a small profit."

"That'll take six months. He's green as spring grass."

At his dejected expression, she reached out, but he withdrew his arm.

"What was I thinking? I don't have what it takes to run Pop's horse breeding business. I made a stupid, rookie mistake."

"Maybe not. Wait until the tests come back."

"It could be too late by then."

"Too late for what?"

"Me returning to the rodeo circuit. There's still time. I haven't missed my opportunity to qualify for Nationals. And if I make it to finals, I can bring home some decent prize money."

"You'd leave?" Macy tamped down the panic rising in her. This couldn't be happening.

"I don't know. This isn't what I expected." Rubbing his forehead, he closed his eyes and let out a long sigh. "When I screw up, I screw up big."

Macy wanted to argue with him. But Dr. Beck chose that moment to return with the testing kit, and Joey wandered over to complain again about wanting to go home.

She didn't get a chance to talk to Everett alone before she had to leave, and when she tried calling him later that evening, he didn't pick up. Finally, before bed, he texted her good-night. That was all. Nothing else. Her panic returned, no longer mild.

EVERETT OWED MACY more than a vague text the next morning saying he'd call later. But he wasn't ready to talk to her. Not yet. She'd ask questions he wasn't prepared to answer. He needed time to think and a reprieve from being pulled in a dozen different directions.

What he had done was call his buddy Rusty who was heading to the Big Timber Rodeo in Tucson. Everett needed an ear to bend, one belonging to someone familiar with his situation. But talking things through hadn't given him the clarity he'd hoped for.

When had everything changed? A month ago, he'd had a plan. Qualify for Nationals, win a title and start a new job as a youth rodeo coach. He'd had no responsibilities beyond taking care of himself.

Now, Pop was depending on him to take over the ranch and horse breeding business and, though he refused to admit as much, help with his eventual care. What if Everett left and Pop didn't propose to his lady love? He certainly wouldn't if they were buried in debt and forced to sell the ranch. His pride wouldn't let him.

Then there was Macy. She and Everett only recently confessed their growing feelings and agreed to start dating. That would come to a crashing end if he returned to the rodeo circuit. She wanted a life partner who stayed home. One who kept his promises.

Except, if he couldn't succeed at the horse breeding business and he was no longer competing, what else did he have to offer her besides a run-down ranch and a pile of bills?

"You're being way too hard on yourself," Pop said. He'd been following Everett around for the past two hours.

"That's a matter of opinion."

"Nonsense," Pop grumbled under his breath. "What about those two appointments you have scheduled this week with my old customers?"

Everett had forgotten about those. "We need more than two customers."

"We'll get them. I've let the business go, and that's on me. But we'll turn things around. I once made a dandy living off this ranch. Isn't Kinsley working on computer advertising?"

Pop was confusing the website and social media accounts. Everett didn't correct him. He was too tired. They'd been going at it long enough that Pop was repeating himself.

Their talk had started during the morning feeding—seeing Hombre stirred a fresh wave of anger at himself and his gullibility—and continued when they'd come inside where Everett ran the vacuum, mopped floors and changed the air-conditioning filter.

These tasks required bending and lifting and standing on a stepladder and were off-limits for

Pop. If Everett returned to the rodeo circuit, he'd have to arrange help for Pop. For Abel, too, since he was staying. Maybe Sheriff Andy could lend a hand.

Another solution would be Pop moving in with Susan. He hated the idea of living in her bungalow, but it was better than a nursing home.

Who was he kidding? There was only one solution. He had to earn money, good money, and fast. Rodeoing was the best way to accomplish that, and the only thing he was truly good at. Except that required him to leave after he'd promised to stay.

"There's always a… What do the young folks call it?" Pop asked. "A learning something or other."

"Learning curve."

"That's it."

They were now outside on the patio where Everett had just finished using the leaf blower to clear off debris from the recent rains. He shrugged out of the machine and set it on the ground by the picnic table. Though only 9:00 a.m., the temperature was already in the low eighties.

Today would be another scorcher, which matched his mood. After a restless night troubled by doubts and worries, Everett's temper was easily riled. Most of it was directed at himself.

Was it only the other day that Macy had told him she believed him capable of anything? How wrong she'd been. He couldn't buy a horse without messing up.

Because Pop was breathing heavily, Everett sat

down at the picnic table. As he'd hoped, Pop joined him. The heat had been getting to him, too. More so these last couple of days.

"We still have Champ," Pop said when he could speak again. "And Hombre."

So much for Everett thinking their conversation was over. "Like I said before, I may sell Hombre."

"You can't!"

Sometimes his grandfather only heard what he wanted to hear. Everett cut him some slack today, however. Susan wasn't feeling well and had canceled their movie date on Thursday. Pop's plan to propose had been delayed, souring his mood.

"What choice do I have?" Everett asked.

"You're always in such a goll-darn rush. Wait till his tests come back yet."

Hearing the rumble of an engine, they glanced up to see a pickup coming into view. Any hopes Everett had of giving the topic of him returning to the rodeo circuit a rest were dashed at the sight of Macy sitting behind the wheel.

COLLECTIVE MEMBERS ARRIVING on a Saturday were expected. Frankly, Everett was surprised no one besides Macy had shown up. Perhaps they had weekend plans and knew he was here to feed and clean stalls.

Another possibility was she'd told them all to stay away. Less interruptions that way. She did have a determined look on her face. Or was that anger?

Drawing in a deep breath, he steeled himself.

He should have called her last night or at least this morning. Too late now.

Pop waved her over the moment her truck door opened and her feet hit the ground. "Morning, Macy."

"Hi, Pop. Everett."

"Hey." He stood.

She opened the rear passenger door. The next moment, Joey bounded over. Unlike his mother, he beamed at Everett. Peanut waddled after him, the opposite of bounding.

Macy brought up the rear. She wore her usual ponytail and ball cap, and her gaze was directed at him. He could feel the invisible daggers she fired at him from where he stood.

"Everett!" Joey reached him and grabbed his legs, his version of a bear hug. "I wanna ride horsie."

Everett bent down and ruffled the boy's hair. "It's a little too hot today to go riding. You can help me put Hombre in the pasture. If your mom's okay with that."

"I'll help."

Everett suspected Joey didn't understand everything he'd said but wanted to go along regardless. As Macy neared, he gave the boy a nudge. "Go to say hi to Pop."

Joey did, taking Peanut with him.

"You're the first to arrive," he told Macy. "No one else is here yet."

She cut right to the chase. "Can we talk?"

For a man in his eighties, Pop had no trouble

reading the room. Or, in this case, the patio. Pushing to his feet, he said, "Joey, you want some lemonade? Come into the house with me. And bring that dog of yours before she has heatstroke."

"Can I have cookie?"

"I'm not allowed to have cookies. How 'bout a bran muffin?"

"No muffin for Peanut," Macy called after them without taking her eyes off Everett.

"It is hot out here," he said when they were alone. "You sure you don't want to have this conversation inside?"

Her reply was to sit at the picnic table.

"I take it that's a no." He joined her, dropping into the seat beside her. "I'm sorry I didn't return your call."

"Calls. Plural."

"Okay."

"Are you avoiding me?" she asked.

"More like procrastinating."

She drew back to study him. "Wow. I didn't realize talking to me was so difficult."

Everett adjusted his cowboy hat, a stalling tactic. Uncertainty and anxiety had plagued him from the moment Dr. Beck had discovered the genetic test results from the seller were for a different horse. No calming exercises or silent talks with himself stopped the building tension.

He'd thought Macy, more than anyone, would understand how he felt. She'd suffered her own bouts with uncertainty and anxiety. Only she wasn't acting like she understood, and that only increased his anxiety.

"Pop's been hammering at me all morning."

"Really?" She gaped at him. "Your response is to deflect?"

"I haven't had a free minute to call you," he said, recognizing how lame his answer sounded.

"Seriously? You couldn't find five minutes?"

"I wasn't ready to answer your questions."

She paused, then nodded. "Okay. That, at least, is an honest response."

"I still don't have any answers."

"About staying?" Her voice rose.

"That. And about what's best for Pop. The ranch, the horse breeding business. Any of it."

"Does that include us?" Her gaze on him didn't waver, although uncertainty flickered in her eyes.

Everett refused to lie again. He'd done that once before and caused her a world of hurt.

"Yes."

"I see."

"Any decision I make," he said, "any direction I turn, I'm going to hurt someone or make them mad or disappoint them. Probably more than one person."

"Don't you think you're being a little dramatic? *Any* decision?" Her brows rose. "Really?"

"Pop's breeding business is a shadow of what it used to be. It needs an experienced person in charge, and that's not me. I proved that when I bought Hombre."

"You'll learn. You're smart."

Everett shook his head, frustrated. She wasn't seeing the whole picture. Or she refused. "Time and money are in short supply. With me living on the ranch, we need to bring in enough income to support two people. And that's in addition to all the upcoming expenses and necessary repairs. And then there's the cost of home health care for Pop, if it comes to that."

"What if you got a job?" Macy asked.

"There aren't many openings in Wickenburg for a retired rodeo competitor."

"What about a wrangler for one of the ranches? Or the Hays might hire you."

He would not ask the Hays for a job. Like Pop, he had his pride. "Neither of those jobs would pay enough."

"So, you'd leave?"

Until that moment, he hadn't decided. As he talked to Macy, the answer became clear. "Yes. Temporarily."

She shook her head. "I'm clearly missing something, because I don't see how abandoning Pop to fend for himself and turning your back on the business and the ranch is a solution."

"I can earn quick money rodeoing. Enough between now and the end of the year to pay the insurance and taxes. Abel's rent will cover Champ and Hombre's expenses. And Pop won't be alone. I'll arrange for Callie to check on him and as of next month, Sheriff Andy will be living here."

"Sheriff Andy?"

"He told me at breakfast the other day that he's selling his house. Until he finds a new place, he's putting his stuff in storage and parking his RV here. It was only going to be until November, but I think I can convince him to stay until the end of the year."

Macy crossed her arms over her middle. "What if you don't win your events?"

"I'll come home." But that wasn't an option he wanted to consider. They needed the money. He had to win.

"The collective can help. We have some funds set aside—"

"No." Everett cut her off before she could finish. This wasn't a subject up for debate. "But thanks for the offer."

"Everett—"

"This isn't your problem to solve."

"It is, in a way," she said. "We have to protect our investment."

"Which is what I'm trying to do. Protect your investment. Pop almost lost the ranch once before because of unpaid taxes. If that happens again and the county forces a sale, you won't have a place for the mares and foals. Then what will the collective do?"

She drew in a long breath before continuing. "I just think there are options other than you returning to rodeoing. Champ has a stellar reputation. It won't take long to bring in customers. You already have two appointments. What about them? Are you going to cancel?"

"Pop will cover for me."

"Talk to the Hays. Not about a job," she hastily added. "Advertising in their feed store. I'm sure they'll let you."

"That's a good idea. I'll stop by before I leave town."

She heaved a sigh. "You are more stubborn than anyone I know. Even your grandfather."

"I'm not stubborn. I'm a realist. I ran the numbers last night." He'd created a spreadsheet on his laptop after Pop went to bed. He was by no means an expert, but he didn't think his calculations were that far off. Sheriff Andy agreed when Everett called him. Much to his dismay, the retired real estate broker had reported his less than encouraging findings from the city about renting out space. It was doable, but the permits would require a lengthy application process, cost substantial fees and take two to three months. "We're going to need twenty thousand dollars over the next few months. And that's a conservative estimate."

When she started to speak, he interrupted her.

"Until the foals are sold and Pop gets his share, which is, at minimum, eighteen months away, this place will be running on a shoestring. And that's only if I can bring in enough income and nothing unexpected happens."

"What if you sold Hombre?"

"You know what I paid for him. At most, I'd get enough to support the ranch for a month."

She lifted her chin. "You're just going to give up, then?"

"I'm not giving up. I'm trying to salvage a bad situation the best way I can."

"Which also happens to allow you to qualify for Nationals."

"This has nothing to do with Nationals."

"But if you do qualify, you'd go."

He tried to slow his rapid breathing. Though they were outside, it felt like the walls were closing in on him. He'd experienced the same sensation before in the months following the accident.

"I would go. If I place in the top three of any event, the prize money would be enough to carry the ranch for six months. That would give us the funds we need to make repairs and me time to learn the business. Also to train Hombre and sell him for a profit."

"You're chasing a pipe dream, Everett, and betting your grandfather's health, his business and this ranch on it."

He heard the bitterness in her retort, and it cut deep, reminding him of a phone call not long after Brody's death when he'd told Macy he wasn't returning.

"If, after a month or six weeks, it looks like I'm not going to qualify for Nationals, I'll come home."

Macy averted her gaze; her posture stiffened. "You got it all figured out."

Everett didn't blame her for being mad at him. "I don't want to sell the ranch and put Pop in a nursing facility. I thought that's what you wanted, too."

"It is."

"Me temporarily returning to the circuit is the best way to accomplish that."

"When would you leave?" she asked.

"Today. I called Rusty earlier. I can still make the Big Timber Rodeo in Tucson."

Team roping was out of the question. Rusty had partnered with Junior. But Everett could enter bulldogging and tie-down roping, both events he excelled at.

Macy's features tightened. She was fighting to control her emotions. "You didn't waste a single second. You must really want to get away."

"I don't." He leaned toward her. She backed away, and he didn't push. "I'll be back. I promise."

"Will you?" She turned to face him then, tears brimming in her eyes. "Because I've heard that line before at Brody's funeral, and then you abandoned me."

"It's different this time."

"Is it? What about us, Everett? What happens while you're competing and saving the ranch? Do we see each other whenever you decide to come home? Are we still dating? On break?"

Here was the hardest part of his plan. "I'm not in a good place right now to make any kind of commitment, and you deserve that."

"I do. I absolutely do." The hurt in her eyes belied the strength of her words.

"I'm sorry, Macy. Try to look at this from my perspective. I don't have much going for me except a ranch that, unless I manage a minor miracle, will soon be in worse debt than it currently is and a business that I may drive into the ground. That's not what you deserve, either."

"My feelings for you don't hinge on how successful you are."

"I won't saddle anyone with my debt. You especially."

She hooked her leg over the picnic table seat and stood. "It sounds to me like your mind is made up. I don't see reason to continue this conversation."

Everett also stood. This hadn't gone well, which was why he'd wanted more time to think things through before talking to her. "I disappointed you before. I don't want to do it again, and I'm afraid I will."

"Right. I get it. A small hurt now rather than a big hurt later."

"Can we talk again in a few weeks? I'll be home after the Amarillo Rodeo."

"No. No." Her composure began to visibly fray, and she waved a hand in the air. "I don't know why I thought this time would be different. You leave when the going gets tough. Just look at your track record."

"This isn't like before." He rubbed his forehead

where a headache threatened to morph into a migraine.

"It's exactly like before. You just refuse to see."

"Macy. Please."

"Whatever you got to do to live with your guilt." She walked away only to turn back.

Any hopes Everett had that she'd had a change of heart were dashed with her next words.

"Please tell Pop I'm going to do the chores and ask him if he'd mind watching Joey and Peanut?"

"I will." His chest ached. Not as much as the pain he'd obviously caused her. How was it possible to mess up so badly when all he'd wanted to do was solve problems?

"You know what hurts the most, Everett? You didn't talk to me first. You made your plans without a single thought of me."

It wasn't like that. He'd felt cornered, and their conversation went sideways. But he didn't say that. "I should have. You're right."

"That's not a quality I'm looking for in a life partner." She walked away then.

He debated going after her only to reconsider. He'd let her down. Nothing he said would redeem him.

Thirty minutes later as he was packing, he mentally replayed the scene between them over and over.

Maybe it wasn't survivor's guilt that had kept him away all those years or not having the courage to face her. Rather, he had a fear of failing. At business and, more importantly, failing those he loved.

And in the end, it became a self-fulfilling prophecy.

CHAPTER FOURTEEN

MACY HAD ABSOLUTELY zero intention of going to the ranch today. In fact, she might not go tomorrow, either. Yes, she was that mad at Everett. Not that he was there. He'd left yesterday for the Big Timber Rodeo. She'd watched him from her hiding place in the mare barn. His truck had hardly disappeared in a cloud of red dust when she headed into the house, grabbed Joey and Peanut, managed to avoid Pop's probing questions and drove straight home.

Fortunately, Larry Hays had volunteered to handle last evening's feeding. He'd been stuck covering for their driver who'd left work early to deal with a family emergency. As the ranch was already on the schedule for their regular hay and grain delivery, he hadn't minded feeding the mares and stallions.

Macy hadn't felt guilty asking Glynnis to handle the morning feeding, as she'd already had plans to take her brother Abel to an early breakfast and then church service. Neither had Kinsley minded when Macy phoned and asked her to feed the horses this evening.

Everett would be home in a few weeks. Maybe

by then Macy's anger at him would have cooled, and she'd see his point of view. Not today, however.

She should have been able to sleep in and spend the morning catching up on things around the house. Except that hadn't happened. Nothing had gone her way since her argument with Everett.

Joey, apparently picking up on her sour mood, had been determined to test her patience from the moment she'd loaded him into the truck yesterday. Her often sweet and biddable little boy was either misbehaving, refusing to cooperate, pitching a fit or tuning her out.

He'd woken her twice during the night with his crying, complaining of a tummy ache. Macy could relate. She'd had her own tummy ache to contend with—namely, Everett.

The thought of him made her groan aloud. It was three years ago all over again. The same emotions she'd experienced back then rose anew to torture and torment her.

In the end, she'd told Joey he could sleep with her, hoping that snuggling with her darling son would ease both their troubles. It hadn't. Not hers. In the morning, splotches stained her pillow, remnants from where her tears had dried.

Why did Everett have to leave? Macy pondered the question while she stowed Joey's toys in the multicolored cubicles lining a wall in his room. In a way, she kind of, sort of, understood his reasoning to put the brakes on their relationship. He did have more pressing priorities, and she had no wish to add to his struggles. But they could have remained friends until the timing was better. She'd have gladly waited.

It was the fact that he was running away that annoyed her. He was putting his rodeoing career ahead of Pop's breeding business and the ranch.

If he'd stayed in Wickenburg, he could have immediately focused his energies on building the breeding business and likely brought in clients quickly. Instead, he'd jumped in his truck and driven to Tucson.

He had better come back, Macy thought and ground her teeth, feelings from three years ago returning. It was one thing to abandon her and Joey. If Everett abandoned Pop, she'd never forgive him.

Finishing in Joey's room, she went to the kitchen in search of Joey, only to stop dead in her tracks. Leaving him alone in his current mood for even a few minutes had been a big mistake.

"Look-it, Mommy." He beamed up at her, so proud of himself. "I fed Peanut."

"Joey. Oh, no!"

Somehow, he'd breached the cabinet's childproof lock, or she, in her preoccupied state of mind, had left it open, and dumped the entire open bag of dog kibble onto the kitchen floor. Peanut, having suffered reduced portions for the last several weeks, now gorged herself. She inhaled each little round nugget with the speed and efficiency of a hand vacuum set on high.

"Peanut. Leave it."

The dachshund ignored her and continued to feast. So much for Sheriff Andy's assurance that she was trained in voice commands.

Macy bent and scooped the dachshund into her arms. Peanut whined and wiggled in an effort to free herself.

"What am I going to do with you?"

The extra food likely wouldn't undo the results of Peanut's healthy diet. But Macy had promised Sheriff Andy she'd take good care of the dog and not overfeed her.

"She hungry," Joey said.

Macy bit her tongue and drew in a calming breath. She would not snap at her son. He was a child. Exactly two years and seven months old this past Friday. He didn't know any better. And she had left him alone in a kitchen with an unlocked cabinet.

"Come on. Be a good boy and help Mommy clean up. But first we need to shut Peanut in the bathroom."

Macy was just returning the broom and dustpan to the pantry when her cell phone rang from where it lay on the counter. She reached it a split second before the call went to voicemail and saw Glynnis's name on the display.

"Hi. How's it going?"

"Fine," the older woman said. "Hey, listen, I was just leaving after dropping off Abel when I heard a distressing sound from the barn."

"What do you mean by distressing?"

"Hard to say. Grunting, I guess? It's Roxie."

Macy's heart rate quickened. "Is she acting colicky?"

"Maybe. I'm no expert. You want me to call Dr. Beck?"

"No." Macy put her earlier determination to avoid the ranch aside. The health of the mares was too important. "I'll be there in thirty minutes. If need be, I'll call him."

"Should I stay? I have to head home soon. My son and his family are coming over for a birthday cookout. But I can hang around here for a little while."

"I'll call Pop. Ask him to keep an eye on Roxie until I get there. You go on."

They disconnected, and Macy rushed to get out of the house. She called her mom on the way and asked if she could drop off Joey. Should Roxie have colic, Macy might be there well into the evening and, more importantly, need to focus all her attention on the horse. Besides, a change might do her cranky son some good.

Once behind the wheel, she phoned Pop and explained things to him. "Do you mind waiting with Roxie until I arrive? I'll hurry."

"Sure." He coughed and coughed again. "No problem."

"Are you all right, Pop?" She didn't like the way he sounded.

"I'm fine. Just tired." His voice trailed off. "Feeling my age today."

"Yeah. I hear you."

He'd probably had a bad night, too, worrying about Everett and sad he'd left for the rodeo. Plus, it was another warm day.

"Thanks, Pop. I'll see you soon."

Having been forewarned about her grandson's mood, Macy's mom greeted Joey with a frozen yogurt bar. He grabbed the treat with both hands and shoved it into his mouth. Macy kissed the top of his head, avoiding sticky smears on her face.

"And nothing for Peanut that isn't on her diet," she said as she climbed back into the truck cab.

The dog sat at her mom's feet, wearing a forlorn expression.

Macy forced herself to remain unmoved and reversed out of the driveway. She really couldn't tell what had her more on edge at the moment: her son's fussiness, Roxie's possible bout with colic, her concern for Pop or her anger at Everett. This was not a good day.

At the ranch, she drove straight to the mare barn, parked and grabbed her medical bag from the rear seat. Pop sat in one of the rocking chairs, his shoulders slumped. Nearing, she noticed his alarming pallor.

"Hi, Pop. Are you okay?"

"Don't bother with me. Go check on that mare."

"You sure?"

She couldn't help herself and put a hand on his forehead. It didn't feel especially warm to the touch. Nor did he sound congested. His breathing was short, however.

"My stomach's been giving me fits all morning," he said. "I must have eaten something that didn't agree with me."

Macy hesitated, torn over what to do. Finally, she said, "Give me a minute. I won't be long."

Inside the barn, she hurriedly checked over Miss Roxie. If the mare had been showing signs of distress earlier with Glynnis, she appeared perfectly fine now. The stethoscope revealed only normal gut noises, and the mare presented alert and interested and calm. She exhibited no signs of pain when Macy palpated her sides, and an inspection of the stall showed normal elimination habits.

"What's up, girl? You just playing games with Glynnis? Getting her upset over nothing?"

Roxie nuzzled Macy's hair, not seeming the least bit distressed.

"All right." Macy sighed. "False alarm, I guess." She shrugged. "Better I came here for no reason than didn't come and you lost your foal. Or worse."

She scratched Roxie between the ears before exiting the stall. There, she returned her stethoscope to the medical bag.

"Maybe I'll come by this evening just to be on the safe side." So much for her vow to stay away.

Lifting the bag by the handle, she started out of the barn. There, she saw Pop still sitting in the rocking chair, his head bent forward. She started toward him.

"Roxie appears fine. I think I'll—" She stopped short. "Pop?" When he didn't respond, she dropped the bag and covered the remaining distance at a run. "Pop! Pop!" She bent over him and shook his shoulder. "Pop, answer me."

"Yeah. Yeah." His voice came out in a strained whisper.

"What's wrong?"

"My chest. It hurts."

She saw then he cradled his left arm. Terror seized her, freezing her insides. "Hang on, Pop. I'm going to call for help."

He didn't object, which Macy took as an indication of how bad he felt.

Straightening, she dug her phone from her pocket and dialed 911.

When the dispatcher answered, she shouted into the phone, "I have an eighty-seven-year-old man with me. I think he is having a heart attack."

EVERETT LIFTED THE saddle off his borrowed paint horse and carried it to the storage compartment in the front of Rusty's trailer. He then grabbed a stiff currycomb and began rubbing the dried sweat from the horse's hide. Tired from a full day's work in the rodeo arena, the paint lowered his head and snorted with contentment. Though tied to the side of the trailer, it was unlikely he'd go anywhere.

"You did good today, boy." Everett patted the horse on the neck.

"You, too," came a voice from behind him. "For

someone out of practice. Second place in tie-down roping was respectable."

He turned to find Rusty's wide, affable grin aimed at him. The lanky cowboy, his plaid shirt and denim jeans dusty from a full morning competing in the arena, carried two foil-wrapped burritos and two cans of soda.

"I've done better," Everett said. He'd been disappointed in his bulldogging performance, coming in tenth. And he didn't want to think about his poor showing in bronc and bull riding. He had no one to blame but himself, thoughts of Macy distracting him.

"Well, that's true." Rusty handed one of the burritos to Everett, along with a soda. "But you kept yourself in the running for Nationals in two events. That's not nothing."

And the tie-down roping prize money would cover his expenses for this weekend and next weekend, too.

They sat down to eat, Everett on the wheel well of the trailer and Rusty in a rickety lawn chair that had seen more than a hundred rodeos.

"Thanks for lunch, by the way." Everett took a bite of his burrito. He wasn't hungry, but he didn't want to offend his friend, who'd been nothing but good to him. That included listening to Everett spill his guts the previous evening in their hotel room when they should have been getting a good night's sleep in preparation for today's competition.

"Mind if I make an observation?" Rusty asked.

"Not at all. I can use some insight."

"Money is replaceable. You can always get more. Family isn't. Once you lose someone, they're gone for good."

"You think I should quit rodeoing."

Rusty's goofy, yet friendly, features fell. "You know my dad died of cancer when I was twenty."

"Yeah." Everett ached for his friend. "Sorry, man. That had to be rough."

"His last wish was for me to win a title. He didn't get it because I spent the last five months of his life home, with him, helping my mom with his hospice care. I set my rodeo career back two years."

"I remember."

"And I've never regretted a single moment. Those five months with my dad meant everything to me. To him, too."

Everett sat back, ruminating that.

"I'm not telling you what to do, pal." Rusty finished off his burrito and crumpled the foil wrapping. "I'm merely telling you what I did. A heart can't be in two places at once."

"Are you talking about my grandfather or Macy?"

"Take your pick."

Everett nodded. The advice had merit. "You sticking around for the bull riding finals tonight?"

"Wouldn't miss it." Rusty hadn't qualified, either. But he'd remain to support his friends and join in the celebrations afterward. "Aren't you?"

"I'm tired. Gonna hit the sack early."

"Suit yourself. It promises to be a good time."

Everett pushed off the wheel well and extended his hand, shaking Rusty's. "Thanks." He didn't elaborate what for, and Rusty didn't ask.

When he reached for the paint's lead rope, Rusty said, "Don't worry about him. I'll take him to the pens with my horse."

Everett smiled. "Sure? You don't want to keep that pretty redhead waiting."

Rusty laughed. "How'd you know?"

"You never change."

Everett got into his truck, turning on his phone as he did. He always shut it off when he was competing, avoiding any interruptions. Beeps and buzzes signaled a slew of incoming voicemails, texts and emails.

Before he had a chance to read even the first one, his phone rang. Macy's number appeared on the display, and his nerves ignited. Why was she calling? Was this his chance to apologize and give a better explanation?

He put the phone to his ear. "Hi, Macy."

"Everett! Thank God. I've been calling for hours."

His heart pounded at the strain in her voice. "What's wrong?"

"I'm with Pop. We're at the hospital."

"Hospital!"

"They think he may have had another heart attack."

"How bad?"

She started to cry. "I don't know. They won't

tell me anything. I'm not family. He was conscious when the ambulance took him away."

"You were there?" He started the engine. "At the ranch?"

"Yes. He didn't look good, and when he complained of his chest hurting, I called 911."

Turning sharply to the right, Everett exited the parking area, the rear wheels of his truck fishtailing on the loose dirt. "I'm leaving right now. I should be there in…" He mentally calculated the drive time. "Two and a half hours."

"I'll stay with him. Call you if there are any updates."

Relief flooded him. "Are you sure, Macy? What about Joey?"

"He's at my mom's."

"Okay. Thank you." He didn't deserve her kindness after the way he'd treated her. In the past and recently. But, he reminded himself, she was doing this for Pop. Not him. "Do you know, does Pop have his phone with him?"

"Yeah. Why?"

Everett merged into traffic on the main road. "Maybe you can ask the nurses to have him call me. If he's able to, that is."

"I will."

"He may not realize he can give permission for you to sit with him."

"Hold on," Macy said. "I'll ask the person at the front desk." There was a lengthy pause followed by muffled voices. After a moment, she said, "They'll give a message to his care team."

Everett let out a long breath. "Good. Good." He'd feel infinitely better knowing Macy was with Pop.

"The woman did tell me it'll be a while. Pop's having some tests."

Everett gripped the steering wheel tight with both fists. Having tests sounded both scary and optimistic. His grandfather was alive, but was he at death's door?

"I hate to ask another favor—"

"Anything, Everett. What do you need?"

"Can you call my mom and update her? I'm about to get on the freeway and don't want to be distracted." Since the accident, he had a strict rule about not using the phone, even on Bluetooth, during demanding traffic situations.

"Of course."

He recited the number for her. "Tell Mom I'll call as soon as I have a chance."

"Drive safe. Don't take any risks."

"Thanks again, Macy." There was so much more he wanted to say, but the access ramp to the freeway was directly ahead, and this wasn't the time. "See you soon."

They disconnected after that. Everett berated himself as he drove along. He should never have left the ranch. His actions had been selfish and thoughtless. The stress he'd caused Pop had likely triggered the heart attack. He'd never forgive himself.

The irony of the situation wasn't lost on him.

Three years ago, he'd been by Brody's side, waiting for Macy to arrive. Now, he was the one driving like crazy trying to get to the hospital before something bad happened, and she was with his loved one.

He clung to hope. Pop had to survive. *Please, God, don't let history repeat itself.*

When his phone rang a half hour later and Macy's number appeared on the truck's dash display, he nearly swerved off the road. Fear sliced through him as he hit the answer button.

"How's Pop doing?"

"I'm with him now," she said. "He's a little groggy from whatever they gave him. We're waiting on the cardiologist to go over the test results."

Relief made him weak. "I'm glad you're with him."

"He wants to talk to you. Hold on a second."

After a pause filled with rustling, Pop's gravelly, slurry voice came on the line. "Hiya, sonny."

"Pop." Everett's throat filled with a burning sensation, and his eyes blurred with unshed tears. "How you feeling?"

"Been better. My ticker's giving me trouble again."

"You're going to be fine."

"Damn straight I am." The feebleness in his voice didn't match the conviction of his words.

"I'm on my way. I'll be there soon."

"How'd you do? Win any buckles?"

Leave it to his grandfather to ask about the rodeo in his condition.

"Second in tie-down roping."

"That's my boy." Pop's chuckled ended on a cough. "We'll talk more when I get there. You rest."

Pop wasn't finished. "Your mom called. She's thinking about flying out here. I told her not to rush. I have no intention of dying anytime soon."

"I'm holding you to that, Pop."

"Susan is, too. I hated telling her I was in the hospital, but when I didn't answer my phone, she got worried and called Macy."

"Susan cares about you, Pop."

"All these folks making a fuss over me." He sighed. "I'm a fortunate man."

He was. Had Everett handled things differently with Macy, he might even now be considering himself a fortunate man, too.

A deep voice abruptly sounded in the background.

"Seems I gotta go. The doctor ordered some more goll-darn tests just to torture me."

"I'll be there real soon, Pop. Wait for me."

"Where would I be going?" The hoarseness in his voice let Everett know his grandfather understood what he really meant.

"I love you."

"Love you, too, sonny. And I'm mighty proud of you. If I'm off getting a test or something when you get here, Macy's gonna give you a hug for me."

"I'll collect that in person when I see you."

Before he could say more, Macy came on the line. "The orderly took Pop."

"Okay." Everett cleared his throat, emotions getting the best of him. "Do you know what kind of tests he's having done?"

"He's had an EKG already and another electro-something. Blood work, and they gave him some medications. I think the doctor said this last one is a cardiac catheterization? He talked fast, and I had trouble understanding him."

Everett didn't know what a cardiac catheterization was and didn't like the sound of it.

"I'll keep you posted if there's any change," Macy said.

"How's he doing? Really?"

"Hard to say. I mean, his spirits are good. But whatever happened definitely took a toll on him. He doesn't seem to be in any pain or much pain. They have him hooked up to oxygen and a heart monitor and a bunch of other machines."

"How are *you* doing? Being in a hospital... It can't be easy for you." Which made her willingness to stay with Pop even more meaningful.

"I'm hanging in there."

"I shouldn't have left yesterday. Maybe this wouldn't have happened."

"You won't get an argument from me," she quipped, and then softened her initial stern tone. "You couldn't have prevented his heart attack, Everett."

"I've put him through a lot the last few days."

"He's been under stress for a long time."

Did she believe that or was she just being nice and secretly holding him responsible for this latest medical emergency? She was still mad underneath her helpful exterior. He could tell. The important questions were, did she hate him and could she ever forgive him?

"Look," he began hesitantly. "Can we talk when I get there?"

"I don't want to rehash yesterday."

"Neither do I."

She sighed, which did nothing to reassure him. Neither did her next comment. "We'll see."

He lost their connection then, having traveled into a mountainous area notorious for faulty cell phone reception. Their call, especially the way it ended, had left Everett with a pit the size of a grapefruit sitting in the bottom of his stomach.

Only seeing Pop, being told by the doctor that he would be all right and talking to Macy would ease his awful discomfort.

CHAPTER FIFTEEN

SHORTLY AFTER POP returned from his latest test, the attending doctor breezed into the ER room to review the results. Macy stood to excuse herself and give them some privacy, but Pop insisted she stay. She supposed he wanted someone with him should the results be grim.

Thankfully, they weren't. Mostly, anyway.

"I initially suspected you had a mini heart attack," the young, haggard-appearing doctor said. "And a mild one at that."

"A *mini* heart attack?" Pop blinked in confusion. "What in tarnation is that?"

"Much like a regular heart attack. Just on a smaller scale and with less damage."

Scratching the two-day stubble shadowing his jaw, he studied the monitors tracking Pop's cardiac vitals. Macy had been watching them, as well, listening to the steady *beep, beep, beep*. Not that she understood what the numbers meant and gave a start whenever an alarm sounded.

"But your tests have all come back normal," the doctor continued. "In fact, pretty good for a man your age. You'll need to follow up with your regular cardiologist as soon as possible. And we'll keep you overnight for observation, just as a precaution."

"What happened to me, Doc? I'm telling you," Pop insisted, "I had a heart attack before. I know what it feels like. I swear to you my chest was about to burst open."

"My guess is a panic attack."

"A what?"

"Panic attacks can mimic heart attacks. Have you had them before?"

"I… I…don't think so. Maybe. When I was first widowed, I had some pretty rough nights. I figured it was grief getting the best of me."

"Did you ever seek professional help?" the doctor asked.

"Nah. I fought my way through."

"Well, panic attacks are common after the death of a loved one. They do occur less frequently in the elderly, and there's usually a cause." He scratched his stubble again. "Have you been under any stress lately or more stress than usual?"

"A little. Yeah." He gave a half shrug. "Something has been weighing heavy on me."

Everett leaving, thought Macy. Pop had been counting on him to stay. Everett returning to the rodeo circuit must have worried Pop to the point that he'd suffered a panic attack.

She'd be angrier at Everett if not for their phone call earlier and imagined he was spending the entire drive to Wickenburg berating himself. Besides, what mattered the most was that Pop would be okay.

"You're going to need to find a way to reduce your stress," the doctor said. "Your health depends on it. Next time could be the real thing."

Pop smiled. "The only way I can think of to do that is to quit procrastinating and get down on one knee."

"What!" Macy's mouth fell open. She had jumped to the wrong conclusion. Everett leaving wasn't to blame. Pop was stressed over proposing to Susan!

"I've gotten myself more tangled than an old fishing line this past week," Pop said. "Ever since I decided to ask my sweetheart to marry me."

Macy clenched her jaw to stop herself from laughing.

The young attending also fought to hide a smile. "Well, I recommend you ask her before you put yourself in the hospital again. And you can consider that doctor's orders."

They chatted for several more minutes with Pop asking questions and the attending patiently answering them. He suggested Pop investigate coping methods to help with stress, such as walks, meditation, chair yoga and breathing exercises.

"I like to nap," Pop said.

The attending couldn't hold back and chuckled. "That works, too."

After he left, Pop drifted off, no doubt a response to his enormous relief. Macy took the opportunity to step outside and phone Everett. When the call went straight to voicemail, she sent a text telling him that the doctor had good news and to please drive carefully. She'd fill him in on the details when he arrived. She figured either he was out of range or his phone battery had died.

She next called Everett's mom and brought her up-to-date. Then she did the same thing with her mom.

"I'm glad to hear that," her mom said. "Panic attacks are no fun, but at least it's nothing life-threatening. What a relief that will be for Everett."

"How's my little man doing?"

The question elicited a long, mournful moan. "Honestly, not great. I'm not sure whose fuse is shorter, his or mine."

"I'm sorry. He doesn't always do well with changes in routine."

"No worries. Your dad and I endured much worse when you were his age."

"You always told me I was an angel," Macy protested, pretending to be offended.

"You had your days."

"Well, Pop should be moved to a room soon. They're keeping him overnight for observation. I won't be much longer, and I'll head home the moment Everett gets here. I'm guessing another hour or so."

"No rush. If you want," her mom suggested, "Joey can spend the night. You'll be tired when you get home."

"But I can't pick him up until tomorrow after work."

"That's all right. I have some errands to run tomorrow. He can come with me. We'll stop by the library for story hour." She paused as if thinking. "You know what? I'll call Fran. She might like to meet us there."

Macy's heart filled with love. Her mom was always thinking of Joey's other grandmother and strove to include her in activities. "You're the best. Have I told you that lately?"

"Not in a week or two."

The orderly appeared then, a short, wide man with a big smile. "Someone here called for a ride?"

Pop instantly roused.

"I have to run, Mom," Macy said. "They're moving Pop."

"Tell him hi from us and to get well soon."

Macy waited outside the new room while the orderly helped Pop change from his clothes into a hospital gown. Once he was settled beneath the bedcovers, she joined him, encouraged by his complaints about not having his own pajamas to wear.

"Darn thing doesn't close in the back."

"I'm going to the gift shop to get you a toothbrush and toothpaste," she said. "Anything else you need?"

He ran his fingers through his thinning white hair. "I could do with a comb, if it's no trouble."

"None at all."

She was about to leave when there was soft rapping on the door. Both she and Pop glanced up.

Pop broke into an enormous smile. "Well, hello, hello."

"Are you feeling up to a visitor?" a gentle voice asked.

Macy immediately jumped out of the chair and moved aside.

Pop levered himself to a sitting position, looking five years younger. "I am now. Come in, come in, my dear."

Susan entered, beaming. She tottered to the side of the bed. "You gave me quite the scare, Winston."

"Gave myself quite the scare, too."

"I'm glad you're all right. What would I do without you?" She bent and kissed him sweetly on the lips. His gnarled hand went up to tenderly stroke her hair.

A lump formed in Macy's throat, and her heart melted.

"You two have a nice visit," she said, feeling like a third wheel. At the door, she paused. "Susan, where's Callie?" She assumed Susan's granddaughter had brought her.

"She went to find some of her nurse friends."

"Okay. Maybe I'll run into her." And be able to extend the lovebirds' private time. "Can I bring either of you a cup of coffee or soda?"

Her question fell on deaf ears. Susan had taken a seat in the chair beside the bed. She and Pop were talking, their heads bent together, their eyes fixed on each other.

Macy started down the hall, her mind on Everett. She'd hoped, for a brief while there, that the two of them might have a relationship like Pop and Susan's. But then her hopes had been dashed.

Was it too late? Seeing Pop and Susan, her optimism had risen. Maybe it was never too late. But if she and Everett were to reconcile, they had to reach a compromise, and therein lay the problem.

THE HOSPITAL'S DOUBLE entrance doors whooshed open as Everett approached. He charged inside as if being chased by a swarm of angry hornets. Cool air-conditioning struck him in the face, but he didn't stop until he reached the information desk straight ahead.

"Which way is room three forty-one?" he asked the woman behind the computer terminal. Macy had texted him Pop's room number a short while ago.

"Down the hall and to that first bank of elevators." The woman pointed. "Avoid the one on the right. That's a service elevator."

"Thank you."

A line was already forming when Everett reached the elevators, including two people in wheelchairs. Five minutes later, he stepped onto the third floor. Glancing at the room number signs on the walls, he turned left. Doctors in lab coats, nurses in scrubs and patients in bathrobes blurred together as he hurried past them.

At last, he reached Pop's room. But rather than enter, he ground to a sudden halt at the door. Susan sat with his grandfather, their hands clasped and speaking quietly. Neither of them noticed they had company.

Everett didn't mean to eavesdrop, but he couldn't help hearing.

"Oh, Winston," Susan said, her voice tremulous. "I'm glad you're all right. Promise me you'll take better care of yourself from now on."

"I promise. We'll take care of each other."

"I know we haven't been seeing each other that long..."

"Long enough to know how I feel about you." He raised her hand to his lips for a kiss. "I love you, Susan. I didn't think I'd ever say those words again to a woman. Can you believe it? An old man like me being in love? But I am. Head over heels."

"I feel the same way, Winston. I love you, too." She rose up from the chair and kissed him full on the lips.

When they parted, Everett saw a handsome young man in the wrinkled face of his grandfather. Susan's smile radiated joy. She must have seen the young man, too.

Everett should step away and give them some privacy. He couldn't, however; the sight of them transfixed him. This was what he wanted for himself. What he might have had with Macy if he hadn't allowed his fears to get the better of him.

"Susan, my sweet." Pop stroked her papery cheek as if it was fine silk. "None of us can predict how much time we have left on this earth. Whether I have a single day or ten thousand remaining, I want to spend every one of them with you."

"Me, too, Winston."

"I had something else in mind, much more romantic than a hospital room. After today, I figure I shouldn't waste another moment."

"Wh...what are you saying?"

"I'd get down on one knee if I could."

"Winston!" Her eyes widened.

"You are precious to me, my love. I realize I have little to offer you other than my heart and a roof over our heads. But I think, between the two of us, we can cobble a wonderful life together."

"I agree." She dabbed at the tears falling down her cheek.

"Will you marry me and make me the happiest man alive?"

"Yes. Of course, I will. I was ready to ask you to marry me if you didn't get around to it."

They laughed and kissed and clung to each other.

"I don't want to wait," Pop said. "You think we can get the minister from your church to come here tonight and marry us?"

"I'm not marrying you in a hospital room, even if it was possible." She gave his arm a playful punch. "I want a real wedding."

"All right. Anything for you. Just don't make me wait too long."

"How about a month?" Susan suggested. "September twenty-second. That's the autumn equinox. The first day of fall, which is my favorite season."

"Sounds like a good day to tie the knot."

Pop and Susan kissed again. Everett couldn't stop grinning. He wanted to bust into the room and shout his enthusiastic congratulations, only he hesitated. This was their special time. The last thing they needed was an interruption.

Retreating a step, Everett turned and nearly knocked into Macy. She held a paper cup of coffee. If not for the lid, she would have spilled the contents all over herself.

"Whoops," she said and pulled back.

"Come on." Everett took her by the arm and led her down the hall. They dodged the same blur of hospital personnel and patients as when Everett had arrived.

"Wait," Macy exclaimed. "What's going on?"

"Pop and Susan need some alone time." He spotted an alcove with visitor chairs. "Let's sit over there."

"That's why I left the room and went to the gift shop and the cafeteria." She raised her other hand, which held a plastic bag. "So they could have some privacy."

"They're not done talking yet." He dropped down into a seat. When she just stood there, he gave her a look.

She sighed and sat. "Fine. Okay."

"Pop proposed."

Macy gasped, only to brighten. "He did? What was her answer? Tell me she accepted."

"She did. They didn't notice me standing there. I saw the whole thing."

"Aw…" Macy looked ready to cry. "That must have been so sweet."

"It was." He relayed the details. "But act surprised when they tell you. They may not like that I overheard."

"Oh, I doubt they'll mind. They're too happy to care."

"Tell me what the doctor said about Pop." With all the excitement of the proposal, Everett had almost forgotten.

"Pop had a panic attack."

"A panic attack? You're kidding."

"According to the doctor, they can present like a heart attack." Macy spent the next several minutes filling Everett in on what the doctor had said and Pop's need to reduce stress.

She smiled. "Pop says his nerves about proposing were responsible."

"Is that really the reason?"

"It's true."

"Me leaving for Tucson didn't help matters."

"Probably not." Her tone was a mixture of teasing and seriousness.

"I regret it. For more reasons than leaving Pop alone," he admitted.

Some of the light in her eyes dimmed. "Well, now that Pop and Susan are getting married in, what, a month you said? You won't have to worry about being gone so much. They can watch out for each other. Plus, Abel and Sheriff Andy will be there," she added. "Along with Callie stopping by."

She didn't understand, Everett realized. *She* was the "more reasons" he was talking about.

"Macy. That wasn't—"

He stopped himself midsentence. What did he intend to say? That, like Pop and Susan, the obstacles he and Macy faced didn't matter? That they cared about each other and they could make it work no matter the difficulties?

No. The fact was, he still had nothing to offer her beyond the hope that one day things might improve if he could pull a rabbit out of a hat. Even if she was okay with a business and ranch barely hanging on, Everett wasn't. He had to bring more to a relationship before committing. A steady, decent income. A promising future. Security. Stability. Dependability. He and Macy could only survive so long on just love.

Before he could take her hand and explain, a loud male voice called out, "Everett. Macy. There you are."

They turned in unison. Sheriff Andy and Kinsley approached, wearing worried expressions. Sheriff Andy carried a thick portfolio.

"How's Pop?" Kinsley asked when she and Sheriff Andy approached.

Everett stood. "Better. He didn't have a heart attack." He gave them the condensed version of what Macy had told him.

"Good to hear," Sheriff Andy said. "It could have been much worse."

"Thanks for coming." Everett once again marveled at the fondness the collective members had for his grandfather. Pop was a lucky man to have so many good friends. Friends, Everett was ashamed to say, that had been there for him when Everett wasn't. That, however, was going to change.

"Can he have visitors?" Kinsley asked.

"Susan's with him now."

The young woman raised a hand. "We don't want to cut in."

"I'm sure it's okay. She's been in there for a while."

"I can check if you want," Macy offered.

"Why don't you go with Kinsley?" Sheriff Andy said. "Pop may not be up to a crowd. We can take turns. Besides—" he clapped Everett on the back "—I've got something to show Everett."

He wasn't the only one who sent Sheriff Andy a curious look. Macy's eyebrows rose high, but she said nothing and just linked arms with Kinsley before they ventured down the hall.

"Let's sit." Sheriff Andy motioned.

"This sounds serious." Everett returned to his previous chair.

"Not at all. I have good news. Made a few calls to some of my old contacts at the city regarding a multiuse permit for rentals on the ranch."

"We can get one?"

"Absolutely. Bear in mind, the fees are the fees. No change to those. But I think we can speed up the application process, thanks to my contacts." Sheriff Andy opened the portfolio he'd brought with him and extracted a stack of papers. "I printed these out for you. Here's the permit application. I can help you fill it out. And a map of the ranch, along with all the acreage." He pointed with his finger. "There are restrictions. A certain percentage of the land must remain natural and untouched. But you can, for instance, turn this parcel here into, let's call it, a mini RV rental park. Running power and water wouldn't be difficult. You'd have to install a second septic tank."

"That sounds expensive."

"It's not cheap." Sheriff Andy named an estimate.

Everett gave a low whistle.

"I have contacts in the construction business," the retiree said, "who will give you the friend discount."

"There's no way Pop or I can afford that. Discount or not."

"I've also included an application for a low interest government-assisted loan for small businesses." He riffled through the stack and removed several sheets from the bottom. "You can't beat these rates. I also threw together a very rough income and expense projection. You should be able to pay off the loan in five years and still bring in a small monthly profit to supplement the horse breeding business."

"You did all that?" Everett was torn between being shocked and impressed.

"Rental properties are one way I used to earn my living."

Everett hedged. "I get this was my idea. But that was before I knew everything that was involved. It's a lot and a big commitment."

"That's true. But it will also bring a big reward."

"But I know nothing about running a rental business, even a mini RV park."

"I do," Sheriff Andy said. "And I'm your second customer after Abel. You just need four or five more of us."

Everett thought of Pop and Susan, Abel and now Sheriff Andy. "If they were all retired, we could have our own senior living community."

"That's a great idea!"

"I was kidding."

"You know what the biggest problem senior citizens have?" Sheriff Andy asked. "We're not ready to be put out to pasture yet. We can still be useful. We want to be active and engaged and learning. It's why I joined the collective and volunteer for the shelter and like helping folks with their investments. It's why Abel would rather stay in his motor home at the ranch where he can interact with people every day than at his sister Glynnis's. Because we're living, not just existing."

Everett studied the older man. "You've given this a lot of thought."

"I looked at where Susan lives, and I realized that's not what I want. Stuck for the rest of my life in a shoebox."

"I hear the place has tennis and pickleball courts and a swimming pool."

"I'm not a man of leisure. At the ranch, I'll be working every day."

"Cleaning stalls and delivering manure to the high school." Everett chuckled.

Sheriff Andy was far more serious. "It's more than that. I'll be part of something bigger. Contributing to the running of the ranch and feeling valued in return. I'm not the only one, either. If you put six RVs on this parcel—" Sheriff Andy again pointed to the map "—you'll change six people's lives for the better."

Everett closed his eyes for a moment and, like Sheriff Andy had suggested, tried to picture it. It wasn't hard. He could see the RVs and their owners living contentedly in a small community. Then, he saw dollar signs.

"The money part scares me," he admitted. "What if this were to fail? Me and Pop would be worse in debt with a loan to pay off."

"There's always risk in every business venture. I won't lie to you and say differently. But ask yourself this. What's the worst that could happen?"

"I just said it. Be in worse debt."

"Then what?"

"Me and Pop go broke?"

"Okay, now you're broke. What next?"

Everett didn't like where this conversation was going? "We'd have to sell the ranch."

"Right." Sheriff Andy smiled. "You'd be no worse off than you are right now. No worse off than before the collective entered into an agreement with Pop."

"That's not true," Everett said. "We'd have put out a lot of money installing a second septic system and utilities to a mini RV park that tanked."

"Okay. There is that," Sheriff Andy conceded. "But what if you succeed?"

Everett knew his limitations. "I can't do this all on my own. There's no way."

"I'll be there to help."

"I can't ask you to do all that for nothing."

"I wouldn't." Sheriff Andy laughed. "I don't work for free."

"We couldn't afford to pay you."

"I'd take my salary in the form of free rent."

Everett picked up the spreadsheet. "Which would reduce the income."

That earned him a huge grin from the other man. "See. Look how fast you're learning. Yes, it would. The loan would take an extra year to pay off. But isn't it worth it to have a manager living on-site?"

A mini RV park that supplemented the horse breeding business. Was it possible without putting the ranch further into debt? Everett worried he'd be taking on too much. But with Sheriff Andy's guidance, he wouldn't be operating blind.

He thought of Macy. Knowing her, she'd love the idea and not only because it meant that Everett would be staying. And with a second business bringing in a monthly income, Everett would feel like he had more value to bring to a relationship.

"I need to discuss this with Pop," he said. "He and Susan...the two of them are serious about each other. Very serious."

The light of understanding shone in Sheriff Andy's expressions. But before they could continue the discussion further, Callie appeared.

"Hey, guys. I'm here to fetch Grandma."

After that, things happened fast. Callie took Susan home. Everett and Sheriff Andy visited briefly with Pop, who was growing tired by then, while Macy and Kinsley went down to the sitting area to wait. At least, that was what Everett assumed.

"You get some rest, Pop," Everett said and bent down to hug his grandfather.

"I love you, sonny,"

"I love you, too, Pop."

When Everett and Sheriff Andy emerged from the room, only Kinsley was there.

"Macy had to go home," the young woman reported.

The stab of disappointment hit Everett hard. He'd hoped to talk with her about the mini RV park. Then again, maybe he shouldn't say anything until he'd discussed things with Pop. For all Everett knew, his grandfather would veto the idea. The ranch was his, after all.

And then what would they do?

CHAPTER SIXTEEN

MACY ENTERED HER parents' kitchen after another long day of work that had started with her observing surgeries. For once, her dad was there. He and Joey sat at the kitchen table and from all appearances were making a mess. A stack of copy paper sat at her dad's elbow, and a pile of crumpled balls littered the tabletop.

"Hey, Dad. Hi, honey."

"Look-it, Mommy. I made an airplane." Joey launched a poorly constructed paper airplane into the air. It nose-dived onto the kitchen floor.

"I see." Though tired from a long day at the vet clinic, Macy plastered a smile on her face. This had to be her dad's idea. "That's...something." She bent and picked up the plane, returning it to Joey and kissing him hello.

"Join us?" her dad asked. He launched his plane, which ascended and sailed across the kitchen to land on top of the refrigerator.

Joey broke into laughter.

She kissed her dad on the cheek. "Thanks, but we should hit the road."

Her mom entered the kitchen in time to hear Macy. "Going to the ranch?"

Peanut waddled after her. Though still over-weight, the dog had lost a pound since being in Macy's care—due in large part to them sticking to her prescribed diet and Peanut following Joey wherever he went.

"I ride a horse!" Joey threw his hands up in the air and rocked forward and backward in an imitation of riding a horse. He had nothing if not a one-track mind.

"Sorry, honey. We're not going to the ranch to-night. Mommy has to stop at the ATM and pick up a prescription on the way home." Not that Joey knew what either of those things were.

He let his arms drop and made a sad face.

"I can't believe it." Her mom opened the re-frigerator and removed a glass pan of marinating chicken, the unnoticed paper airplane inches from her head. "You've never gone four days without checking on the mares."

"Sheriff Andy and Kinsley are keeping me up-dated."

"How long are you planning on avoiding Ever-ett?" Her dad launched another plane, this one at Macy.

It hit her in the arm, bounced off and crash-landed at her feet. Peanut pounced on the plane, snatched it in her teeth and ran under the table where she promptly shredded the plane into tiny pieces. No one stopped her.

"I'm not avoiding Everett." Macy removed the

plane from atop the refrigerator and, crumpling it into a ball, tossed it into the pile of rejects.

Her dad winced. "Ouch. That was my best design yet."

"I thought you and Everett had a nice conversation at the hospital the other day," her mom said.

"We talked. And we were nice to each other."

But, Macy thought grumpily, the conversation hadn't gone anywhere. At least, it hadn't gone where she'd hoped it would—namely a discussion of where they stood. She'd thought he'd been about to say something when they'd been interrupted by Sheriff Andy and Kinsley.

"And he hasn't spoken to you since?" Her dad helped Joey fold a piece of paper into another plane.

Her mother emitted a soft sound of distress. "That doesn't sound like Everett."

"He's texted me a few times," Macy said, disgruntled. "Stuff about the mares or repairs he's making to the mare barn."

He hadn't suggested they continue their conversation. Nor had there been a declaration of love. Not that she'd expected one. An invitation to coffee, perhaps.

Whenever she wasn't preoccupied, she'd replay their last conversation in the hospital, searching for clues and finding none.

Why had Everett abruptly clammed up? What changed? Was he expecting her to make the first move?

"He must be mad at me," she mused aloud. "I did leave the hospital while he was in with Pop."

"Without saying goodbye?" Her mom moved the chicken to a baking sheet.

"I couldn't stay. He knew that." Did he? In hindsight, she should have stuck her head in Pop's room and at least motioned to him that she was heading home.

"Texts." Her dad harrumphed. "Why do people these days have such a problem with calling?"

"You should go to the ranch," her mom said. "I don't understand why you refuse. This is a simple misunderstanding."

Macy should probably call, like her dad suggested. Give Everett an opening for that talk.

She blew out a long breath. "I wish I knew for sure if he was staying or not."

"Ah. So now we're getting to the heart of the matter." Her dad demonstrated to Joey how to launch this newest plane. "You want assurances."

"Is that so wrong?"

"Of course not, sweetheart," her mom said. "What's the last thing he told you at the hospital?"

"He was saying how him returning to rodeoing might have contributed to Pop's stress."

"I imagine he felt guilty."

"But he wasn't responsible for Pop's panic attack," Macy insisted. "I told him that."

"Guilt can't always be rationally explained away."

"He's waiting for you to show up in order to talk to you in person," her dad said. "And you're avoiding him."

"You're not acting like someone who likes him," her mom added. "The exact opposite, in fact."

"Do you want him to chase you?"

"No!" Macy glared at her dad. "I'm not insecure. I don't need a man's attention to feel good about myself."

"What then?"

"I'm confused. He hasn't exactly given me a reason to feel confident in us."

Her mom nodded. "That's reasonable, and, frankly, you should tell him as much."

"You should ask him what he was doing at Town Hall the other day." Her dad passed Joey a fresh piece of paper.

Macy was certain she'd misheard. "What are you talking about?"

"I ran into Everett on Tuesday. I was submitting my company's bid for the new park project's zero maintenance landscaping."

"Why was Everett at Town Hall?"

"He said he'd dropped off a permit application for the ranch."

"What kind of permit?"

"He didn't tell me, and I didn't ask." Her dad pushed back in his chair. "Why don't you call and find out?" He exchanged glances with Macy's mom. "Do we sound like a broken record?"

"Joey can stay with us," her mom offered.

Macy was wild with curiosity about what kind of permit Everett had applied for. "If I ask him, he'll know you told me."

Her dad shrugged. "He told me why he was at Town Hall. He didn't act like it was a secret."

True.

"I just wish he'd reached out to me." The insecurity Macy had denied having coursed through her. She must really care for Everett for him to be able to put her through such an emotional wringer.

"I'm not defending Everett or his actions," her mom said. "He's made mistakes. He should have come around after Brody died. But he hurt almost as much as you after the accident and carried a terrible burden with him."

"I've forgiven him for that."

"Okay. But let's look at all he's dealing with. His grandfather's health. Running the ranch and the business. Stepping up and doing the right thing after being absent for three years."

"I get that."

"Then cut him some slack and stop playing games." Her dad wagged a finger at her, which Joey mimicked.

Games? Macy ground her teeth together. Was she?

Her mom came over and put an arm around her shoulders. "It's normal that the idea of a new relationship can cause some hesitation. Especially for you. Anyone in your shoes would be afraid of losing someone again."

Macy wasn't sure she liked how her mom saw inside her to her greatest fears.

"I'm fine with spending the rest of my life alone."

"Were fine," her mom said. "Then Everett returned, and you started thinking maybe you didn't want to do that."

"It's not just me anymore. I have Joey to consider. He's fond of Everett and could wind up hurt if things go badly."

"But think how much his life could be enriched if things go well." Her mom smiled encouragingly. "I'm willing to bet Everett is going through all kinds of uncertainties of his own. And if he's anything like your dad, he's putting unnecessary demands on himself."

Everett *was* like that, Macy conceded.

"Go to the ranch," her mom urged.

"We men are proud creatures," her dad interjected. "Everett's always had only one thing, and that was rodeo. He measured his success by how well he does in the arena. By leaving rodeo behind, he's venturing into unfamiliar territory. That can be pretty nerve-racking for guys like him who have always been confident in their abilities."

How was it that her parents seemed to know Everett better than her?

"Okay." Macy drew in a deep breath. "You win. I'm off to see Everett. But I'm taking Joey with me."

"Are you sure?" her mom asked. "We're more than happy to keep him."

Macy paused. If she was doing this, if she was putting herself out there, then she had to go *all out*. None of this "let's see how Everett reacts first" or hinting at her feelings. She'd tell him what was in her heart, her expectations in a relationship with him, and if he wasn't interested or couldn't reciprocate, then that was the end for them.

Though her stomach clenched in anticipation, she squared her shoulders.

"Joey's my son. Can't have one without the other. If Everett and I are going to discuss a potential future, he needs to understand that."

"I'll send some peanut butter and jelly sandwiches with you," her mom said.

"Thanks, Mom." No amount of protests would stop her mother from feeding her and Joey.

Ten minutes later, they were on their way to the ranch, Peanut riding alongside Joey in the back seat.

Macy mentally rehearsed what she'd say during the entire drive. Every word flew out of her head when she pulled into the ranch and saw the layout of stakes and yellow tape to the west of the pasture. Parked beside it sat a bright orange machine used for digging trenches.

Hombre stood in the pasture, staring at the machine as if it might come to life and devour him.

Macy hit the brakes on her truck. What in the world…?

CHAMP STOOD IN his stall, his large brown eyes glued to Everett and his ears pricked forward.

"Don't worry, boy." Everett paused in his work and rolled his shoulders, trying to ease the kinks.

He then removed a red handkerchief from his back pocket and wiped off the sweat dampening his brow. He'd been hard at one task or another for the last four days. "Nothing bad is happening."

Champ snorted and shook his head. He clearly didn't agree.

"If this plan has any chance of succeeding, Sheriff Andy and I need a place to work. There's no room in the house for an office. Not with Pop and Susan getting married soon and her moving in."

The newly engaged couple had set a date and were busy arranging their small church wedding. Their days were also filled with packing Susan's belongings and moving the items she was bringing with her to the ranch. The rest would either be given away to family members, donated to charities or sold.

Pop was clearing out space in the house for her and getting rid of the junk, as he called it. He wanted his new bride to decorate to her liking and make the place her home. Everett went along, his one job to help with their combined garage sale this coming Saturday.

Sheriff Andy was coming out of retirement to not only manage the mini RV park but to help Susan sell her bungalow.

"Glad I kept my broker's license current," he'd told Everett the other day.

Champ suddenly pivoted and trotted through the connecting door to the paddock. Like Hombre, the big chestnut had been keeping watch on the construction staking and delivery of the trencher.

Hombre had recently discovered the mares not far away and was fascinated with them, though he was too young to understand the root of his fascination. Dr. Beck had called Everett to let him know the genetic testing results should be available either late today or tomorrow morning. Everett's nerves jumped every time his phone pinged with an email notification.

Whether as a second stallion in residence or a gelded saddle mount, Everett had decided to keep Hombre. His training was coming along, and Hombre showed a keen aptitude for learning. Thanks to their early morning lunge line lessons in the round pen, he was already responding to voice commands and had accepted a bareback pad.

"Hello? You around, Everett?"

"Hey." Hearing Macy's voice, he straightened. At the sight of her entering the stallion's quarters, his pulse rate spiked. "I didn't hear your truck."

"I parked at the house. Pop and Susan said I'd find you here."

"Um…yeah."

An awkward silence fell on them. That hadn't happened since they were teenagers when he'd returned to Wickenburg and learned she was dating his best friend.

He should have done more than send a few short texts. More than that, he should have prepared himself for this moment.

"Where's Joey?" he asked, breaking the silence.

"Inside with Pop and Susan."

Everett nodded, still tongue-tied.

Macy hitched her chin toward the outside. "What's going on with all the yellow tape, and is that a trencher? My dad said he saw you at Town Hall. Something about a permit application."

This he could talk about without any awkwardness. "Come on. I'll show you."

He started toward the cordoned-off area. Hombre trotted to the pasture fence, his long tail swishing side to side. Whatever was happening, he wanted in on the action. Champ whinnied a greeting to them from the paddock.

At the edge of the yellow tape barrier, Everett gestured. "Welcome to Rocking Chair Ranch."

Macy turned to stare at him. "Rocking Chair Ranch?"

"That's what Susan is calling it, and Pop likes the name. I like it, too. It fits our vision."

"Your vision?"

"This is going to sound crazy." He gave an anxious laugh. "Considering I was the one insisting I have no business experience."

"I'm confused."

"It started with Abel staying in the motor home and then Sheriff Andy in his RV. He's parking his RV alongside the garage until construction is done and Rocking Chair Ranch is officially open."

"You're building an RV park?"

"A small one. Six spaces for very specific residents."

"Now I'm really confused," she said.

"We're going to be a retirement community for senior citizens. That's what the permit is for. Abel and Sheriff Andy are our first two renters."

"I'm...speechless."

"Sheriff Andy is going to handle the books and all the office work in exchange for free rent. I'm in charge of construction, maintenance, sales and everything else." Everett summarized the plan for running power and water lines to the parcel, the digging for a septic tank, and the pouring of concrete pads. Also, what he imagined Rocking Chair Ranch would look like when it was up and running. "This won't be your standard retirement RV park. We'll have one big difference."

"What's that?"

"All the residents will have part-time jobs," Everett added with a grin. "Rather than get paid, they'll receive reduced monthly rent. They'll work as many or as few hours a week as they want or can, in whatever capacity they're able. Feeding and cleaning stalls, maintenance and repairs, groundskeeping, tending the community garden."

"A garden?"

"That was my idea. Gardening is good for mental health. That's something older people struggle with. Even Pop admits to having bad days."

"You've been researching again." Macy's eyes sparkled.

"Some."

"You mentioned the horses. The collective takes care of them."

"There'll be more soon," Everett said. "Clients boarding their mares here for breeding. I can't ask the collective to care for them. That's not part of the agreement."

"We don't mind."

"Sheriff Andy insists the residents will like caring for the boarding horses," Everett said. "And we're all here to help each other. I also have a long list of improvements I'm going to start on when money becomes available. I plan on building a gazebo with an outdoor barbecue area and picnic table. Maybe even a hot tub."

"I can see that."

"The idea is for Rocking Chair Ranch to be a real community with the residents more like one big extended family. Rather than sitting around in a nursing home, the residents will be active and, in a small way, contributing to their support by helping around the ranch. If all goes well, Callie and one of the male caregivers from Total Home Nursing Services will visit weekly to handle any of the residents' medical needs. We won't abandon anyone just because they're old or ill."

Macy glanced around, taking everything in. After a moment of silence, she exclaimed, "I love it! Oh, Everett. I have goose bumps. I'm serious."

"I thought you might."

"You are a kind and wonderful man." Her voice broke.

"Well, it's still business, and I hope a profitable one. The monthly income should enable me to fund the repairs to the ranch and expand the horse breeding business. That's my goal, anyway. With eleven available stalls in the mare barn, I can start right away. My first client is bringing his mare by this weekend."

"All this in just a few days." Macy shook her head in astonishment.

"There's a lot of work ahead."

"Rocking Chair Ranch is going to be a huge success. I always knew you had it in you."

Her praise warmed him. "This isn't a one-man show. Pop has to stay healthy because I need his expertise. And Sheriff Andy's, too."

"Can I ask a financial question? And you're not obligated to answer," she hurriedly added.

"Sure."

She waved her arm to encompass the entire staked-off area. "Doesn't all this require money?"

"Which is why I almost didn't agree. Sheriff Andy had to convince me a low interest loan was the way to go and agree to walk us through the process." Everett winced. "I worry about making the monthly payments."

"I would, too," Macy agreed, more somber now.

"Though, because the ranch is in Pop's name, he's the one who ultimately decided. And the low interest rate was too hard to pass up."

"How long until you open?"

"Optimistically, two months. Realistically, more like three. Which is about how long it will take to obtain the permit, assuming there are no hiccups. In the meantime, Larry Hays's brother-in-law has agreed to start digging the trenches for the power and water lines. Sheriff Andy is obtaining bids for the concrete pads and the septic tank."

"How can I help?" Macy asked.

"You and the collective are already doing enough."

"Come on, Everett," she insisted. "What else?"

"Spread the word. If you know of anyone looking for a quality, proven quarter horse stud, send them our way. The horse breeding business is the quickest source of income, and we need some."

"I saw that Kinsley has your web page and social media accounts up and running. That should help. Did you ever talk to the Hays about advertising in their store?"

"Brenda said to bring over a stack of flyers and she'll put them on the counter by the register."

"You have flyers?"

"And business cards. They're on order. Kinsley designed them. Said I needed them. And she created our new logo."

Macy brightened. "I can't wait to see it."

Until now, Everett hadn't realized how much her support meant to him. A kind of contentment settled around his heart.

"And what about rodeoing?" she asked.

"I'm hanging up my spurs and lariat for now.

Maybe for good. I think I'm ready to settle down in one place."

"Settle down," she repeated as if not quite believing him.

"It's true, Macy. I've given you reason to doubt me, but I'm serious this time. Too many people are depending on me."

She considered that before asking, "How do your parents feel about Rocking Chair Ranch?"

He tried not to read too much into her unenthusiastic response. Clearing his throat, he said, "Mom's thrilled. She's eager to see the changes when she and Dad fly out for the wedding. My aunt, on the other hand, is concerned. And I understand. She's worried Rocking Chair Ranch will be too much for Pop and hard on his health."

"I think it'll be just the opposite. Pop will thrive. He's a people person."

"I agree."

"Does him marrying Susan have anything to do with your aunt's concerns?"

"It might." Her astuteness impressed Everett. "My aunt isn't entirely on board with the engagement."

"Why? Susan is a lovely person."

"She worries they're marrying for financial reasons."

"Financial reasons?" Macy frowned. "What? She thinks Susan's a gold digger?"

"Well…"

"Nothing could be further from the truth."

"I told my aunt as much," Everett said. "And that Susan's willing to sign a prenup. But Pop won't hear of it. He says they don't need a prenup, as he's still planning on transferring ownership of the ranch, half to me and half to my mom and aunt."

"I'm sure your aunt is just looking out for Pop," Macy conceded. "Older people can be susceptible to scammers and swindlers. That isn't Susan, however, and your aunt will change her mind once she meets her. She's coming out for the wedding, isn't she?"

"Insisted she wouldn't miss it. And I think she'll feel better when gets a look at the place."

"She will. This will all work out." Macy took a step back and gave Everett a long once-over. "I have to say, you've impressed me."

"Pop and Sheriff Andy are the brains behind this operation. I'm just manual labor. In fact, I was clearing out the storeroom in the stallion quarters for an office when you arrived."

"You're a lot more than manual labor. You're the driving force behind this new venture."

Her words lifted him in a way nothing had in a very long time. Taking a chance, and uncertain of her response, he closed the distance between them.

"About that talk I wanted to have."

She surprised him again with her answer, and not in a good way.

"First, I have a question."

"What's that?"

"Let's get out of the sun."

Without answering, she walked in the direction of the mare barn. Everett's heart began to hammer. The short walk gave him just enough time to wonder if this was what Pop had experienced when he'd had a panic attack.

CHAPTER SEVENTEEN

INSIDE THE MARE BARN, Macy pivoted to face Everett. She hadn't planned on confronting him when she first arrived at the ranch. But then he'd made what stuck her as an overture, and she'd seen the eagerness in his expression. It had reminded her of the look he'd worn at the hospital the other day right before they were interrupted.

No way could she go on another moment without clearing the air between them and, more importantly, getting reassurance on where the two of them stood. If they stood anywhere at all.

"Why didn't you tell me about Rocking Chair Ranch before now?" she asked. "Honestly, Everett, if I hadn't come here today, I'm not sure when I would have found out."

"That's a fair question." He cleared his throat. "I wanted to tell you."

"What stopped you?"

Around them, the mares shuffled in their stalls as if vying for the best position to watch the entertainment. The sun drifted slowly toward the mountaintops, taking the remaining daylight with it and casting the interior of the mare barn in shadows. Sparrows pecked the ground in a last search for food before darkness fell while owls stirred from their hidden roosts, readying for the night's hunt.

"Is it because I left the hospital while you were in with Pop?" she asked, giving him an opening.

He lifted in a shoulder, more in surrender, it seemed, than uncertainty. "I figured you took off because you didn't want to talk."

"That's not true, Everett. But I can see where you'd jump to that conclusion. My mistake."

"Then why did you leave without saying goodbye?"

Now it was her turn to say, "Fair question." She released a long breath. At her parents earlier, she'd claimed her reason was to get home to Joey. She realized now that wasn't true. "When you left for Tucson, that hurt."

"I know. I'm sorry."

"It makes no sense, I know, but when Brody died, it felt like he abandoned me. Same when you didn't come home after promising you would. Though, that was a genuine abandonment. Then you left for Tucson. I couldn't take it a third time. I'm not that strong. I need someone in my life I can depend on."

"I wish you'd told me."

"Would you have stayed?" she asked.

"I'd like to say yes. The truth is, I'm not sure. I was in my head at the time and doubting myself."

Macy swallowed, stalling for time. His honest

answer had thrust her right back into that day they'd argued, and the awful pain coursing through her.

After a moment, she spoke. "I wasn't ready to hear you ask for another chance. I needed more time, and I was afraid that was the reason you wanted to talk."

"It was. You're right."

"I didn't want to agree to something I wasn't ready for, because, and I mean this sincerely, I can't live in fear that you'll leave one day just because we hit a rough patch."

"I'm not going anywhere. Pop has given me an incredible opportunity. And with Sheriff Andy's help, I can build a life and a career. I'm learning to forgive myself for the accident and accept I wasn't to blame. I'm repairing burned bridges with Brody's parents. And I'm committed to caring for Pop as he ages."

He hadn't said what she most wanted to hear. "What about us, Everett?" She needed to know. She wasn't jumping off this ledge alone.

"I care about you, Macy. More than that. I can see us together forever."

"Really?" A thrill rose in her.

"I'm staying. Not just for me and Pop, but for us." He was cut short by his phone dinging. "Sorry. I need to check this email."

"Really, Everett? Now?"

"Hold on." He tapped on his phone screen. "This will just take a second."

"I don't believe this is happening." She started to walk away.

"It's from the equine genetic testing facility. Doc Beck told me to expect it."

She came to a grinding halt, her annoyance instantly fleeing. "What does it say?"

"The print is small." Everett's features knit in concentration as he enlarged the document and continued reading.

"Everett?"

"The seller wasn't lying!" He broke into a spectacular grin. "She did just send the wrong results. Hombre tested negative across the board."

Macy let out a delighted gasp. "That's wonderful news."

Everett whooped and, grabbing hold of Macy by the waist, swung her in circles. "We have two healthy stallions. I didn't make a mistake buying Hombre."

"I'm so happy for you." Her head spun and not just from Everett twirling her. When he finally set her down, she blurted, "Maybe Dusty can be his first mare."

"He won't be ready for another six months, and the collective may have other ideas."

"I can ask."

He smiled tenderly at her. "Let's wait until next year. I'm planning on entering Hombre in some halter and saddle classes if his training continues to go well. He needs a few wins under his belt to raise his value."

"I guess we'll use Champ, then, and modify our agreement with Pop."

"With me," Everett said, grinning. "Pop transferred ownership of him to me."

"Ooh. I like the idea of us joining our businesses."

She didn't need to worry about Everett misreading her signals. Looping an arm around her waist, he pulled her flush against him and lowered his mouth to hers. "I like the idea of that, too."

She stopped him with a finger to his lips. "I need to hear it. What exactly are you saying? Because I won't settle for anything less than a committed relationship."

"We pick up where we left off and start with dating. See if you can stand my company for more than thirty minutes at a time."

"If I can't?" she asked jokingly.

"That's the end for us, I guess."

"And if I can?" She tilted her head and wrapped her arms around him.

His voice lowered, his meaning clear. "We're going to spend so much time together, you'll be sick of me."

"I doubt that."

"Let's test your theory." Again, he lowered his mouth to hers.

And again, she stopped him before he could kiss her. "There's something else you need to know. A condition, actually."

He paused. "Should I be worried?"

"It's Joey. He and I are a package deal."

"I wouldn't have it any other way," he said before claiming a kiss that let Macy know in no uncertain terms he was in this with her for the long haul.

When, minutes later, they broke apart, Macy swore her feet weren't touching the ground. A pleasant sensation bloomed inside her. No, that wasn't quite right. It emanated from her heart and spread to the tips of her fingers and toes. She realized this was the beginning of love. Or, more likely, the young teenage love she'd once felt for Everett evolving into a mature love.

He nuzzled her cheek, seeming unwilling to release her. She wasn't all that eager herself to end their moment. This was once in a lifetime, and she wanted it to last as long as possible.

"I'm falling for you, Macy. If you haven't figured that out yet."

She nuzzled his cheek in return, enjoying the outdoorsy scent of him, the strength of his muscled arms and, most of all, the look in his eyes that reflected his words. "I'm getting that impression. Which is a good thing," she added, "because I'm falling for you, too."

"The first of many things we can agree on."

Several of the mares abruptly snorted and tossed their heads in alarm. The next second, Joey came racing into the mare barn, bursting with energy.

"Mommy, Mommy. Where are you?"

Macy slid from Everett's embrace. "I'm right here, honey."

"Hey, sport. What are you up to?"

"Everett!" Joey ran straight for him.

Everett grabbed him under the arms and swung him in a circle, not unlike he had Macy. When he set Joey down, the boy cried out, "Again."

He obliged, then asked, "Where's Pop?"

"He is coming." Joey pointed.

The three of them stepped outside the mare barn just as Pop was helping Susan into one of the rocking chairs, which were sitting in a white circle cast by the exterior floodlight.

He glanced at them and called out, "Sorry, Joey got away from us."

"No worries." Macy reached for Everett's hand and clasped it in hers.

He sent her a look that asked if she was sure about this. Pop and Susan might be in their eighties, but they were both sharp as tacks and would notice.

Her answer was to squeeze his fingers.

"Well, lookie there," Pop said, easing himself into the other rocking chair. "Appears there's gonna be another change around here. Though I can't say I'm surprised."

"Took the two of you long enough." Susan delivered her comment with a mischievous wink.

Joey looked at Macy's and Everett's joined hands and took hold of Everett's other hand.

A sentimental lump formed in her throat as she leaned her shoulder into Everett. Her gaze took in the ranch and the many new beginnings. Pop and Susan. Rocking Chair Ranch. Hombre. The revived horse breeding business, which would soon rival what it once was in the past.

Best of all, there was her and Everett and their freedom from past secrets and guilt. No longer afraid to face the future, her emotions soared. Thank goodness her rodeo cowboy had returned.

EPILOGUE

Three Months Later

AT A LOUD banging on the door, Everett hollered, "Hold your horses. I'm coming."

He examined his freshly shaved face in the tiny mirror over the compact bathroom sink. Satisfied, he placed his new Stetson on his head and adjusted the fit. For a final touch, he stuck his lucky turkey feather in the hatband. Pop had insisted Everett look the part of a business owner when meeting with customers for the horse breeding business or Rocking Chair Ranch.

The Stetson and feather must be working, for there wasn't an empty stall in the mare barn, and that included the horses owned by the collective. Champ's services were booked for the next several months, and before long, Hombre would be ready for those who wanted to cross their mare with a striking gray with distant thoroughbred bloodlines.

The young stallion's training was starting to pay off. Last weekend, he'd won his first ribbon at a local horse show. Third place, which wasn't bad for a start. Soon, Everett would advance Hombre from the lunge line to light saddle work, depending on when the vet cleared him for riding. The bones of a two-year-old horse needed to be well developed before bearing extra weight.

The banging sounded again, and a deep voice hollered through the door, "What in tarnation is the holdup? You're keeping everyone waiting."

Everett recognized his caller as Abel. "All right, already."

He opened the door, allowing a blast of brisk November air inside the horse trailer's compact living quarters. He'd been looking for a way to move out of the house after Pop and Susan married two months ago, wanting to give the newlyweds their personal space. When his buddy Rusty asked if Everett could store his horse trailer at the ranch until he found a buyer—he didn't have a place for it in Oklahoma with the Twisters —Everett had made his friend an offer on the spot.

The living quarters were cramped, but they were also temporary. Susan had insisted on using a portion of the money from the sale of her bungalow to build an attached suite onto the ranch house for her and Pop with its own separate entrance. Pop had balked at first, refusing to let her spend any of her own money. Eventually, he'd agreed when Everett suggested they reimburse Susan with regular payments out of the business proceeds.

Construction was scheduled to start after the first of the year. That way, after Pop and Susan moved into the suite, Everett wouldn't feel like he was living on top of them or that his irregular hours interfered with their quiet routine.

Eventually, sometime next year, once they were on steadier financial ground, Everett planned on building a small rodeo arena on a back acre of land. Besides giving lessons, he'd rent out the arena for those needing a practice facility or a venue for their event.

"Let me get my jacket." Everett retrieved it from the hook beside the door.

Abel shuffled back a step, giving Everett room to climb out of the trailer. "It is a might nippy out today. Hope that doesn't keep the guests from showing up."

"Not a chance." Everett had checked the weather forecast a dozen times during the past few days. "Going to be a clear and sunny day."

He donned his jacket as the two of them walked from the spot where Abel had once parked his motor home behind the stallion quarters. The ancient vehicle had been replaced with a newer, larger RV with all the bells and whistles.

Abel's was the first RV in Rocking Chair Ranch, moved in weeks before the grand opening—which was today. Sheriff Andy's was next after he moved out of his house and put it on the market. All six spots were now rented, the residents having signed year-long leases. The proceeds were enough to cover taxes and insurance and meet the small business loan's payments.

Everett drew a small salary from the horse breeding business while Pop and Susan had their social security and modest investment incomes. They weren't rich, but they had more than enough to get by. And once Hombre was old enough to start breeding, and the foals were sold in a year or so, they might actually be doing well for themselves.

"You look spiffy," Everett told the older gentleman as they approached the patio, where rented tables and chairs had been set up to accommodate the over one hundred expected guests.

"Not every day I get to attend a big shindig. Had to pull out my best Western shirt and jeans. Glynnis bought me this jacket special for the occasion."

"I don't suppose our new retired schoolteacher resident, who just happens to be single, has anything to do with it."

"Not just a schoolteacher. Did you know she taught equine science classes at the community college?"

"I did. She'd going fit in just fine here."

"She promised to save me a seat at the party."

Everett chuckled. "So, it's serious between you two?"

"We'll see." Abel's steps were a little less wobbly, and his shoulders a bit squarer.

Amazing what effect the prospect of romance had on a person's health.

A couple dozen people were already milling about. Just as many were inside, judging by the noise level. The collective members had spent the past three days helping Everett, Pop and Susan prepare. The house had been cleaned top to bottom, furniture rearranged to accommodate folding chairs, and the family room decorated for a belated wedding reception. Banners and streamers hung on the walls. Gold and silver confetti covered every flat surface. Helium-filled balloons had been tied to the backs of the kitchen chairs. A four-tier wedding cake with a pair of ornamental white doves for a topper sat on the counter. Bottles of champagne chilled in the refrigerator.

Pop and Susan had stuck to their original plan and gotten hitched two months earlier at her church in a small, intimate ceremony. Afterward, they spent four days honeymooning at a charming inn in Wickenburg. Today, their many family members and friends were here to wish them well on their journey as a married couple.

Upon seeing how happy Susan made Pop and his improved health, Everett's mom and aunt had fallen instantly in love with her and given their full support of the union. Susan, in turn, couldn't be happier in her new role as stepmother and step-grandmother.

The newlyweds had one strict rule for their guests: no gifts. They had everything they possibly needed. Instead, they asked for donations to the animal shelter where Sheriff Andy volunteered. Already, a stack of multicolored envelopes filled a crystal bowl on the side table, some of them quite thick and likely containing a cash donation or gift card that could be used to buy food and supplies for the shelter.

Everett motioned for Abel to go ahead of him onto the porch. The older man made a beeline for Rocking Chair Ranch's newest resident. The former teacher sat in a chair, holding a cup of punch in one hand and a plate of nachos in the other.

Sheriff Andy and Glynnis's husband supervised the grill. Before long, they would be serving fajitas to hungry guests. The outside banner, strung along the wall, featured Rocking Chair Ranch's new logo, which Kinsley had designed and that resembled a livestock brand.

Fielding greetings and congratulations, Everett wound his way to the back door. It opened just as he was reaching for the knob, and the woman who emerged threw her arms around him.

"Everett. Don't you look handsome."

"Hey, Mom." Giving her a quick kiss, he released her. They stepped out of the way of other people coming and going inside. "Thanks again for flying out so soon after the wedding. It means a lot to me and Pop."

"Are you kidding? I wouldn't have missed the grand opening for the world. I'm just sorry your dad couldn't be here. Work wouldn't let him take more time off."

"It's all right." Everett glanced around. "The party's livening up."

"Pop says to expect another fifty or sixty people. I'm not sure where you're going to put them all."

She stood on her tiptoes and leaned close. "I really like Macy. I always did, but I like her more now."

"Me, too."

"And Joey is so cute. Such a charmer." She nodded at the door. "He's in there, wrapping everyone around his little pinkie."

"Takes after Macy. She has me wrapped around hers pretty tight."

His mom touched his arm. "I know you haven't been dating long, but I'm hoping it's serious."

"It is."

"Really serious?"

"Really serious, Mom," he answered.

"Because if you two were to…" She let the sentence drop.

"I promise, if we were to, you'll be the first to know."

"No pressure," she said on a wistful sigh. "I'm just excited for you. And proud enough, I could burst."

"Thanks, Mom. That means a lot to me."

"I have to run. I told Susan I'd check on the ice in the coolers. See if we need to make a run to the store for more bags." She dashed off, and Everett went inside.

"Everett!" Joey scurried over to him. "You're here."

"Hey, sport." He scooped the boy up into his arms as naturally as if he'd been a part of Joey's life since the day he was born.

"I'm gonna ride Dusty later." The gentle mare had become his favorite.

"We'll see. That's up to your mom."

"What's up to me?"

Macy appeared from around the corner, a vision in a turquoise sweater that brought out the flush in her cheeks. Everett fell for her again, as he did every time he saw her.

He opened his arm and she went to him, fitting perfectly against his side as if they were made for each other.

"Joey wants to ride Dusty," he said.

"Not today, honey." She tweaked his nose. "We're having a big party."

"Tomorrow?" Joey asked, his expression hopeful. He'd recently learned the word and used it to counter almost every no Macy delivered.

"Okay. But not too early." She snuggled closer to Everett. "We're going to need our rest after today."

Suddenly, he couldn't wait another moment to be alone with her. "Hold on a second." Carrying Joey into the family room, he deposited him on the couch with Susan and Pop, who were holding court among the guests. "Can you watch him for a second?"

"Of course." Susan patted the boy's head.

"Be right back, sport." Everett grabbed Macy by the hand and drew her down the hall to a secluded nook.

"What are you doing?" she asked, a laugh in her voice.

"This." Cupping her cheeks in his palms, he lifted her face to his for a searing kiss that left no doubt about how much he wanted to be with her today and for the rest of their lives.

"What was that for?" she asked, slow to pull away and a little breathless.

"We've been taking things slow. And that's fine. I've had a lot going on. You've also been busy and are going to get even busier when your classes start up again in January. But you need to know something, sweetheart. I'm in love with you. Not falling. I'm there. Totally. All the way up to my ears."

"Love." She said the word as if savoring it. "Is that so?"

He touched his forehead to hers. "This is the part where you say it back."

"It is?"

"Yes. Unless you don't—"

"I love you, Everett. More than I ever imagined."

He kissed her again, long and hard. "Don't ever tease me like that again. My system can't take the shock."

"I won't. I swear."

"Good. Because when I propose someday in the future, I'm going to need a straight answer from you."

She drew back, her eyes wide. "Propose?"

"Someday," he repeated. "Just giving you fair warning." He dropped his hands only to wrap his arm around her. "Nothing would make me happier than being your husband and Joey's stepdad. It's not my intention to replace Brody in Joey's life. He has a father, and I will do all I can to keep Brody's memory alive. But it would mean the world to me to help raise Joey in the way Brody would have if he was still with us."

Her features softened. "Oh, Everett. I do love you."

As if hearing his name, escape artist Joey came running down the hall toward them, his sneakers pounding on the hardwood floor. Seeing them, he pulled up short.

"Mommy. Everett. There you are."

"Here we are," Macy said, sending Everett a look that said they'd continue this conversation later when they were alone.

They returned to the party then, Joey walking between them, Everett and Macy each holding one of Joey's hands. Judging by the tender and sentimental expressions on every face, there wasn't a single person in the room who didn't recognize what Everett knew with complete certainty.

He, Macy and Joey were a family, now and forever, and nothing would ever change that.

* * * * *